THE END OF THE RAINBOW

BY

BRIAN   WRIGHT

1

THE END OF THE RAINBOW

SCHEDULE OF CONTENTS

CHAPTERS

PART ONE

THE PROBLEM IS UNFOLDED

CHAPTER ONE

THE UNEXPECTED VISITORS

MARCH 1993

It was nearly half past seven when Louise Mercier turned into the road where she lived. As private secretary to a business executive she had had a long and tiring day. Not that there was anything unusual in this. Her boss was a workaholic and he expected other people to work as hard for as long a time as he did. Thank goodness it was Friday and she could look forward to two less stressful days. Whilst many women would have been unwilling to work for such a demanding and, apparently unappreciative, boss Louise actually found the work stimulating and she had got used to being taken for granted.

Her house, which she had inherited from her late father, was about half way down the tree lined road. She turned in at the gate and walked down the short brick pathway to the front door. As she was about to put her key into the lock, she became aware of a low noise that seemed to be coming from her back garden. Crossing the grass to the concrete path that led from the side gate to the back of the house she was surprised to find the gate unlocked. She walked carefully down by the side of the house and, as she reached the far corner, she was startled to see two people sitting on the garden chairs under the old apple tree.

'Bethany!' she exclaimed, 'what on earth are you doing here?'

'Visiting my big sister' replied the young woman with long fair hair, blue eyes and a sun-tanned face.

'You could have at least have told me you were coming.'

'I could have I suppose but we didn't know when we would get here. That is the problem with hitch hiking. Oh, by the way this is Tod Grimhausen.'

'How do you do mam' the young man got to his feet. He was over six feet tall and had brown eyes and shoulder length hair.

'No need to call her mam' giggled Bethany 'she's my half-sister not my aunt even though she is much older than me.'

'Call me Louise otherwise I shall start to feel like Bethany's great aunt. So, what are doing here Bethany? And are you planning to stay here?'

'The usual Louise, my wardrobe needs sorting out and I could do with a trip to a good hair stylist. I presume the funds are available.'

'They are.'

'Talking about funds' said Tod, 'do you think I could make a phone call?'

'Its OK Louise 'grinned Bethany, 'if he is planning to phone home, which is in New York State, he will reverse the charges or get them to ring back.'

The phone is in the hallway. I'll open the door for you.'

As Bethany had said she and Louise were half-sisters . Louise's mother had died when she was fifteen. Her father had remarried two years later and his new wife, Catherine, was some twelve years younger than him. Three years after the marriage she gave birth to a girl, Bethany Laura. Louise had always got on well with her stepmother even though, given the short age gap between them, they were more friends than mother and daughter. Sadly, Catherine died when Bethany was fifteen and her father just two years later. Catherine had inherited a substantial amount from her parents which she left to her husband, when he died his Will made provision that the funds that he had inherited from his second wife should pass to his younger daughter and be paid to her when she reached twenty-five. He named his solicitor and Louise to be the trustees of Bethany's trust fund. After the lawyer retired from practice and the trust, Louise continued on her own as, by this time Bethany was of age and did not need two trustees.

Bethany had gone to university to study the history of art but had given up the course after two years and gone to live in a kibbutz in Israel. That did not last long and the next that Louise heard of her was that she trekking in Nepal. When she arrived back in England she turned up at Louise's house dishevelled and under nourished. To her dismay Louise learned that Bethany had been taking drugs in Nepal. Fortunately, she had not become addicted, and with careful nursing she returned to full health. Despite all that Louise could do to persuade her to take a proper job, she vanished one day without leaving any forwarding address. The next time she turned up it seemed she had been living in various squats with groups of what could only be described as anarchists. Once again Louise set her on her feet and, once again, she disappeared as suddenly as he had reappeared. This had turned into the pattern of her life until this latest visit.

When Tod had disappeared inside Louise turned to her sister. 'Where did you meet him?'

'I spent a couple of weeks on a dig in the Orkney Islands. Tod was another of the diggers. We left the site at the same time and have been hitching our way south. We stopped for a couple of weeks at a place called The End of The Rainbow near Richmond in Yorkshire. It's a new type of Community where people who become members live a total communal life. It is certainly different.'

At this point Tod returned.

'There should be a call coming through for me in a minute or two' he said. In fact, he had hardly spoken when the phone rang and he ran back into the house.

'What's all that about?' asked Louise.

'Tod's something like me' Bethany replied 'he has a family fund back home on which he can draw. It seems his family are successful investment bankers in New York.'

'Does he know about your trust?' asked Louise concernedly.

'Only in very general terms. We don't speak about money. It's just something that you need to get by in this crazy world.'

'Don't forget that your fund will pass to you on your twenty fifth birthday which is just about a year away. And don't forget that I am going to need to be able to contact you at that time. So, no more wandering off into the wide blue yonder and just popping up like the demon king in a pantomime.'

'That's all fixed', Tod grinned when he reappeared.' All I need to do is go to the office of the Anglo American Bank tomorrow. 'One thing about the States being five hours behind us here is that they can fix the transfer for today.'

'What about accommodation for Tod?' asked Louise.

'He'll stay here of course' replied Bethany. 'We can have the parents' old room, that is if you haven't moved into it.'

'No, I am still in my own room' said Louise trying to hide her embarrassment at the idea of the two younger people sharing a bedroom without being married.

'There is still the question of food for tonight. I wasn't expecting to have to feed three people.'

'No problem' laughed Bethany 'we can either order a Chinese takeaway or a pizza delivery. We can do the rest of the shopping tomorrow.'

Over the next four weeks Louise saw that Bethany had sufficient money from her trust fund to buy the clothes she wanted, have her hair restyled and had spending money as she and Tod played the tourists in London. Louise, who lived an ordered life, had to let them do their own thing and sometimes she did not see them for two or three days.

On the second Friday of their visit Louise came home looking particularly tired and distraught.

'What's up' asked Bethany. 'Is Ebenezer Scrooge being particularly difficult?'

'Who is this Ebenezer Scrooge?' asked Tod.

'He's Louise's boss, not the character out of Charles Dickens' laughed Bethany. 'I call him that because he is a slave driver and Louise, poor woman, has to work all hours that are sent as his private secretary.'

'You really should not call Mr Lewis names like that Bethany. You have never met him.'

'Nor do I want to. I have never understood why you put up with him. Surely someone like you could find a more congenial boss.'

'I like working for Mr Lewis.'

'What's he done now that's upset you?'

'Today he was appointed the Group's Chief Executive Officer.'

'And he's dropped you like a hot potato. Typical of the man!'

'He has done nothing of the sort. In fact, he told me he wanted me to continue to be his private secretary.'

'Then, what's the problem? No pay rise?'

'The problem is that half an hour after he was told of his new job he collapsed in his office and has had to be admitted to hospital.'

'That's tough' Tod acknowledged. 'What was it a heart attack?'

'I am not sure. I think it was a stroke. I was the one who found him.'

'Not nice' consoled Tod.

'I may not like him, said Bethany 'but I hope it's not too serious.'

Whilst he was in the clinic used by the firm's medical insurance plan Louise was the one who had tidy up his flat and see that it was kept clean and tidy and that his mail was forwarded to the clinic. She was the only person who visited him, a reflection of the general level of dislike with which he was held by all his colleagues.

During their stay she listened as Bethany and Tod talked about the Community that called itself The End of The Rainbow. It appeared that it was based in an old woollen mill in North Yorkshire. It was a kind of modern-day arts and crafts centre in that it produced furniture, ironwork, fabric, pottery and artwork all of which were hand produced. It seemed to base itself on a sort of William Morris concept. Whatever it was it certainly sounded better than most of the places that Bethany had been associated with and Louise found herself hoping that perhaps her sister had found, at last, somewhere worthwhile where she could live and work.

When she returned home that Friday, she found the house empty. Bethany and Tod had gone. All that was left was a lovely bouquet of flowers with a note in Tod's handwriting that said "Thanks for everything". As she tidied up the house the next day Louise found herself wondering when she would see her sister again.

CHAPTER TWO

TODAY IS THE DAY

MARCH 1993

The face that had looked out of the mirror at Peter Graham Lewis showed a man in his late forties. His hair was light brown and carefully styled, his eyes were blue and his gaze was icy. There were deep furrowed lines between his eyebrows and at the corner of his mouth which was thin and tight lipped. The overall picture was of a man of determined character, who it would be as well not to cross. Peter Lewis would not have described himself in those terms. To him he was a man who knew what he wanted and was prepared to do what was necessary to ensure that he achieved his objectives. He was what he was and made no pretence to be anyone other than himself.

Today was the biggest day in his life. The day he had worked towards for over twenty-five years. At two thirty the non-executive directors of Folkingham Investment Group were to meet to confirm the appointment of a new Chief Executive Officer. That they would select Peter Graham Lewis was an almost forgone conclusion. He had worked with that one goal in mind from the day he had joined the company. He had worked his way up the clerical, then the managerial ladders and finally the executive ladder with a grim determination. If such a thing as a company man existed, he was Peter Graham Lewis. About five years ago the Folkingham Investment Group had experienced very troubled waters. Its investment performance had slipped badly, a fact that, to Peter Lewis, was due to weak management at the top of the company. He was the one who had produced and implemented the recovery programme. The non-executive directors had accepted his recommendations which resulted in a wholesale clear out of most of the senior management starting with the Chief Executive Officer. For the immediate future, this role was integrated into that of the chairman. Peter Lewis oversaw the total reorganisation of the investment management team and the fundamental review of all the group's administration activities. He had been ruthless in carrying out his plan and spared no-one when it came to removing them for lack of what he considered to be adequate performance. For investment managers this was based on how they performed against the stock market indices, for administrators it was the efficiency and cost consciousness of their areas of responsibility. The plan had been a success. The group's investment performance put it back firmly into the top quartile, the administration ran smoothly and efficiently. The group profits and its share price reflected that success. Peter Lewis might have been a hard task master but he had driven himself as hard, if not harder, than anyone else.

Even before he had taken on the job of restructuring the group, he had worked tirelessly on behalf of his employers. An average working week for him was never less than one hundred hours. He took no more than two weeks holiday a year and only took that time because it was an inviolate rule of the group that everyone should be absent for two weeks so that if they were being dishonest in their work this would come out as no-one was allowed to simply let their work stop for two weeks. Another person had to take over their work and, if there were any defalcations going on, the odds were firmly stacked that they would come to life in those two weeks. Peter Lewis circumvented these rules by ensuring that he was in constant touch with whoever was doing his job and with the firm as a whole so that he could keep his finger firmly on the pulse of the organisation. Dedication at this level did not come without a price but it was one that he paid without the least resentment. That price was the breakup of his marriage, his wife finally tiring of being married to a corporation rather than a husband. She had walked out on him, had divorced him for mental cruelty and married a nonconformist minister who had counselled her during the break up of her marriage. Also, he had wilfully neglected his two children to the degree that they wanted to have nothing to do with him as they grew older. As far as they were concerned, they had no father.

At work he was respected for his undoubted abilities but, as a man, he was either feared or actively disliked. He was an autocrat and made little or no effort to be a good manager of people. There was probably only one person who, in addition to respect for his abilities, had a personal regard for Peter Lewis the man. That person was Louise Angela Mercier who had been his secretary for fifteen years. Although he hardly ever treated her as another human being, more as a robot designed to carry out his instructions, she enjoyed working for him and recognised that, although he would never admit it to her or to anyone else, he relied heavily on her loyalty and efficiency. On the credit side was the fact that as he rose up the ladder, she followed on his coat tails and her salary increased accordingly.

That morning Peter Lewis carried out his work as if the meeting of the non-executive board members did not exist. Having worked through his correspondence he called Louise into his office and dictated replies to his letters or gave her instructions as to whom they were to be forwarded and with what instructions. This might be the age of the computer and, while Peter Lewis made use of it as and when he wished, he remained attached to direct dictation to a secretary. After a cup of coffee and two biscuits he had chaired a meeting to consider the latest updating of the group's Compliance Manual. One of the managers who should have been present was absent as she had been forced to make an urgent dental appointment. Peter Lewis made no attempt to hide his displeasure and later dictated a memo to the person concerned pointing out that her dental health came a very poor second to her work responsibilities and tearing to shreds the draft that she had submitted to the working party, requiring that it be rewritten and placed on his desk by the close of business the following day. He ensured that a copy of that memo was sent to all the other members of that group.

Unless there was a business lunch Peter never went out of the office at lunchtime or went to the canteen or director's dining room. Instead, he ate two rounds of sandwich and an apple and drank a small bottle of mineral water that had been obtained for him by Louise. While eating he read the Financial Times. After a break of thirty minutes, he studied a report he had commissioned from the group's auditors on the tightening of the internal audit and compliance functions. Two thirty came and went and, as far as anyone could tell if they had seen him, this fact had no impression on him. It was four o'clock before his door opened and Sir Richard Deal, the group chairman entered. Richard Deal was in his mid-sixties, a man of medium height with white hair and grey eyes, dressed in a dark blue suit, a white shirt and a club tie. Before joining the Folkingham Investment Group Sir Richard had been a senior civil servant finishing his career as secretary to the Prime Minister.

'Afternoon Peter' he said with a smile. 'I suspect that you have a good idea as to the reason or this visit'

'Possibly, Sir Richard' Peter allowed a rare grin to cross his face.

'Then there is no point in beating about the bush. The board of the American Group has accepted the recommendation of the non-executive committee and have confirmed your appointment as Chief Executive Officer of the UK group of companies. Congratulations! It is a well-deserved promotion' Sir Richard held out his hand and shook Peter's firmly. 'We shall have a good deal to discuss in the coming days but now I have to dash off. I have been summoned to meet my former chief who is writing his memoirs and requires my help over some point or other. He says he needs my memory which is hardly surprising from a man who had a problem knowing which day of the week it was.' Sir Richard turned to go but paused. 'Oh yes, Press Department have been instructed to make an announcement and the Finance Director is advising the Stock Exchange. And here' and he produced an envelope from his pocket, is the official letter confirming your appointment.'

With that he was gone, leaving Peter to savour the success that he had worked so hard towards over all those years. He had no-one he could ring and give the news to so he returned to his work. A quarter an hour later he picked up the internal phone and rang the Personnel Director.

'Peter Lewis here Victor' he said and accepted the obviously insincere expressions of congratulation. 'I would like to have the files for all the senior managers please. Perhaps your girl could bring them to my secretary right away.'

That would set the cat among the pigeons he thought. There will be more than one of them who will have an uncomfortable weekend. Sure enough, ten minutes later his door opened and Louise Mercier entered carrying a pile of files.

'I gather you asked for these Mr Lewis.'

'Yes, put them on the desk will you. I expect you have heard the news.'

'About your promotion? Yes, it's all round the building. May I offer my congratulations.

'Thank you, Louise. I shall want you to come with me to my new role.'

'Thank you. I shall be pleased to do that.'

'We can talk about your salary revision next week. Now, I expect you want to get off home. Good night.'

As Louise left the room, Peter got to his feet and stretched out his arms. It was then that there was a sudden searing pain across his head and the darkness overcame him as his body slipped to the floor. Fortunately for him, Louise was only on the other side of the door and heard him hit his chair as he fell to the floor. She rushed into the room, took one look at him, and rang the Medical Sister who took care of minor ailments and accidents. Without waiting for her to arrive, Louise rang 999 and asked for an ambulance. It was only then that she rang the Personnel Director.

Ten minutes later an unconscious but alive Peter Lewis was on his way to St Bride's Clinic which was the hospital used by the Group Health Scheme.

The day that had promised so much had ended in a way that no-one had anticipated.

CHAPTER THREE

NEW ARRIVALS AT THE COMMUNITY

JUNE 1993

Not far outside the small market town of Netherton in the Swaledale valley there stood an old cotton mill. The arched sign over the gateway to the site was painted in seven distinct colours and the black wording read "The End of The Rainbow". Passing underneath the sign you entered a large cobbled area, at the end of which stood a big, three story stone building facing four square to the road. It had been built originally in the middle of the nineteenth century as a woollen mill and had closed for business only some fifteen years previously. The family company, that had operated the mill for over a century, were no longer able to compete with cheap cotton from India and the Far East and so went into administration until all the equipment and fittings had been sold by the administrators, leaving only the shell of the building. Adjacent to the mill were a number of other buildings, which stood at right angles to it. These included the house of the original mill owner and later the home of the mill manager. The other buildings had been used as offices and workshops. Passing by the side of the mill you entered another large cobbled area, around whose edges were buildings that had been used as stables and then garages. In the centre of these buildings was an arch that led through to yet another square. This one was edged by three ranges of houses and cottages that had housed the mill's employees.

The mill had originally been powered by a giant water wheel, but over the years this had been replaced by a steam boiler and, later, by its own electric generator before being joined to the national grid in the late thirties. There was little or no demand for buildings of this size in this northern valley in the Yorkshire Dales. For ten years it had remained empty and was starting to deteriorate with each passing year. Then, out of the blue, the administrators received an offer for the whole site. Admittedly it was a low offer but it was the only one they were likely to receive and there were no funds available to maintain the buildings. It was hardly surprising the administrators accepted the offer without argument. The buyer was a company that called itself 'The End of The Rainbow'. They applied for, and received, permission to convert the site to one for use as a craft and light industrial workshop together with living accommodation for the people employed on the site.

When the Commune purchased the property there was a considerable amount of work needed to convert the mill into the workshops for the light industry and crafts. The industrial activities such as architectural metal work, blacksmithing, furniture design and construction as well as other woodworking plus pottery were located on the ground floor while things such as art, textile design, weaving and clothes making were located on the upper floors. A separate shop was set up which sold the goods manufactured on site and there was a café and restaurant for visitors. Some of the other outbuildings were used for storage and the remainder of the properties were converted into living accommodation. A gymnasium and indoor swimming pool were also created and the grounds were made into lawns and flower and vegetable gardens the produce from which was sold in separate shops. Overall a separate and separated community was created.

It was a wet and windy afternoon when Bethany Mercier and Tod Grimhausen arrived just outside Netherton at the End of The Rainbow building. They found their way to the Reception

19

area where a middle-aged man was seated at a desk.

Can I be of assistance?' he asked.

'I hope so' replied Bethany 'We are interested in becoming members of this Community.'

'In that case' replied the man 'I must pass you on to one of the senior members. If you would take a seat over there, I will ask someone to come and talk to you.'

They were left sitting on a couple of plastic chairs for nearly fifteen minutes before a door at the end of a corridor opened and a youngish man wearing tweed jacket and twill trousers came up to them.

'Good afternoon' he said 'would you like to come with me.'

He led them down the corridor and through the door by which he had come to where they found themselves in another corridor. He opened a door on the left and ushered them into a room furnished with a table behind which was a big office chair and in front of which were two armchairs.

'Let me take your coats' he said and hung them on a coat rack. 'Not the best of weather is it?'

'You can say that again' grunted Tod.

'Now how can I help you? By the way, my name is Colin.'

'As we told the man at reception 'Bethany replied 'we are interested in becoming members of the Community.'

'Can I ask you how much you know about our Community and why you think you would like to join us?'

'We stopped by here about two months ago' said Tod 'and stayed for about a week doing casual work in your gardens. That was how we learned about the set up you have here. The more we have thought about it the more we have liked the idea.'

'We have both spent a good deal of time moving about this

country and abroad' added Bethany 'but we think the time has come for us to put down some roots.'

'The usual sort of life of a nine to five job with a house and a mortgage doesn't interest us. We are looking for something different and reckon this place offers it.'

'You must understand' said Colin 'that becoming a member of this Community is not like joining the local library. There is a great deal more to it than that. You would be drawing a line under your past lives and all that entails. As members of the Community you are joining a co-operative as far as all aspects of your life are concerned. Do you understand that?'

'Yes' replied Bethany 'we understand.'

'The best analogy I think I can give you is that we are like a non-religious medieval monastery.'

'But they were single sex institutions' said Tod.

'Mainly they were, but there was one order, the Gilbertines, who had both nuns and monks. However, that does not concern us. What does is that a monastery was based upon a dual foundation. There were people who worked for the monastery but were not full members. They were called lay brothers or sisters. It was only when they had completed a period of acclimatisation that they could ask to be admitted to full membership and a new way of life. Membership which will be for the rest of their lives. Let me explain. But first, would you like a cup of tea or coffee?'

'Coffee for me' said Tod.

"And me' added Bethany.

Having passed their order over the phone Colin continued his explanation.

'Those wishing to join The End of The Rainbow Community must, at first become lay members. This means that they live and work here but are not considered to be full members. For example, they are paid a salary from which they contribute to the cost of their housing and feeding etc. The Community treats them as employees as far as things such as tax and national insurance are concerned. Only after a period of some six months can they apply, if they so wish, to become full members. By then, as you will understand, they will have been able to decide whether or not this is the life for them. Becoming a full member involves letting go of all contacts with an earlier life. For example, the new member is given a Community name. The name given to me was Colin. In this we are following the ways of the medieval monastery or nunnery. No further contact is permitted with friends or relations. Instead of being employees the person becomes a member of the co-operative that is the Community which means that they are housed, fed and clothed free of charge. They continue to work for the Community but do not receive and wage or salary. The Community deals with all contacts with local and national bureaucracy as regards taxes and insurance contributions. In other words, they are relieved of all the usual burdens of everyday life. At the same time, they relinquish all personal property and any that accrues to them, from say the death of a parent, passes to the Community.'

'How does one start the process of becoming a full member?' Tod asked.

'The sooner we can begin the sooner we will be admitted' added Bethany.

'What we have to do first of all' said Colin 'is to take down some details. 'First of all can I have you full names and addresses.'

'Bethany Laura Mercier and I don't have a fixed address. I haven't done since I left home years ago.'

'Patrick Tod Grimhausen and I am an American citizen. My home town is New York but, like Bethany, I have no permanent home either here or in the States.'

'Do you have any special qualifications or skills?' asked Colin.

'I was studying art history at university but I didn't complete the course.'

'And I studied to be a furniture designer and repairer' said Tod.

'Both skills which fit in well with the Community' replied Colin. 'What about financial resources?'

'The only thing I have is some occasional money from a family fund' said Bethany. 'My only relative is a half-sister who lives in London.'

'I am much the same except I have parents and two sisters who live in New York State.'

'The first thing to do' said Colin 'is to sign you up as lay members of the Community which means that you will be employees and that we will provide you with accommodation and food etc. Now this bit requires some form filling I am afraid.'

The next hour was spent on these administration formalities after which Bethany and Tod were handed on to a woman called Sarah who took them on a tour of the Community and showed them where they would be living and working. She also explained about how they could get their meals in the canteen.

By the end of the day Bethany Mercier, who was given the Community name of Claudia and Tod Grimhausen, who was given the Community name of Kirk, were lay members of The End of The Rainbow.

CHAPTER FOUR

NEW HORIZONS

JANUARY 1994

Peter Lewis stood at the foot of his front steps and looked around at the rolling countryside, the rolling hills and the view of a church spire in the distance. If anyone had asked him a year ago if he would be living in the rural Yorkshire Dales within twelve months, he would have said that they were out of their minds. Yet here he was. At times he would have found it hard to explain how it had all come about.

He had spent his entire working life with one aim in mind. He was determined to get to the top of the tree. To do that he was prepared to do whatever it took and pay whatever price even if that was working a hundred hours a week, never taking a real break from work and sacrificing his marriage and family. It had taken all those things and, unknown to him, something else. His health. The day he had reached his goal and been appointed Chief Executive Officer he had collapsed in his office and been rushed off to St. Brides Clinic where he had been told he had suffered a stroke.

Eventually, he had come to accept that his good fortune had not abandoned him entirely. He had suffered none of the side effects that he could so very well have suffered. He was not paralysed in any part of his body nor had he lost his power of speech or any mental capacity. After a month of examinations and tests he had been told by the consultant that he was a very fortunate man. A view that Peter thought was complete rubbish seeing what he gone through during the past four weeks. However, when the consultant went on to say that if he returned to his former way of life, he would be dead within five years, it had been like a bucket of cold water being poured over his head. He had worked in that one way for so long he doubted if he could do it in any other way. He would just have to take his chances; nothing was ever gained without some form of risk.

Much against his wishes he was ordered to take a two-month break during which time he was not to contact his firm. This was underlined by the fact that all the employees were told that to enter into any form of contact with him would be considered a major breach of company regulations. Realising that he could not stay in his flat in London all that time he set out in his Mercedes car, on a leisurely tour of his native land. At the end of a month, he had landed up in the north Yorkshire Dales. Here he found a very comfortable and superbly furnished Georgian farmhouse that had been converted into a bed and breakfast whilst the old farm buildings had also been converted, this time into single story holiday lets. Originally, he had intended to stay just a few nights but he so enjoyed the locality and his excursions into the surrounding countryside that he stayed the rest of his holiday. Feeling better and more relaxed than he could ever remember he returned to London ready to take up the duties as Chief Executive Officer.

To his amazement he was told on the first morning that although the British medical advisers had passed him fit for work those of the American parent group had recommended that he be retired on grounds of ill health. As the British group of companies had no power to reject a ruling of the parent company's board with the result that by lunchtime, he was escorted off the premises. To say that he was angry at the treatment he had received was the understatement of the century. His first reaction was to sue the Group for every last pound it possessed and for the return of his job. It took the wise advice of his solicitor to convince him that this was a no-win policy. What was a far better policy was to secure the most advantageous settlement in the form of compensation for loss of office and pension rights and health cover. While this would remove any need for him to work again it would not stop him accepting some lucrative non-executive directorships nor to his setting up as a business consultant. So, he settled down to plan a new life. Whilst waiting to see his solicitor one morning he picked up a Rural Life magazine and, to his surprise, saw a photograph of the guest house that he had stayed in a few weeks before. It was for sale. At which point he was called into his meeting.

The next morning was spent on working on the Business Plan he was developing for his proposed venture as an independent director and business consultant. After a salad lunch, he was trying to eat more healthily, he decided to take a walk. He crossed the park and went into the large supermarket with the intention of buying the latest edition of the Economist. It was there that saw the magazine entitled Rural England which said that it contained an in-depth report on the Yorkshire Dales. As he had been there recently Peter bought the magazine to find out what it said. Back at his apartment he returned to work on his Business Plan. During the evening he read the Economist and the article in the other magazine on the Dales. He was surprised to see in the current magazine a repeat of the advertisement he had seen in his solicitor's waiting room and read it with considerable interest.

What caused it he never discovered but when he sat down to work the next morning, he found that suddenly he had lost all enthusiasm for his Business Plan. Not only that but he had somehow come to the conclusion that now was the right time to make a complete change in his way of life. Putting the Business Plan aside he put a blank piece of paper in front of himself and began to put his thoughts into words. This led him to make a series of telephone calls all of which provided him with further details. Having completed this work, he went for a long walk. After sleeping on the idea, he found he had decided to follow it up. The plan was to sell his London apartment, which had increased enormously in value during the twenty years he had owned it, and move to the north where he would buy the guest house and the holiday lets he had stayed at and start a completely new life. Provided the property was in a good state of repair, and as far as he could recall it was, and it produced a reasonable profit it would mean that, together with the handsome pension he would receive from his former employers, he would have more than enough to live on comfortably. The first thing to do was to tell his solicitor of his new plan so that he had the necessary information when negotiating on his behalf. Then he would go north again and make some detailed local enquiries including obtaining a full survey on the property if his bid was accepted. Before he left London, he would put his present apartment on the market.

In all these negotiations he kept his keen business mind and experience in full operation. Eventually, despite the usual ups and downs of any such negotiations, he was able to put his plan into force. Which was how he came to be standing where he was, in front of an old Georgian farmhouse now converted to a luxury bed and breakfast with six attached holiday lets.

As he stood before his new home and his new business Peter looked back as well as forwards. Nothing could take away from him all that he had achieved but that success had been bought at a price. He did not regret what he had done and what he had tried to do. But he had had to accept that the price he had paid had been a heavy one, which underlined the need to draw a line under that part of his life. It would have been a mistake to try and create what could only ever be a poor substitute for what it was seeking to replace. The only sensible thing to do was to change direction and give himself a new challenge. However, the man who had accepted that new challenge was a different and he hoped a more rounded person than the old one.

It had not been easy for him to recognise that he had been a very difficult, if not downright unpleasant, man as he had driven himself and everyone he came into contact with such relentless ferocity. It was true that he had not courted popularity but, looking back, he could see no justification for much of his behaviour. It was no excuse to say that it had become a way of life. No-one had required him to behave like that. It was his free choice. The consequence of his behaviour was that in reaching his goal he had very nearly destroyed his health and put his own life at risk. There was no point in arguing that it had given him financial success. That was not he had wanted. He had wanted power. His illness had shown him quite clearly that his grip on that objective had proved very poor. He may have got to the summit but he had very quickly fallen off it. The greatest benefit that he had got from what was happened was the time and the chance to draw up a personal balance sheet. That and the discovery that life could be lived in a very different way and still provide a high level of satisfaction. He had made a complete mess of his personal relationships up to now, but he was determined to see that he did not make the same mistakes a second time.

Turning round he went into the house to start on the second part of his life.

CHAPTER FIVE

A FATAL FALL

MARCH1994

Police Constables Owen Headlow and Noreen Abbott were on their routine patrol when they received a call directing them to The End of The Rainbow just outside Netherton where a fatality had been reported. A doctor and the ambulance were on their way to the location.

'Do you know a place called The End of The Rainbow?' Headlow asked as his partner switched on the car siren and flashing lights.

'I think it's some sort of Craft Centre' Noreen replied 'you know the sort of thing; they make and sell all kinds of hand produced arts and crafts. According to what I have heard it's an attempt to recreate the Arts and Crafts movement of about a hundred years ago. It's based in what was originally the biggest woollen mill in the area. You must have seen it.'

'I know the place you mean. Sylvia has been there a couple of times buying the odd thing for the house. And when I say odd, by the look of them, that is exactly what they are.'

'The trouble with you Owen is that you have no taste for anything artistic. You wouldn't know a Rembrandt if you fell over one.'

'What kind of fatality are they going to have in a place like that?'

'We'll soon know it is just about two hundred yards along this road on the right hand side.'

As they pulled into the car park, they saw that the ambulance was already on site and they had no sooner stopped than the police doctor's car pulled up alongside them.

'What have we got here Owen?' asked Doctor Lucas Constatine who was a fellow member of Netherton Cricket Club.

'All we know is there has been a fatality reported. The Ambulance chaps seem to have got here first. By the way, this is Noreen Abbott.' He pointed towards his colleague.

'We had better go and see what's happened' the doctor said striding towards a knot of people that could be seen through an arch that led into a courtyard.

'Keep back please' Headlow said as he pushed his way through the people looking on.

The doctor had dropped to his knees by the side of a body that lay crumpled on the cobblestones.

'I don't think there is anything we can do' said one of the ambulancemen. 'She's gone as far as we can tell.'

'Yes', agreed the doctor 'she is dead. Been dead under half an hour, I guess. Looks like a broken neck. You will want to call in your people I guess, Owen. I can't wait around for the pathologist as I have a surgery in ten minutes, so I will leave things to you.'

'Rope off the body and surrounding area will you Noreen while I call base. Then you might ask if anyone saw what happened and take a statement from them.'

Half an hour later the police surgeon had viewed the body and agreed it could be moved. The ambulance had carried it off to the mortuary. Detective Sergeant Quentin Barbour had arrived and taken charge of the enquiry. The first thing was to try and obtain an identity for the victim. Here a middle aged man who introduced himself as Martin Delaney came forward.

'I am the director of the Community' he said.

'Are you able to identity the young lady sir?' asked Barbour.

'Yes, she was called Bethany Mercier and she lived in the Community.

'Do you know if she had any next of kin sir?'

'No, I don't. Perhaps the best way I can explain this is to compare the Community with an abbey in the middle ages where the members of that community gave up their previous lives and identities to enter a cloistered lifestyle. They cut themselves off entirely from their previous lives. When someone wishes to become a full member of our Community similar rules apply. They surrender their past life and enter one in which all their needs are met by the Community. Like the earlier monasteries and abbeys, we also have the equivalent of lay members. They are people who work here but are not full members. They are paid a wage and live off site.'

'Does that surrender of a past life include any next of kin?'

'There is nothing to prevent them from informing their family where they are and what they are doing but, if they do that, they are required to say that all future communications will not be answered. What you must understand is that this Community is a completely separate lifestyle. Our lives here are all inclusive and have no connection to what may have happened in the past.'

'Therefore, you have no information other than her name? For example, you don't keep a note of their next of kin?'

'If someone wishes they can give that information and it's noted in our records against their name. I will have to check to see if Bethany did that.'

'Perhaps you would do so. However, before you do so, can you tell me anything about how the young lady came to fall to her death?'

'As you can see, 'Delaney said pointing upwards, 'there is an open door on the third floor and above it there is a hoist that

31

was used when this building was a woollen mill. It seems as if Bethany must have been standing in that opening and either have become dizzy and lost her balance or tripped over something causing her to fall to the ground.'

'Why should she be there in the first place?'

'I may be able to help there, sergeant,' said Constable Headlow. 'we found this where the body fell

He held out a jumble of twisted metal.

'This was once a camera. It seems she may have been taking photographs when she fell and she landed on top of the camera.'

'Why would she be taking photos from up there?' asked the sergeant. 'Is there a special view?'

'Bethany worked in our art department. She was an accomplished water colour artist and might well have wanted to take a photo that she could turn into a picture' replied Delaney.

'Very well sir, would you kindly check your records and let us know what information you have about the deceased and also you might ask all your members to contact us if they have any information about the young lady and what she was doing before her fall. There will have to be an inquest and you will be called to give evidence. We will let you know when and where that will take place.'

'Excuse me Sergeant' said Headlow 'but Mr Delaney refers to the young lady as Bethany but I noticed she was wearing a badge with the name Claudia.'

'Can you clarify that point sir? asked the Sergeant.

'Certainly. Members of the Community are given a new name when they join us. It signals the separation from their previous lives. Bethany's Community name was Claudia. When I was told that it was Claudia that had fallen, I checked for her birth name.'

'Thank you, sir, that clarifies that.'

'What about funeral arrangements sergeant?' asked Delaney

'When the post mortem has been completed then, assuming there is no reason for a delay, a death certificate will be issued and permission to hold a funeral granted.'

A full report was submitted to Inspector Seagrave who visited the site of the fatal accident and satisfied himself that what the sergeant had reported appeared to be a fair summary of the tragic event. He conveyed his opinion to the Coroner.

The post mortem confirmed that the cause of death was injuries suffered during a fall from a great height. Forensic tests failed to show any evidence of alcohol, drugs or other dangerous substances being present in the body.

The inquest on Bethany Mercier was held in Richmond and ruled that it was a case of accidental death. There being no record of any next of kin, the Community arranged for there to be a civil ceremony at the crematorium and the ashes were scattered in the grounds of the Community. So ended the brief life of Bethany Laura Mercier.

CHAPTER SIX

A ROAD TRAFFIC ACCIDENT

MARCH 1994

It was a misty morning as Gordon Whitton cycled along the narrow lanes from his home in St Gwennep in the far south of Cornwall towards Penzance where he worked at a local farm produce wholesaler. Normally, at this hour, he had the lanes to himself as he started work before most people even got out of bed. He turned a sharp left-hand bend in the road and almost collided with something laying against the grass bank. He skidded to a stop, dismounted and approached the shape carefully. When he saw that it was a human body and it was not moving, he hurried forward and knelt down beside it. Fortunately, Gordon had been on a first aid course at work and he realised immediately that there was nothing he could do for this young man. He must have been dead for some hours. He was debating what he could do, the problem being that if he left things as they were some motor vehicle could come round the bend and hit the body. At the same time, he knew that he should not try to move it. Luckily for him he heard the sound of an approaching tractor and moving back round the corner he was able to signal it to stop.

'What's up me old friend?' asked the middle-aged driver looking down at him.

'There's a man laying by the edge of the road just round the corner. He's dead.'

'Been hit by a car, has he?'

'Seems like it. The difficulty is we shouldn't move him but if we don't do something to warn people another vehicle could hit him. Also, we need to contact the police.'

'You're in luck mate. I have got a couple of red warning triangles that I use when I am hedge trimming. We can put one either side of the corner in the middle of the road to warn people. There is a policeman that lives in St. Crowan. I'll go on there and give the alarm. Have you got a torch or a lamp?'

'There's one on my bike.'

'Then you base yourself on the corner and use that as a signal to slow down anyone who comes along.'

Having set up these arrangements the tractor moved off to drive the two miles to St. Crowan. Over the next hour a police car, the doctor and an ambulance arrived at the site and the police had set up a diversion thus closing the road between St Gwennep and St Crowan. Gordon Whitton managed to arrange for the police to tell his employers why he was late for work. The doctor gave it as his opinion that the man had been hit by a car or other motor vehicle and had been dead about eight hours. What he had been doing walking along that road at that time no-one could say. It was thought that maybe he had a car that had broken down but a search of the road revealed no such stranded vehicle.

Before the ambulance took the body to the mortuary, the police officers looked through the pockets of the deceased. There was not much in them. A few coins and one five pound note, a hand-kerchief but no wallet or credit or bank cards. All they found was a card that said 'The Rainbow Craft Centre, Trescowen Cove, Cornwall and a name embroidered on a handkerchief that said P.T.Grimhausen.'

'Sounds a German sort of name' said one of the police officers.

'Could be, I suppose, that his father was a prisoner of war over here, married an English girl and this is the son.'

'Do you think he has been robbed? I mean it's odd that he doesn't have any folding money or bank or credit cards.'

'It's possible. We shall have to include that in our report.'

Once the ambulance had gone the police having searched the road and found nothing to indicate how an accident had oc-curred, took down their barriers and re-opened the road. An-other officer was sent to The Rainbow Craft Centre to make enquiries about a P T Grimhausen. The Rainbow Craft Centre was up a narrow lane that had led originally to a tin mine. There was an open gate across the narrow track over which was a sign The Rainbow Craft Centre and at the very apex of that sign was a painted rainbow. Having parked the car the police officer headed towards what seemed to be the main building and knocked at a door with a sign Reception. His knock was answered by a middle aged woman dressed in a patterned skirt and a red blouse.

'Can I be of help?'

'Police madam', said the officer showing his proof of identity. 'I am making enquiries in connection with a Mr P T Grimhausen.'

'You had better talk to our director' she said and closed the door. Two minutes later it was opened by a man in his forties, with long fair hair, blue eyes and a small moustache. He was wearing a tweed suit, a check shirt and a bow tie.

'Good morning 'he said 'what can I do for you?'

'I am making enquiries about a Mr P T Grimhausen. Does that name ring a bell?'

'I am afraid not. You see here everyone is identified by a com-munity name. I shall have to ask our manager to track if this P T Grimhausen is known to us.'

He disappeared into a room and they heard him talking on the phone. When he came back, he was asked if he had identified the man. At this point he was joined by a middle aged man who identified himself as Nigel Threlfall the director of the Centre who said:

'Mr Grimhausen runs our furniture restoring workshop. He is known by the community name of Hank. Why are you asking for him?'

'Is Mr Grimhausen available?'

'I understand that he is not. He sometimes goes into Penzance to collect items needed for the workshop.'

'Could you describe Mr Grimhausen for me please?'

'What is all this?' asked the man.

'A description if you please sir.'

'He's aged in his twenties, about six feet tall, has brown hair and grey eyes.'

'What was he likely to be wearing?'

'Probably a jacket and trousers and a check shirt. Will you please tell me what this is all about?'

'I am sorry to have to say sir that it seems that Mr Grimhausen has met with an accident.'

'Is he badly hurt?'

'I am afraid he is dead. His body was discovered this morning lying by the side of the road between St Gwennep and St Crowan. It appears he has been the victim of a traffic accident.'

'This is terrible news officer. You had better come into my office.'

The office was a small room with a desk and two chairs and a row of filing cabinets. When they were seated the police officer took out a notebook and opened it.

'Do you have any information as to next of kin sir?'

'I am afraid not.'

'Did Mr Grimhausen never mention any relatives?'

'I had better explain the nature of this community, officer. The Rainbow Craft Centre is, as its name implies, a place where a number of traditional crafts are practiced. These include, pottery, wood carving, glass making, painting, picture frame making, wrought iron work and furniture restoring. The people who live and work here are part of a closed community. On joining the Centre, they give up all contacts with their previous lives including their legal names. The Centre is a true community in that none of us own any personal property. Everything is held communally. The nearest analogy I can give you is that we are a secular order not a religious one but our structure is very much that of a monastery or convent. Like those bodies people joining us are given new names.'

'Does that mean that Grimhausen was not his real name?'

'Not at all. We do keep a record of their birth names against which is recorded their Centre name. That is how I was able to trace that we did indeed know Mr Grimhausen, although I am puzzled to know how you came to know it.'

'It was embroidered on a handkerchief. May I ask your name and position here sir?"

'I am Nigel Threlfall and I am the director of the Centre.'

'Thank you Mr. Threlfall. I am afraid that, given the information you have provided, I shall have to ask you to attend the police mortuary and formally identify the body. As you will understand there will have to be a post mortem and an inquest at which you will be required to appear.'

Mr Threlfall identified the body as that of Patrick Tod Grimhausen known within the Rainbow Craft Centre as Hank. The cause of death given by the pathologist was that the deceased had died from a broken neck. The injury was in line with his having been hit by a van or small lorry. The inquest gave a verdict of accidental death. The police were unsuccessful in tracing the vehicle that had been the cause of death. The fatality became just another number in the road deaths statistics.

There being no next of kin the Craft Centre undertook the funeral arrangements and the body was cremated and his ashes scattered out at sea.

So ended the short life of Patrick Tod Grimhausen.

CHAPTER SEVEN

DO YOU KNOW SOMEONE CALLED TOD?

MARCH 1994

Louise was watching a film on television one evening when the telephone rang.

'May I speak to Louise Mercier please?' a male voice asked.

'Speaking.'

'My name is Gilbert Ravendale, I represent Capital Enquiries a private investigation service. I was wondering if you could spare me a few minutes.'

Instinctively, Louise was on her guard. She had no means of knowing who this person was. It could be some form of scam to try and get information about her.

'I am sorry but it's not convenient at the moment. If you will give your phone number, I will call you back tomorrow evening. Who did you say you were?'

'My name is Gilbert Ravendale of Capital Enquiries and my phone number is 01-743-619253.'

'Very well Mr Ravendale I will call you at seven thirty tomorrow. Now I must go. Good evening.'

Louise went back to her film. When it had finished, she turned on her computer and logged on to the internet. There she did indeed find an organisation called Capital Enquiries whose web site said it provided a range of investigatory services. The phone number given was not that provided by Mr. Ravendale. In addition, she found there was a trade body that covered private investigators and she made a note of its number. The next day she telephoned the trade body and asked if they recognised Capital Enquiries as an authentic inquiry bureau? They confirmed that the firm had a solid reputation although she was advised to make further enquiries before employing any agent. After that she rang Capital Enquiries and asked for Gilbert Ravendale only to be told he was not available. She was told, however, that the gentleman did indeed work for the organisation. Satisfied that she had done all she could, later that day she telephoned the number she had been given.

'Thank you for ringing Miss Mercier' she recognised the same voice as that of the caller the day before. 'I am hoping that you may be able to help me with some enquiries I am making. Could I call round to see you please?'

'I would prefer to meet on neutral ground Mr Ravendale. Tomorrow is Saturday so perhaps we could meet in the café at the National Gallery at, say, eleven in the morning. I shall be reading a copy of Good Housekeeping.'

If Gilbert Ravendale thought her suggestion odd, he did not admit it and agreed to what she suggested. At the stated time a voice said to her:

'Miss Mercier?'

Louise found herself looking at a middle-aged man about fifty she guessed. He was of average height, with a rounded figure, a bald head and horned rimmed glasses. He was wearing a striped shirt and a plain green tie. He looked like one of the thousands of office workers you could see in the City any day.

'Gilbert Ravendale' he held out a hand and took the seat opposite her. 'My card.' It was a plain white card with his name printed on it with the phone number he had given her. There was no address.

'You said you worked for Capital Enquiries' she said looking at the card.

'That's correct.' And he produced a plastic covered identity card which hung from a ribbon round his short neck. This showed the name of Capital Enquiries and had a photograph of the man sitting opposite her.'

'Thank you', she said 'I am sorry if I appear over cautious.'

'Not at all.'

'How can I help you?'

'Miss Mercier do you know a man called Patrick Tod Grimhausen?'

'I have met someone of that name. He is a friend of my half-sister. May I ask why you are looking for him?'

'His family in New York are concerned because they have not heard from him for some time, nor have they been able to contact him.'

'If he is a friend of Bethany's, that is my half-sister, that does not surprise me. Bethany is what you might call a rolling stone. She never has a fixed address and I never know where she is or where she has been until she suddenly appears at my house out of the blue. If Tod is anything like her I then I am not surprised his family have not heard from him.'

'Have you heard from your half-sister since her last visit?'

'No, but as I say that does not surprise me. Over the years I have learned, after the event, that Bethany has been in Israel, in Nepal, in Spain and in France as well as various parts of the United Kingdom.'

'How close friends were Tod and your half-sister ?'

'They were what today is called an item.'

'I see. Then, you have no idea where to find your half-sister?'

'I am afraid not. But tell me, Mr Ravendale, how did you come to contact me?'

'That was not too difficult. Tod Grimhausen's family made some phone calls to your home when he was staying there. Their telephone bill gave your number so all I had to do was to ring that number. Tell me, do you know of any other friends of your half-sister, who might have information about her?'

'I am afraid I do not. Bethany is some twenty years younger than me and we have never shared friends. Added to which the life she has led these past years means that I would have had little, if anything, in common with the people she has associated with.'

'Have you no idea where they had been before they visited you?'

'Not really, though I do seem to recall they had been on an archaeological dig in the Orkneys and had done some casual work at a craft centre in Yorkshire. I have no idea where exactly this dig was located. I don't think they ever said. As far as the place in Yorkshire is concerned, I remember it had an odd name. When I try to recall it I find all that happens is that I am singing The Yellow Brick Road. Odd isn't it the tricks one's memory pays on one. Sorry I can't be of more help.'

'Well, thank you anyway Miss Mercier. If you do get any news of Tod or your half, I should be grateful if you could let me know.'

'Of course. And, if you are in contact with Tod's family, tell them not to worry. They will turn up sooner or later. Probably when they are in need of money.'

CHAPTER EIGHT

A LETTER OUT OF THE BLUE

MAY 1994

Peter Lewis looked at the hand addressed envelope which would normally be an enquiry for accommodation or perhaps a booking. However, the hand writing looked familiar and for the moment he could not place it. Rather than open it first he decided to put it to one side and open it last. Having gone through the rest of the mail and sorted it into various classifications he picked up the one he had put aside and, using a paper knife, opened it. It was indeed a letter and when he turned to the end to see who had written it he received a considerable surprise. The letter came from his former secretary Louise Mercier who had never written to him previously. He expected she was seeking a reference but he was in for a surprise.

"Dear Mr Lewis

I hope that you are keeping well and that your new business venture is proving successful.

I must apologise for bothering you but I am wondering if it is possible that you may be able to help me with a problem that is worrying me. Briefly, this problem relates to my half-sister who is some twenty years younger than me. Ever since she dropped out of university six years ago, she has led what I can only describe as a nomadic life. I never know where she is or has been until she appears out of the blue at my house where she stays for a few weeks and then disappears again without saying where she is going. My problem is that she will be twenty-five in the near future and its vital that we are in contact as she is due to be paid a trust fund of which I am the sole trustee and which was set up by our late father.

I saw her last some months ago and have no idea where she went after she left me apart from the fact that she did mention a craft community in Yorkshire that she had visited and found enjoyable. For a long time, I could not remember its name but eventually it came to me it was The End of The Rainbow. By searching the phone books, I found it at an address in Netherton, Yorkshire. I wrote to Bethany at that address but got no reply even when I sent a stamped and addressed envelope. When I tried to phone them, I was told that they never gave any information about their members as they were a closed community.

I am wondering if you have ever read or heard anything about this community or know anyone who has had any dealings with them. If so, can they give me any idea how I can find out if my half-sister is there? I am sorry to bother you but I don't know anyone else who lives in that area. If you cannot help, I shall quite understand.

I am attaching a photograph of Bethany in case anyone recognises her.

Yours very sincerely

Louise Mercier"

Peter smiled at the reference to 'that area'. A typical idea of someone who lived in London about anywhere north of Watford. He had never heard of a place with the odd name of The End of The Rainbow nor indeed did he have any idea of the exact location of Netherton. He studied the photograph and noted the resemblance of the young woman to his former secretary. He put the letter to one side while he got on with his work. During the day he did ask members of his staff if any of them had heard of The End of The Rainbow. Most of them had not although one of the ladies who cleaned the bedrooms and cottages came to him and said;

'Were you asking about The End of The Rainbow, Mr Lewis?'

'Yes, I was. Do you know it?'

'I visited it once as part of a day out organised by the Women's Institute. We went to Richmond and stopped at this place for coffee. It sells a whole lot of different art and craft things from mugs to furniture or garden gates made of wrought iron. Its leaflets said it was a closed community of people who worked as a co-operative in the making of good quality arts and crafts goods.'

'When did you go there Mrs Abbott?'

'Oh, it must have been four year ago at least.'

'Thank you very much for that information. A friend of mine was asking if I had heard of it and I hadn't.'

Later that day Peter sat down to reply to the letter.

"Dear Louise

It was a very pleasant surprise to receive your letter. I am pleased to say that I am very well and that the business is running smoothly.

I had never heard of The End of The Rainbow or Netherton which I find is about forty five miles away from here. I asked the people who work here if any of them knew of this craft community and one of the lady cleaners tells me she visited it some time ago as part of a day trip to Richmond. All she could tell me was that it was rather like a shopping centre that sold a whole range of arts and crafts which doesn't' increase our knowledge very much.

It so happens that I am planning to go to Richmond this coming week to attend an auction that has one or two items that I am looking for. I will make it part of my trip to call in at The End of The Rainbow and see what I can find out for you. I will contact you again after my expedition.

I hope you are keeping well.

By the way, do you have an email address as it might be easier to communicate that way than rely on the post.

Yours very sincerely"

Peter was able to buy the two items that he had earmarked in the sale catalogue at what he felt were very reasonable prices. On his way home from the auction, he made a small detour to Netherton and to The End of The Rainbow. Parking his car in the car park he entered the retail part of the building which was made up of a variety of sections each of which handled a different type of handmade items. In each of them he browsed the stock and then engaged one of the staff in conversation. He then produced the photograph of Bethany Mercier and asked if the person recognised her. On each occasion he got a polite denial but had the feeling that he was being given a stock response. He was on his fourth such enquiry when a man came up to him.

'Excuse me sir' he said 'but would you be good enough to come this way.'

He led Peter into a small office. Then man was in his forties and dressed in plaid shirt and twill trousers. He had black hair and brown eyes.

'I understand sir that you have been making enquiries as to whether members of the community know someone in a photograph.'

'That is correct. I am trying to trace the sister of a friend of mine who lives in London.'

'I am sorry but we do not permit such enquiries to be made here.'

'Why not?'

'Because this is a closed community and our members have renounced all contact with the outside world.'

'If they are not allowed to answer my questions who can do so. There must be someone who is authorised to speak to me. Do you recognise this young lady?'

The man pushed the photo away without looking at it.

'I am afraid that you do not fully understand the nature of this community. In some ways we are similar to a religious order although we are fully secular. When we become a member of the community, we cut ourselves off from our past lives, that includes friends and families. Like a monastery or a convent, we give up our birth name and are given a community name. None of us know the birth name of any other member so we cannot possibly reply to your question. It is a fundamental rule of the community that we do not give any information, positive or negative, about persons who may or may not be here or have been here. You are entirely free to continue shopping but you can only do so by agreeing not to ask any questions. If you are not prepared to give me that undertaking then I must ask you to leave this community.'

What is known as the bum's rush Peter thought as he was escorted back to his car. All in all, he could only hope that Bethany Mercier had steered clear of such a place. When he returned home, he found another letter from Louise thanking him for offering to help and giving her email address. His reply set out in some detail his impression of the place he had visited and what had happened. He apologised for his lack of success and said that all he could suggest was that Louise publish a short notice in the local press asking that anyone who knew Bethany to contact her. He ended by saying that she should be very careful of people who did reply because there was a real risk that they might be trying to trick her out of money. The best way to avoid this was to use a box number in the advert. If he could be of any further help, she should not hesitate to contact him.

CHAPTER NINE

NEWS OF BETHANY

JUNE 1994

Peter Lewis was called to the telephone while he was talking to some guests.

'Mr. Lewis, this is Louise Mercier.'

'Hello Louise, how can I help you?'

'I have received a most disturbing letter about Bethany. It's from a firm of solicitors in Richmond who say that Bethany is dead.'

'I am so sorry to hear that. Do they say when and where she died?'

'Yes, it was on the 21 April and it was at The End of The Rainbow. It seems she fell from a high window and died instantly.'

'Do they say why you weren't told at the time?'

'They say that it was because, at that time, they did not have any information about next of kin. They only found my name and address when they discovered her Will which was hidden taped under a drawer in her bedroom. The Will names me as her executor.'

"Are you also the beneficiary?'

'No, that is the odd thing. She left all her money to something called the Arcus Foundation which has an address in Luxembourg. I have never heard of them. Another strange coincidence is that her date of death is one week after her twenty-fifth birthday which means her trust fund had become her property.'

'Can I ask how much is involved?'

'About three hundred and seventy thousand pounds.'

'A large sum by anyone's standards. Did they send you a copy of the death certificate? If I were you that is the first thing I should ask for. If what they say is right there should have been an inquest and you need to get a copy of what happened at that inquiry.'

'How can I do that?'

'I think you are going to need the help of a lawyer.'

'I don't know any I am afraid. Also, it sounds expensive.'

'Don't worry about that I think you will find you can charge the cost of legal assistance to the trust fund. As to the name of a solicitor, leave that with me and I will have a word with my lawyer in London. He should be able to recommend someone.'

'It's very kind of you I am sorry to be such a nuisance.'

'You're not. It's an intriguing situation. I will send you an email as soon as I can.'

When he rang Louise the following evening Peter asked her;

'Did you get my email?'

'Yes, I did thank you. I will contact Mr Branton in the morning. I really am very grateful for your help in all this.'

'I only hope that Roger Branton will be able to help you. If there is anything else I can do please let me know.'

It was over two weeks before Peter heard from Louise again. This time her email read;

'I met with Roger Branton and he is representing me both as executrix of Bethany's estate as well as trustee of my father's trust. He has been in touch with the firm who wrote to me and obtained the original Will and a copy of the death certificate. In addition, he has obtained details of the Coroner's Inquest and is making enquiries about the Arcus Foundation.

When he asked the other firm, who had instructed them they tried to claim client confidentiality but he says he does not think it could have been anyone other than The End of The Rainbow. He has written to that organisation asking how it was that the Will was undiscovered for such a long time and how it came to be discovered. Also, he has asked them why they did not contact me direct. It all seems confusing and worrying and I am only glad I have Mr Branton to help me. Thank you, once again, for all your help.'

According to Roger Branton the Community said that the Will had not been found in an initial search of Bethany's room but by the person who took possession of it after her death. It was only when a drawer became stuck and it was necessary to remover the one below it that the document had been found. They had passed the Will to a solicitor thinking that it was the correct way to proceed especially as the Community made it a rule to have no contact with the next of kin of members. They had no prior information about Bethany having made a Will and could add nothing to the fact that it had been found in the place they stated. The only unusual thing about this, according to Roger Branton, was the method of selecting the witnesses who were apparently strangers. It should not have been difficult to find witnesses from other members of the community. The other odd thing about the Will was that it seemed that Bethany did not have any property of her own apart from her clothes and personal effects which had been of marginal value and, in any event, had been disposed of by the Community who had met the cost of the cremation. There appeared to be no reason why Bethany should have wanted to make a Will other than she wanted the Arcus Foundation to benefit if she died before her twenty fifth birthday. If she acted on that assumption, she had made a mistake because her father's Will had specifically provided that in such an event the funds held for her were to pass to Louise rather than to her estate. There was no need to prove the Will as things stood at the moment.

With all this going on It had escaped Louise's mind to wonder about Tod Grimhausen. When she did think about him, she was surprised to realise that there was no mention of him in any of the communications from the Community nor in the report on the inquest. Did this mean that he was not at The End of The Rainbow. She found that worrying because when they had been at her home Bethany and Tod had seemed genuinely fond of each other. She had not seen their relationship as one of those causal affairs that one heard so much about these days. These thoughts brought to her mind the contact that she had had with Gilbert Ravendale of Capital Enquiries. Uneasy in her mind about all this she rang the private investigator.

'I am not sure you will remember me, Mr Ravendale' she said 'but we met a short while ago when you were trying to trace a Tod Grimhausen.'

'I do indeed remember Miss Mercier. Does your call mean that you have some news for me?'

'Yes, I do have some information but no I don't think it helps in tracing Tod. Tell me, did you contact The End of The Rainbow and were you able to find if Tod was or had been there?'

'I contacted them but was unable to get any information out of them. They hid behind a stated rule that they never gave any information as to whether or not someone had been living at their place.'

'That does not surprise me. It is the same response that I got to my enquiries.'

'Did you go there?'

'No, a friend who lives fairly close went for me and was escorted off the premises.'

'So, what is the news you have Miss Mercier?'

'I received a solicitor's letter telling me that Bethany was dead. She had died as a s result of fall from the third floor of a building while trying to take some photographs. An inquest had ruled accidental death and she had been cremated and her ashes scattered. All this happened some time before I was contacted. The reason being, so I was told, that her Will was only found by accident. It was taped to the underside of a drawer in her room.'

'I am sorry to hear of your loss Miss Mercier. It must have been a great shock to you.'

'It was. In fact, it quite drove from my mind your search for Tod Grimhausen. It's only now that the thought has struck me that it is strange that there has been no reference to Tod in all this. When I saw them together, they seemed to be on excellent terms and I should have imagined that if Bethany was at this Community then Tod would be there as well. If that was so why was there no mention of him and why didn't he, who knew of my existence, contact me to tell me what had happened. That's why I am contacting you, to see if you have been able to trace Tod?'

'I haven't found any trace of him, Miss Mercier. Not only that but his family have not heard from him which they say is unusual as he has always sent them at least a postcard every month. Of course, if he parted from your half-sister, he may have gone off anywhere from Oslo to Santiago.'

'So many things keep coming back to this strange community in Yorkshire. It would make all our lives so much easier if they would only answer our questions.'

'I quite agree. Well, if you come across any other information about Tod you might let me know.'

'I will and, for your part, I hope you will let me know if you find him.'

CHAPTER TEN

NEWS FROM AMERICA

JULY 1994

Louise Mercier found her telephoning ringing as she came in from work.

'Louise Mercier'

'Ah, Miss Mercier, this is Gilbert Ravendale of Capital Enquiries. You may remember we met a while ago.'

'Of course, you were trying to trace Tod Grimhausen. Have you made any progress?'

'Only in a negative sense. All my enquiries ran into brick walls and I was left with the only option being that he had left this country and gone overseas. It appeared that he had disappeared into the wide blue yonder.'

'I am sorry. What can I do for you now? I am afraid I have heard nothing of Tod since we last spoke.'

'I was in the same position until a week ago. Then, I had a call from his father. They had received a letter from a firm of lawyers in England telling them that Tod was dead and enclosing a copy of what was claimed to be his Will.'

'O dear, this all sounds rather familiar.'

'It does, doesn't it. It seems that Tod was the victim of a hit and run accident.'

'In Yorkshire?'

'No in Cornwall, quite close to Land's End. He was working as a wood carver at a craft centre down there."

'Cornwall, but that's the other end of the country from York-shire.'

'I know, but the interesting thing is that he was based at a place called The Rainbow Craft Centre. Sound familiar?'

'You mean it was another place like the one at Netherton?'

'Very much, but on a smaller scale. Once again, they claimed to know nothing of any next of kin. They arranged the funeral and he was cremated and his ashes scattered at sea.'

'How do they say the Will was found?'

'This time things were different. Two months after his fatal accident one of the other people at the Centre produced an envelope written by Tod which said 'Only to be opened two months after my death.' Inside was another envelope addressed to a local Catholic priest. He was contacted and said that Tod had left a sealed envelope with him. This envelop produced a third one. This was addressed to the manager of the Anglo-American Bank in Threadneedle Street in London. That envelope contained a typed letter saying it was to be taken as authority to open the sealed envelope he had deposited with the bank. That was where the Will was found.'

Am I allowed to ask what the Will said?'

'It had been drawn up by a lawyer familiar with American requirements when he must have been staying at your house. It gave his parents address in New York and left them the proceeds of an insurance policy for five thousand dollars. The rest of his estate was left, and wait for this, to the Arcus Foundation in Luxembourg.'

'The same people to whom Bethany left her estate.'

'Exactly. Were you aware that he had made a Will while he was in London?'

'No. He and Bethany went their own way. They simply used my house as a bed and breakfast. Neither of them said anything about making a Will.'

'I assumed that was the case but thought it worthwhile to ask.'

'Does this mean that the same thing happened to Tod as to Bethany?'

'I would like to say that it was unlikely Miss Mercier but who can tell.'

'What about the person who had the envelope? Was he able to throw any light on why Tod had asked him to look after it?'

'That's another interesting point. I went down to Cornwall to interview him but was told that he had left the Centre three days after handing over the envelope. They had no idea where he was. When I asked for his name, they refused to give it to me, citing confidentiality.'

'What about the priest?'

'He was simply doing something that he was asked to do by someone who had worshipped at his church.'

'And I suppose the bank couldn't help either?'

'No. Tod's family have been valued clients for years and they were happy to offer their services to him.'

'What do you do now?'

'Tod's family have appointed me as an attorney to act in all matters involving this country that are connected with his estate. May I ask that if, from dealing with Bethany's affairs, you come across anything that throws any light on things you keep me posted?'

'I will do so with pleasure and no doubt you will return the favour?'

'Of course.'

CHAPTER ELEVEN

DISCOVERY OF A BODY

AUGUST 1994

A hiker walking across the northern Dales heard the sound of a sheep bleating. Looking around he could not see any sheep nearby. Then he realised that the sound was coming from one of the gaps or sinkholes as they were known in the limestone outcrops. Further investigation showed that there did appear to be a sheep trapped down the sinkhole. Looking around, he saw some farm buildings about two miles away and he set off in that direction. When he told the farmer what he had discovered the latter got into his four by four and drove out onto the hillside to confirm the discovery.

'So that's where she got to the stupid beast' he said. 'I shall have to call out the mountain rescue people to get her up.'

'Will you need me anymore?' asked the walker.

'I shouldn't think so lad. You get on your way and leave this to me.'

Two hours later a small group of men and women arrived in their vehicles, bringing with them the equipment needed to get a sheep out of a hole in the ground. They were the local mountain rescue team. Having examined the sinkhole they decided that one of them would be able to be lowered down on a rope and to put a harness on the animal so that it could be raised to the ground. When their arrangements were complete one of the members, a man in his forties, was carefully lowered into the hole with his ropes being held and controlled by a winch fitted on to one of the rescue vehicles. It took him nearly fifteen minutes to make his way down the steep sides of the narrow sinkhole.

'OK' he called 'I can see her. All I have got to do now is get the harness round her and there is not much room to do that. Come here you stupid animal. How can I help you if you insist on wriggling about like an eel?'

It took ten minutes before he had secured her and then he called for the beast to be winched up. He would stay down until she was safe and sound. While he was waiting to be lifted up, he looked round the sinkhole and noted that it got very narrow which was just as well as heaven only knew how deep it was and if the animal had fallen much further there would have been no way it could have been recovered. It was just before he expected to be winched up that he saw something almost immediately below where he was standing.

Hang on a minute' he called up, 'there is something else down here. By heck! I reckon it's a body. Can you lower a more powerful lamp down to me?'

When it arrived, he turned it on and saw that he was right. Below him was a human skeleton.

'It's a body alright' he called up 'this is a job for the police. You had better pull me up, there is nothing I can do now.'

When he got to the top again, he turned to the team leader.

'One other thing I noticed. The body is tied at the wrists and ankles.'

'Hells bells Tony, are you saying it's a murder?'

'It looks like it. I don't see why anyone should tie their hands and feet together and then jump down that hole. If the sheep hadn't fallen in the body may never have been found. Where is the animal by the way?'

'When it was released from its harness it gave a couple of bleats and trotted off to find its chums.'

'You mean it didn't even say thank you?' Tony laughed.

'No, but its owner did promise us a cheque for our funds.'

It was over an hour later that two police vehicles arrived at the site. They had come from Barnard Castle and were led by a detective inspector who proceeded to question the members of the rescue team before shining a powerful lamp down the chasm where it was just possible to see the body.

'The first thing we need is some photographs' he said. 'Could the chap who found it go down again and take some pictures?'

'What about it Tony' asked the leader 'are you game to go down and take some photos?'

'I don't mind. I assume that you have a camera. The one's we carry aren't designed for that kind of work'

'Give him the camera sergeant and show him how to operate it.' Then he added for Tony's benefit, 'for God's sake don't lose it those things cost an arm and a leg. When you are down there, I want pictures of the whole body and its position and the wrists and ankles if they are, as you say, bound up. We'll start with a couple from the top and then please take some at various stages of your descent."

'I can tell you one thing right now' said Tony. 'Whoever it is has been down there some time. There are only bones remaining and I don't reckon we will be able to get that skeleton up in one piece.'

'That's why I have asked for a forensic anthropologist from Durham University to get here as quickly as possible. If we have to bring it up in pieces, I want the job done by an expert.'

The next hour was taken up with Tony taking the photographs and with the police examining the pictures by plugging the camera into their portable computer.

'Well done Tony, you've got us some first-class shots' the Inspector said. 'Looking at them it's my guess it's a woman.'

'How do you arrive at that' Tony asked.

'I've seen more than a few skeletons in my time. Looking at the top of the eye sockets I would say it's a female. Also, the shot of the pelvic region seems to say the same thing. Now we must wait for that anthropologist to tell us if I am right or wrong.'

To the surprise of the rescue team and the police officers the forensic anthropologist proved to be a young woman.

'Dr Tracy Long' she announced as she got out of the vehicle. 'Where exactly is the body?'

'It's down this sinkhole in the rocks doctor' replied the Inspector. 'As you can see it is not exactly easy to get at?'

'How was it discovered?'

'A sheep fell down the hole and when the mountain rescue team were releasing it they found the body.'

'Has it been moved or is it in situ?'

'It has not been moved but we have taken some photos of it that you may like to see.'

'Thank you, that will be useful.'

Dr Long spent several minutes studying the photographs.

'The first thing to say Inspector is that I very much doubt if it will be possible to get the body out in one piece. That means I shall have to take it to pieces bone by bone, package those bones and then reassemble the body back in the laboratory.'

'You will have noticed that it is bound at the wrists and ankles which indicates a homicide.'

'Yes, I did see that and I will take care that the rope or whatever it is not lost. The first thing I need to do is suit up. I hope it will be possible for the rescue team to lower me into the hole. I shall take a bundle of plastic bags into which I will place the bones so as we know what goes where. This is going to mean that I shall need one other person just above me to take those bags and send them to the surface. In addition, we need to get as much light as possible down that hole so that I can see what I am doing. Perhaps you can make the necessary arrangements whilst I get ready.'

It took a further three hours before the parts of the skeleton were separated, bagged and sent to the surface. Dr Long did not find anything else in the sinkhole and was returned to the surface.

'Did you notice anything particular about the body, doctor?' Inspector Northcott asked.

'It's a female aged somewhere between twenty and forty I should think. The only other thing of particular interest is that the skull shows signs of blunt force trauma. In other words, she was hit over the head before being dropped into that hole. I might be able to tell you more when I have reconstructed the skeleton.'

'There was nothing else that might help with identification?'

'Nothing at all. All the flesh has gone so there is no hope of obtaining any finger prints. Her teeth were in good order so I doubt if you will have much luck in tracing any dental records.'

'How long do you think the body had been down there?'

'To answer that we have to consider the extent to which the environment down that hole will have affected the rate of decay. My initial guess is that she has been down there at least a year, but I would not want to be held to that at this stage.'

The formal report, when it was received, confirmed virtually all the anthropologist's original diagnosis. The victim was a woman in her twenties or early thirties in good health. She had not had any children. Her teeth were in a very good state and it was unlikely she had had dental treatment that would help identification. Such information as was available was published in the local press and on radio and television and while this led to people contacting the police about friends or relatives that they knew who had gone missing these leads led to nowhere. The physical description of the people concerned did not match the body closely enough to provide a positive identification. At the same time the police checked the physical description of the victim with all reports of missing young women on their books but, again, there was no-one who appeared to match the body.

It was at this stage that the police decided to ask the anthropologist and an artist to see if they could create a picture of the woman. As a result of detailed measurements and careful discussion of what these meant the artist was able to produce a drawing of a woman that the anthropologist felt was probably a reasonable likeness to the deceased. This was published and, once again, brought in a large number of responses from people who said they recognised her. The main problem was that many of these suggestions turned out to be people who were still alive and well. There was only one that offered more definite evidence.

CHAPTER TWELVE

A FLOATER

AUGUST 1994

It was a fine morning with high fluffy white clouds and little in the way of wind. John Woodcote parked his car in the car park at Bentwood Down Reservoir. It was one of John's favourite fishing spots. Unlike some of the other reservoirs in the area it had not been developed for sailing, swimming or family outings. It lay in a valley where trees came down to very close or to the edge of the water. This provided greater privacy and gave the tranquil atmosphere something special. John collected his fishing gear from the boot and made his way round the side of the reservoir to a point where there was a group of trees that stood right on the edge of the water. It was one of John's preferred locations because he had found by experience that, in the deep pools created by the erosion of the bank which had been caused by the tree roots, you could find some unusually large fish. He put up his stool and umbrella and sorted out his rod and bait and before casting he studied the water to look for a suitable spot to try his luck.

It was then that he noticed it. At first, he thought it was just a piece of floating rubbish caused by some thoughtless individual throwing away something he should have put in one of the wastebins that were provided. Taking his landing net and stepping into the edge of the water he tried to haul the package ashore. It was bigger than he thought and much heavier. Whatever was in it had been tied in with rope. Getting a hold on the rope he pulled the package nearer. Suddenly a bit of the black sack gave way and, to his horror, John found himself looking at a human hand. Without waiting he turned on his heels and ran back to the car park and the site office which had just opened. He panted out to the man at the pay desk what he had seen and then had to wait while a phone call was made and the police were summoned.

When the police and ambulance arrived, he led them to the spot he had chosen to fish and pointed out the black package that was held tight against some tree roots by a thick rope. When it was pulled ashore and the packing opened, John had to beat a hasty retreat from the overpowering stench and to find somewhere the air was fresh and he could gulp it down into his lungs to prevent him throwing up. He stayed out of the way whilst the police photographed the package and its contents, a doctor had viewed the body and pronounced it to be a male who had been dead for some months at least. The decayed remains were then placed in a sack which was zipped up and placed on to a stretcher that was transferred to an ambulance on its way to the nearest mortuary.

John had to explain to the police how he had come to make his unfortunate discovery. Eventually he was allowed to pack up his fishing gear and go back to his car. He had no appetite for fishing that day and drove carefully home to tell his wife, but not his children, what had happened to him and to have a stiff whisky.

At the mortuary, the body was examined by the police surgeon who confirmed that the body was that of a Caucasian male aged under thirty. He estimated death had taken place at least four months earlier. The man had been in excellent health. However, his death had not been caused by drowning as there was no water in the lungs. Tests brought to light no signs of drugs or alcohol. The difficulty that the pathologist faced was in trying to determine how he had died. First there was the natural deterioration over the period since the likely date of death, then there was the damage that it had suffered during its immersion in the water. As there was no water in the lungs, he must have been dead when placed in the water. He could hardly have bound himself into the plastic sacks so must have been a victim of foul play. It was only after very careful and detailed examination that he decided that an injury to the head was not the result of a natural event but rather that the young man had been hit very hard by a metal object right behind the left ear. His verdict was one of homicide.

Apart from the question as to who he was and who had killed him the police were faced by the question as to why the body had been hidden in a couple of black sacks, tied to a tree root and weighted down. It was only when the water rotted through one of the ropes that the body had floated. It was felt that best chance of identifying it was by checking up on all missing persons from an area across northern Yorkshire and Durham County.

One thing the pathologist who carried out the post mortem noted was that the deceased had received some sophisticated dental treatment. He suggested that enquiries be made to try and get a more specialised analysis of this treatment. The x-rays taken of the teeth were forwarded to a professor of dentistry at Liverpool University. As he was considering the x-rays, he was introduced to a visiting professor in odontology from a university in New York State. He joined in looking at the x-rays and immediately said that he recognised the work that had been done as that of American origin. This meant either that the body was American or someone who had consulted an American dentist, possibly in Britain. Enquiries of American dentists practicing in Britain brought no results. That led to the enquiries being directed towards reports of missing American citizens who had been living in Britain at the time of their disappearance. This line of enquiry had not produced any useful leads and days had drifted into weeks and then into months. The case was rapidly heading towards being classified as unsolved when the police in

Durham received a phone call. It was now late October.

In his contacts with the Grimhausens, Gilbert Ravendale had sought to try and find out as much as he could about the young man as reflected by his life in the United States. For this reason, he obtained his medical and dental records. As part of his search, he had contacted all the police forces where there had been an unidentified body reported. Most of these were either female or were much older than Tod. There were only three which were young males of the right age but the information available did not offer any proof as to identity. When he received the medical and dental records, he contacted those three areas again and offered them the chance to study these records to see if they helped in identifying the body. Thus, it was that he rang the police in Durham and offered these records. His offer was pounced upon eagerly because of the potential American dental treatment that had been revealed. After an anxious wait of ten days Gilbert had a phone call from the police.

'Thanks to those records you sent to us Mr Ravendale we have been able to make a formal identification. The body that was found in a reservoir was that of Patrick Tod Grimhausen. Will you inform the next of kin or do you wish us to do so? I should mention that the deceased was dead when he was put in the water. He had been killed by a blow behind the ear.'

'I will inform them. However, there is something that you need to know. Patrick Tod Grimhausen was killed in a hit and run road accident in Cornwall earlier this year. His death was subject to a Coroner's inquest and the body was released for cremation. I am looking at a copy of the death certificate as I speak.'

'But that is impossible. You can't have two identifications for the same individual and our forensic dental specialist is in no doubt that the body found here is that of Mr Grimhausen.'

'There is something else that I think you ought to know. There is a similar case in Yorkshire where a young woman died in a fall which was recorded as an accidental death at the inquest. Her body was also cremated. Sometime later a skeleton was found in a rock sinkhole in the limestone hills. That has been formally identified as being the same person who died in the fall. Not only that but she was murdered. I can provide you with her details and the name of her next of kin'

CHAPTER THIRTEEN

WHOSE BODY IS IT?

OCTOBER 1994

Among the newspapers delivered each morning was the Northern Reporter. As Peter Lewis picked up the papers and laid them out for people to collect, he noticed on the front page a drawing of a woman. He paid no particular attention to it other than thinking that it was vague enough to be any of thousands of people. In fact, he had a vague feeling that he had seen someone like that somewhere at some time but he had no idea as to whom or when or where. It wasn't until some hours later that he had a sudden insight as to where he had seen someone who resembled the picture. When he had finished the tasks he had been doing he went into his private lounge and opened up his desk. There, looking straight at him, was a face that seemed very much like the picture in the paper. He hurried out to find if the paper was still where he had left it but it had gone. It wasn't until the lunchtime local news came on to the tv screen that he saw the drawing a second time and was able to compare it with the photo he had found in his desk.

'It can't be!' he exclaimed. 'It's just a coincidence. It's certainly an eerie one but still a coincidence.'

The thought returned to him several times during the afternoon and he turned on his computer and found the site for the newspaper. He stared at the drawing and the more he did so the more he saw a likeness to Bethany Mercier. There was only one thing to do and that was to get Louise Mercier to see it. He picked up the phone and dialled her number.

'Louise Mercier here.'

'Louise, its Peter Lewis. How are things?'

'They are OK thank you.'

'Louise something rather odd has happened at this end. Can you go on to your computer and find the site for the Northern Reporter. It's a regional paper. Go on to the site and look at today's front page. I will ring you again in fifteen minutes. Alright?"

'It all sounds very mysterious.'

'Just what I thought. I'll speak to you again shortly.'

A quarter of an hour later he telephoned again.

'Louise, have you been able to find that page?'

'Yes, it's right in front of me now.'

'What do you make of the drawing there?'

'It gave me quite a shock when I first saw it. I could have sworn it was a drawing of Bethany, but it can't be. She's dead, just like this woman, and I have a death certificate for her. It must be a coincidence. I suppose all of us can look like someone else and it is only an artist's impression.'

'I agree, but if someone who had met Bethany sees it but doesn't know she is dead they could tell the police it is her and quite innocently send them off on a wild goose chase. Look, if you will allow me, I will take the photo you sent me to the police and explain the situation. That way we can save them from being misled.'

'Yes, that does seem like the best idea. You'll let me know what they say?'

'Of course. I will ring you tomorrow evening.'

After a few minutes' general conversation, they rung off. The next morning Peter Lewis drove into Barnard Castle and called at the police station. He explained that he was calling about the drawing in the previous day's Northern Reporter and was shown into an interview room where he was joined by a man who introduced himself as a detective sergeant. He explained briefly the reason for his call and put before the police officer both the newspaper and the photograph.

'Excuse me a minute sir while I see if Inspector Northcott is available.'

The Inspector was available and listened to what Peter had to say.

'The main problem is that the drawing really does look like Bethany Mercier yet I don't see how that is possible as we have been told she is dead. In fact, her sister has been given a copy of her death certificate.'

'When and where did Bethany Mercier die?'

'It must have been about seven months ago. She was living at a place called The End of The Rainbow just outside Netherton. It was said she fell while taking photographs from the top floor of an old mill. No-one apparently knew of any relatives and, after the inquest, she was cremated and her ashes scattered. My friend, her sister, knew nothing about it until four months later when she received a letter from a firm of solicitors in Richmond.'

'What I don't quite follow Mr Lewis is your own involvement in this matter.'

'I had better explain. Bethany Mercier's half-sister, Louise, was my secretary for fifteen years when I worked in the City. After I was retired on health grounds I moved to this area where I run a guest house with associated cottages. Louise Mercier is nearly twenty years older than Bethany, who was apparently something of a rolling stone with no fixed address. When she reached twenty-five, she was due to inherit a large sum of money from a trust fund administered by her sister. When Louise tried to contact her just before her twenty-fifth birthday, she got no response. The last she knew, or thought she knew, was that Bethany and an American friend were planning to visit something called The End of The Rainbow at Netherton. Letters to that address got no response and when she telephoned, they denied all knowledge of Bethany. Louise asked if I could make local enquiries but I fared no better. They declined to tell me, a non-relative, anything. It was not until some four months after Bethany had died at that Community that Louise was told of her death. The lawyers who had been instructed said that the Community did not know that she had any relatives. She had said nothing about her half-sister. The main problem for Louise is that she feels the drawing is an exact picture of her sister and that other people who knew her may contact you without knowing that she is dead which could cause you a lot of wasted work.'

'Thank you, Mr Lewis, that is very helpful. As you say it could assist in avoiding unnecessary enquiries if someone does come along claiming that it is Bethany Mercier.' I wonder if we could take a copy of that photograph as it might be useful if someone does come forward claiming it is that young lady.'

After Peter Lewis had gone Inspector Northcott said to his sergeant, 'Send that photo across to the Crime Lab and ask them what they make of likeness between it and the skeleton. Also, get in touch with Richmond and ask them if they knew that the deceased's half-sister had been told of her death some four months after the event.

At the regional crime laboratory, the Assistant Director looked at the photograph of Bethany Mercier and called for the file on the case. Having read it through together with the note from Barnard Castle police he went to find one of his staff who specialised on skeleton identification.

'Roger,' he said to Dr Roger Marlborough, who was a palaeontologist, 'Are you familiar with the case of the young woman's skeleton found down a sinkhole on the dales?'

'Not beyond the fact that it has not proved possible to establish an identity.'

'Read this file and look at this photograph and the artist's impression of the woman, then let me know whether or not the two are related.'

Roger Marlborough returned to his desk and started by reading the file then he examined the photograph under a powerful lens. Having done that, he transferred a copy of the photo into a computer program and brought up a picture of the skull of the woman found down the sinkhole. He spent several hours studying both of these pictures before returning to the Assistant Director's office.

'Excuse me sir but I wonder if you could come and look at this.'

He led the way back to his desk and the computer screen on which was an image of the skull. Then he brought up a copy of the photograph and laid them side by side. Next, he slid the two together so that photo covered the face of the skull.

'As you can see sir,' he said, the eye sockets, the nose and the mouth of the photo fit exactly over the skull. It's as perfect a match as I have ever seen. To my mind this skull belonged to the woman in the photo.'

'Let me see' said the Assistant Director easing Marlborough from his seat and taking his place and looking at the two images separately and together. 'Well I'll be a monkey's uncle' he exclaimed' I do believe you're right. If so, someone is going to have to try and explain how the skull of a woman who was killed and thrown down a sinkhole matches a photo of one who is said to have died in an accidental fall and who was cremated. But before we go public, I want our analysis checked by an expert. Get in touch with Doctor Tracy Long at Durham University, who is reckoned to be an expert on skeleton reconstructions, and get her opinion. She was the person who extracted the body from the ground.'

At five o'clock the next afternoon Dr Marlborough returned to the Assistant Director's office.

'Excuse me sir but I have just heard from Dr Long. She is one hundred per cent certain that the skull belongs to the woman in the photograph.'

'Well, that's put the cat among the pigeons.' He reached for his phone and buzzed his secretary. 'Will you get me Inspector Seagrove in Richmond please.'

CHAPTER FOURTEEN

WHAT HAPPENED TO BETHANY?

OCTOBER 1994

When Inspector Northcott received the detailed report from the Crime Laboratory, he did three things. Firstly, he contacted his colleagues at Richmond to get all the information they had available about the case of the young woman who fell to her death at The End of The Rainbow; secondly, he set about trying to find as much as he could about both Louise Mercier and Peter Lewis and, thirdly, he arranged for the mountain rescue team to return to the sinkhole where the skeleton had been found and to make a search with a metal detector to see if anything had fallen from the body as it decomposed.

A study of the first of these did not add very much to his knowledge. The case had seemed open and shut and the inquest had brought nothing to light. So, his next move was to undertake enquiries about The End of The Rainbow and whilst this proved to be an unusual organisation there was nothing that caused him to think that the death there was other than an unfortunate accident. Equally, his inquiries about Louise Mercier and Peter Lewis showed that they were exactly what they said they were. Louise had been a secretary all her working life, was unmarried and lived in the same house that she had been born in over forty years ago. Peter had been a highly successful businessman whose health had given way under the pressure of his lifestyle and he had moved north to run a small but profitable hospitality business. The search of the hole in which the body had been found produced a number of coins from a period of over two hundred years, evidence of people dropping or throwing them down the sinkhole. The only other item was a silver earring which might very well have fallen down the hole like the coins.

When he had gathered all this information, Northcott decided that the time had come to talk to Louise Mercier and Peter Lewis and to reveal to them what had been discovered about the skeleton. When he told Peter, that he wished to see him he added that he wished to see Louise as well. Peter said he would invite Louise to stay at his guest house so that they could attend the meeting together. He passed on this information during a telephone call.

'Why do they want to see us?' asked Louise. 'We have told them all we know.'

'I have no idea. It's possible, I suppose, that they have discovered something more about either Bethany's death at that Community or about the person in the sinkhole in the dales. Look, why don't you come up here, I can put you up at the guest house and we can go to the meeting together? It's only by doing that we are going to discover what is bothering the police.'

He didn't add that it might be that they wanted to see if they should eliminate either or both of them from their enquiries into these two deaths.

He arranged to meet her at Darlington Station. He recognised her at once as she came off the platform and advanced to greet her.

'Welcome to the north' he smiled and when she held out a hand, he shook it but, at the same time, leaned forward and kissed her lightly on the cheek, something he had never done when they worked together. It was a signal that their relationship had changed and was no longer that of secretary and boss.

'It's lovely to see you' Louise said. You are looking very well.'

'I am very well thanks and more than happy to be away from the grindstone of the City. I must say you don't look a day older.'

'But I am' she laughed. 'It's very kind of you Mr Lewis to allow me to stay at your Guest House.'

'It's my pleasure and it's Peter now not Mr Lewis.'

He drove her down the A1 and past Richmond out into Swaledale.

'Do you know this area?' he asked.

'No, I have never been here before.'

'I think you will find it an attractive part of the world.'

Louise certainly enjoyed the drive through the largely unspoiled countryside with its small villages and stone walled fields and its rolling landscape. Peter drove to the village which was closest to his new home where he turned off up a lane and into a short driveway and a courtyard.

'This is it' he said as he parked the car.

'But it's beautiful' Louise exclaimed.

'I'm glad you like it. It was originally built as a farmhouse and outbuildings in the eighteenth century. In fact, the same family went on farming here for about two hundred years. They gave up when the old man died and none of the children wanted to be farmers. It was then that it was converted into a high-class bed and breakfast and a number of holiday lets. I bought it from those original purchasers. '

'It's so different to what I imagined.'

'If you like the outside, I think you will enjoy the interior. Come on, let's get your suitcase and do the half-crown tour.'

He was right, Louise found the interior enchanting with its fine period furniture and decorations which were, if anything, enhanced by the modern benefits of electricity, central heating and plumbing. The room allocated to her was not only comfortable with a built-in bathroom but had lovely views from the window. When she returned to the lounge Peter explained that as well as bed and breakfast, he offered an evening meal to those who pre-booked it.

'You must have a big staff to help run a business such as this' she said.

'Not really, I have someone who comes in to prepare the breakfasts and someone to act as waitress, then there are two who act as chambermaids and deal with the bedrooms and two who come in at weekends to handle the changeover of the holiday lets, plus a handyman to deal with all the small jobs and keep the garden tidy.'

'What about the dinners?'

'Oh, I am the cook for those, nothing fancy or nouveau cuisine, just basic food. The breakfast waitress returns to handle the front of house. And there is one other woman who deals with the dishes etc.'

Very different from life in the City' smiled Louise.

'Very different and much more enjoyable.'

After an excellent evening meal of Chicken Provencal with Olives followed by a Tarte Tatin and cream they adjourned to Peter's sitting room to discuss what had brought Louise to the north.

'Before we get down to considering tomorrow's meeting with the police, I feel I should ask you how things are at Folkingham Investments?'

'I don't work there anymore.'

'Why did you leave?' Peter asked in a surprised voice.

'I didn't. After you had to retire the Americans brought in a man from New York to fill the job of CEO. He set about a thorough shake-up and your old job disappeared, so I was technically re-dundant. I was given six months gardening leave and a generous redundancy package.'

'I am sorry' Peter said 'I feel somehow to blame.'

'It wasn't your fault you were taken ill.'

'In a way it was. I should have had more sense than to think you can work one hundred hours a week without paying the price. I am sorry it caused you to lose a good job. What are doing now?'

'I am attached to an agency that has very good contacts with the literary and educational fields. I am virtually self-employed. I type up learned papers and lectures and book drafts, working largely from home. Actually, it's very interesting work. Now about tomorrow, do you know why the police want to see us?'

'They haven't said but they are faced with a case of someone dying some months ago and then finding that a body down a sinkhole could be her double. They are probably hoping that we can help them.'

'You don't think they suspect me of being involved in all this?'

'Good lord no. Why should they? They can have no evidence that suggests such a thing. All we can do is wait and see what they have to say and answer their questions. What we mustn't do is to try and answer questions they do not ask.'

The next morning, they arrived at the police station in Rich-mond promptly at ten thirty and were shown into an interview room. Inspector Seagrave as a tall man with fair hair and blue eyes and was wearing dark grey suit, a blue shirt and striped tie. Peter guessed he was in his forties.

'Thank you very much for coming in this morning' he said after the necessary introductions had been completed. 'Please sit down. We will be joined in a minute by an officer who will take notes of what we discuss.'

The officer proved to be WPC Noreen Abbott who had been one

78

of the first officers at the site of the fatal accident.

'The first thing I need to do is to thank you for the information that you gave to my colleague Inspector Northcott. This was of considerable assistance to him in identifying the body that was found up on the dales. I am afraid that what I have to say will not be good news for you Miss Mercier. Following detailed scientific examination and tests we are satisfied that the body was that of your half-sister Bethany.'

Hearing her gasp and seeing her shut her eyes Peter reached out and took hold of her hand.

'But how is that possible?' Louise said in a tight voice. 'You were satisfied that the young woman who died at Netherton was Bethany. Not only that but her Will was found where she had been living. The signature on the Will definitely was that of Bethany. I would know it anywhere.'

'At the moment I am afraid we don't have an answer to that question.'

'What do the people at that place in Netherton say?' asked Peter.

'They say they are fully satisfied that the person who died there was a person who gave the name of Bethany Mercier and their records confirm this.'

'Does that mean that the body from the Dales was not in fact Bethany?' Louise asked.

'I don't think so' replied the Inspector. 'Since we had the first identification, we have had a facial reconstruction carried using a computer image of the skull. Experts can take the skull and using scientific knowledge of the physiology involved can make a model of what the person looked like in life. I am going to show you a photograph of what they have produced. I appreciate that it may be a shock to you but can you tell us if this is a true likeness to your half-sister?'

He placed a photograph on the desk face down and slowly

turned it face up. Louise gave a sharp intake of breath and her face went white.

'it is Bethany' she gasped. 'The hair style is different so is the colour but it is her. Poor Bethany to end like that in some hole in the ground.'

'There is one other thing Miss Mercier. Do you, by any chance, recognise this' and he produced a silver earring.

'Why yes, 'gasped Louise 'it is one of a pair that I gave to Bethany for her twenty first birthday. Where did you get that?'

'It was down the same hole as the remains. I think that underlines that it was your sister who was there.'

Inspector Seagrove, noticing Louise's pale face and trembling hands looked at Peter silently asking if he thought she could take any more.

'I think Inspector that we need to know all that you know.'

'Very well' the Inspector spoke in measured tone. 'Certain information has not been released to the public. When the body was first discovered it was tied at the wrists and ankles. Not only that but I am afraid that the cause of death has been ruled as blunt force trauma, in other words, she was hit over the head. Your sister did not die in an unfortunate accident. I am sorry to have to tell you that she was killed and her body deposited where it was found. If it had not been for an unfortunate sheep that slipped and fell the chances of it being found were virtually nil.'

'But why?' cried Louise leaning back in her chair with closed eyes.' Why would anyone want to kill her, She was a harmless person who never did anyone any deliberate harm'

'That is what we are hoping you may be able to help us with Miss Mercier.'

Over the next hour and a half, the Inspector took both Louise and Peter through all the events starting with the arrival of

Bethany and her friend at Louise's house in London right up to Peter seeing the picture in the paper.

'Thank you very much' said Northcott. 'I appreciate your coming in and I am only sorry I had to give you such bad news.'

'The thing is we already thought that Bethany was dead. What we could never have imagined was that the person we mourned was not my sister' replied Louise, 'nor that the real Bethany had been murdered.'

'There is one other thing that I think you ought to tell the Inspector, Louise' said Peter. 'Tell him about Tod Grimhausen'

Louise then told Northcott how she had been approached by a private investigator trying to locate the young American who she had last seen when her sister had left her house in London. She then went on to recount how he had been killed in a road accident in Cornwall and how his Will had turned up later. Not only that but he had been working at The Rainbow Craft Centre when he was killed and he had left his estate to the same beneficiary as Bethany. She gave Northcott details of Gilbert Ravendale's address and phone number.

'I think I had better contact my colleague in Cornwall.' he said.

PART TWO

THE PROBLEM

IS RESOLVED

CHAPTER FIFTEEN

AN INVESTIGATION IS OPENED

DECEMBER 1994

Following the receipt of a statement made by Gilbert Ravendale at a London police station the facts were reported to the Chief Constable of County Durham Police who, in his turn, contacted his colleagues in the Devon and Cornwall and North Yorkshire forces. He outlined the situation regarding the body found in his area and how it appeared to have the same name as a hit and run victim in Cornwall. When his Yorkshire colleague asked how that affected his area, he drew attention to the similarity with the case of Bethany Mercier.

'The link between these cases seems to be that yours in the north involves something called The End of The Rainbow and yours in the south west a place called The Rainbow Craft Centre. Not only that but both these young people left their estates to the same beneficiary.'

'Was there much involved?' asked Roderick Johnson of Devon and Cornwall.

'Our young woman had just inherited over three hundred thousand' replied David Newton of North Yorkshire.

'The young American had a trust fund approaching half a million dollars' said Oliver Treaton of Durham. 'The question is, gentlemen, do we investigate separately or do you think it better there is one, unified, investigation?'

'Tell me', said Roderick Johnson 'did these young people know each other or were they strangers?'

'They certainly knew each other' replied David Newton,' in fact the last time they were seen alive by anyone who really knew them, was at the home of the girl's half-sister.'

'My feeling is that there should be a single investigation. If we have three forces involved the costs are going to be much higher and, as we all know only too well, we are under continual pressure over costs. I suggest that we do what our forces do to us. Pass the buck up the line and earn some brownie points for being cost conscious.' said Roderick Johnson.

'I agree' said David Newton.

'So, do I, added Oliver Treaton.

It was Oliver Treaton who, by agreement, drafted the report to the Home Office asking that the cases of Bethany Mercier and Tod Grimhausen be assigned to a single police authority in order to save duplication of effort and the allied increase in costs. Thus, it was that Assistant Commissioner Gordon Barnwell of the Metropolitan Police called Commander Richard Buxton to a meeting in the early afternoon.

'Have a read of this' he said pushing a file across the desk.

While Richard Buxton was reading the file, the Assistant Commissioner carried on with working on some papers that lay on his desk. When he saw that the Commander had finished reading, he pushed aside his papers and removed his glasses.

'What do you make of that Richard?' he asked.

'Interesting. There are two cases of accidental death, one in Yorkshire and one in Cornwall, confirmed by inquest and the remains cremated. Sometime later documents purporting to be the Will of the deceased come to light. Nothing particularly untoward in that. However, quite some time after these people die in an accident two bodies are found. In the first case it is down a rock sinkhole in Yorkshire and in the second the body is washed up in a reservoir. Forensic investigation brings to light that these bodies are in fact those of the two young people it is claimed died in those accidents. Not only that but the deaths of the two who were discovered have been recorded as homicides. In the cases of the accidents, one happened at a sort of community called The End of The Rainbow and in the other the victim worked at a place called The Rainbow Craft Centre. Their Wills, and they both had sizeable estates, bequeathed their assets to the same Luxembourg foundation. Not only that but it seems the two young people knew each other. As I said it is an interesting story sir.'

'And one that has just fallen into your lap Richard. The three Chief Constables involved have asked the Home Office to appoint a single authority to handle any investigations. The Home Office, in its wisdom, has chosen the Met and I have chosen you.'

'Then I had better get on with it, sir'

'Who do you want to work with you?'

'I think my preferred choice is Chief Inspector Thomasson. We have worked together before when we were both attached to the Sussex Police.'

'Right, I will see that he is released from anything he is working on at the moment. I shall be interested to see how this all works out. Meanwhile you had better clear your desk. Baddeley can take on your current work.'

It was the following morning that Richard Buxton and Robert Thomasson had their first meeting to consider the case of the two murders.

'You are probably wondering what all this is about Robert' Buxton greeted his colleague.

'It had crossed my mind to wonder, sir'

'Briefly, the Home Office has decided that the Met should investigate two murders, one in North Yorkshire and one in either Cornwall or County Durham, it is not entirely clear at the moment where the victim actually died. The case has landed in my lap and I have asked for your help. Read this file while I pop along the corridor to have a word with Commander Baddeley.'

'Well, what do you make of it?' Buxton asked when he returned.

'It's certainly not a run of the mill enquiry sir. Two people meet an accidental death. They are both cremated and their ashes scattered. Then Wills turn up made by the deceased in which they leave their entire estate to the same foundation in Luxembourg. Not only that but first a body is found in Yorkshire down a rock sinkhole. I said a body but it's a skeleton. Following a series of somewhat odd events it's identified as a woman who is supposed to have died months before in a fatal fall. Then a body is washed up in County Durham and, again as a result of some rather odd events it is identified as that of a young man killed in a road accident in Cornwall. The question is how can you have two bodies scientifically identified as known people when those self-same people died deaths ruled as accidents by a coroner's inquest whereupon the remains, in both cases, are cremated. Do we know how much was left to this foundation in Luxembourg?'

'I gather it's about six hundred thousand in total.'

'You can imagine someone thinking that worth killing for sir.'

'The first thing we are going to have to decide is how we are going to approach this investigation. I think we will start in the centre and work out. There are two important people who are based in London, the half-sister of the woman and the private investigator employed by the man's family in the United States. Let's see what they can tell us. At the same time, I want you to see what you can find out about this Arcus Foundation. I am going to contact the various police forces that have been involved and get them to copy all their appropriate files to us here. This will let us review them and see if anything new comes to light. It will also allow us to plan the next stage of the investigation.'

CHAPTER SIXTEEN

BUXTON AND THOMASSON MEET RAVENDALE

DECEMBER 1994

Thomasson had arranged for Buxton and himself to meet with Gilbert Ravendale at the latter's office. Capital Enquiries was situated on the top two floors of a glass tower in Thames Street and the room that they were shown into had a bird's eye view of the river. Obviously, a meeting room it was furnished with high class modern furniture and the tastefully decorated walls had a number of impressionist prints in chromium frames. The two visitors were standing by the window taking in the view when they were joined by Gilbert Ravendale.

'Commander Buxton, Chief Inspector Thomasson' he extended a hand to his visitors 'welcome to Capital Enquiries.'

'Pleased to meet you Mr Ravendale' said Buxton. 'I appreciate your sparing the time to see us.'

'Not at all Commander. I assume this is about the Grimhausen affair?'

'It is indeed. I had better explain that the Home Office has decided that the cases regarding both Bethany Mercier and Tod Grimhausen should be handled by a single police authority and they have asked the Metropolitan Police to do that.'

'I must admit that I did wonder how Scotland Yard had become involved. Make yourselves comfortable gentlemen' and he pointed to the chairs that surrounded a pine-coloured table.

'To begin at the beginning Mr Ravendale perhaps you could tell us how your firm came to be involved?'

'We were approached by a firm of lawyers in New York for whom we have acted on previous occasions. They had been instructed by a Mr and Mrs Grimhausen, who were longstanding clients of theirs. It transpired that the Grimhausen family control a long established firm of investment and financial advisers based just off Wall Street. The Grimhausens, particularly Mrs Grimhausen, had become concerned because they had not heard from their only son for some months. The last they had heard of him he had been in London. They went on to explain that the son, called Patrick Tod, was a young man who had declined to enter the family business. Instead, he had decided to see the world, had taken himself off and was living the life of a nomad. As his father pointed out they always heard from him every month or two, if only to ask for his bank account to be fed. It seems that his grandmother, that is his mother's mother, was a wealthy lady in her own right and left Tod some half million dollars with the caveat that the capital was not to be paid to him till he was twenty five. In the meantime, he had use of the income generated by the fund.'

'Sorry to interrupt you Mr Ravendale ' said Thomasson ' but, as you will understand, we are generally familiar with firms of private investigators who operate in London but I have to confess Capital Enquiries is not a name that was familiar to us.'

'I am delighted to hear you say so Chief Inspector' Ravendale smiled. 'You see this firm does not undertake criminal cases. Therefore, I should have been somewhat concerned if we had come to the notice of Scotland Yard. We deal exclusively with commercial and personal enquiries many of which involve probate matters. Let me hasten to add that we are not involved in divorce cases. You could call us a private firm of private investigators. Discretion is our watchword.'

'Thank you for clarifying that Mr Ravendale' said Buxton. 'You mentioned that Tod Grimhausen was what you called a nomad. Do I understand that he tended to move from one country or even one continent to another?'

'I gather he has been known to visit Asia, Australasia and Africa as well as Europe. However, the latest information his parents had was that he was in England.'

'Yet, I suppose he could have left here and gone virtually any-where?'

'That is possible. However, an approach to his bankers by his parents did not give any indication that he had left this country. What puzzled them was how he was managing to live without his usual requests for money.'

'He might have obtained employment I suppose' pondered Thomasson.

'That is very true but again there was no evidence to support such a contention. I gathered that the young man showed a dis-tinct disinclination to work for his living.'

'Without giving away any trade secrets' said Buxton with a grin 'how did you go abbot tracking Tod?'

'The family gave me one piece of information. It was a London telephone number. I traced that to a Louise Mercier. She told me that Tod, together with her half-sister, had stayed at her house. As was usual for her sister she arrived unannounced and, after about a month, they both left without saying where they were going. Since when she had heard nothing of either of them.'

'Was that all she could tell you?' asked Thomasson.

'She did say that the couple had visited an artistic community in Yorkshire but she could not recall its name. All she had was a vague idea that it was connected with the old film The Wizard of Oz. The most famous thing about that film is a song called 'Over the Rainbow'. After a great deal of fruitless searching, I came across somewhere called The End of The Rainbow.'

'Did you contact them?'

'I did more than that. I went up to a place called Netherton and visited them.'

'Did you learn anything useful there Mr Ravendale?'

'I did not. They refused to answer any of my questions about a Tod Grimhausen.'

'Why was that?'

'They told me they were a closed community and that those who joined it gave up their previous identities and all contacts with family or friends. They even took a new name. They were prohibited, under the rules of the community, from contacting people they were related to or knew. Equally, the community undertook not to divulge information about them to any outsider. To all my questions they simply repeated those rules. As I was neither family nor friend I was completely off their list. I was politely shown the door.'

'May I ask what else you did to try and trace this young man?'

'I used all my usual lines of enquiry and I put up photos at all the ports and airports but they all came up blank. I could only imagine that Tod was in that commune in Yorkshire or had left the country unobserved. That was the state of play until I had a call from Miss Mercier to tell me that her half- sister had met with a fatal fall at the community in Yorkshire. There was no mention of Tod Grimhausen which was odd as they seemed to be pretty close when they were in London.'

'Did she tell you how she had learned about the accident?' asked Buxton.

'She said that they had found a Will naming her as executor but it had not come to life for some time after the accident. As a result, Bethany had been cremated and her ashes scattered.'

'Did that seem odd to you Mr Ravendale?' asked Thomasson.

'Yes and no; in the context of normal deaths then it was strange it took so long to find a Will, but in the context of that community nothing would surprise me.'

'I presume you had virtually given up on finding Tod Grimhausen by this stage' said Buxton.

'That's right. I couldn't go on incurring costs for our clients with no prospect of success. It had become what you would call a cold case. It remained that way until I had a further call from Mr Grimhausen in New York. They had heard from an English lawyer that Tod had died in a road accident in Cornwall some time ago. He had been living and working at a place called The Rainbow Craft Centre near Land's End.'

'What was your reaction to that news?'

'I assumed that Tod had split from the Mercier girl and gone to Cornwall. I went down there but got no change out of the people at the craft centre other than the fact that Tod had worked there. I was not allowed to talk to any of his colleagues. It was against their rules they said. I asked specifically to speak to the person he worked with most closely but was told that he had left the centre three days after Tod's accident and they had no idea where he was.'

'Did you give up your search at that point Mr Ravendale?' asked Thomasson.

'No, I didn't exactly give up because I was appointed attorney by his father to act in all matters relating to Tod's estate in this country. The next thing was that Miss Mercier told me of the discovery of a skeleton in Yorkshire that had been identified as her half- sister. Not only that but that she had been murdered. I began to wonder if the same ting had happened to Tod so I started making enquiries about unidentified bodies found during the past months. I was able to eliminate most of these very easily they were either the wrong age or wrong sex. There were just three or four that might be possibilities but how was I to be certain. That was when I asked the Grimhausen's for details of Tod's medical and dental records. I offered these to the police in the areas where there was a possible body. The authorities in County Durham took me up on the offer and were able to confirm that the body they had, which had been tied in a parcel in a reservoir was that of Tod Grimhausen. He had been killed by a blow to the head. Now we had two cases of people who were said to have died in accidents but whose actual remains turned up months later. Then I received your phone call Commander.'

'I must congratulate you Mr Ravendale, said Buxton 'on the persistence and thoroughness of your investigations. Without you I doubt very much if anyone would have connected a washed up body in County Durham with a young man supposed to have died in Cornwall. May I ask what you make of all this?'

'That, if I may say so Commander, is where your expertise comes in. As I said we do not handle criminal cases and I am not qualified to make a judgement' laughed Ravendale.

'I can't think that you have not formed some opinion.'

'I suppose the obvious question is qui bono. It seems both these young people had funds to leave. Whilst I can imagine that the body found in the Yorkshire Dales might have some connection with that place in Netherton I can't see how Tod Grimhausen turned up in County Durham. I didn't try to find out if these Rainbow people have any of their communities there.'

'Thank you, Mr Ravendale that's very interesting.'

CHAPTER SEVENTEEN

WHAT DOES LOUISE HAVE TO SAY?

DECEMBER 1994

Louise Mercier was surprised when her doorbell rang at nine thirty one morning. Keeping the security chain in place she opened the door.

'Good morning Miss Mercier' said the elder of the men.

'Who are you and what do you want?' she asked, keeping the door on a chain.

'My name is Commander Richard Buxton and this is Chief Inspector Robert Thomasson. We are officers in the Metropolitan Police. We should like to speak to you if it's convenient.'

'Can I see your identification please?'

'Of course.'

The two men held out cards from which Louise could see that they were who they claimed to be. She undid the chain and opened the door wide.

'Please do come in. I am sorry if I was less than welcoming but you have to be careful these days especially when you live alone.'

'That is quite understandable Miss Mercier and, if I might say so, very sensible.'

Once they were in the hallway the elder one held out his hand.

'Commander Richard Buxton' he said with a smile.

'Chief Inspector Robert Thomasson' said the other holding out his hand.

Louise led them into a pleasantly decorated and furnished lounge with French windows leading on to a neat garden.

'I had better explain the reason for this visit' Richard Buxton said when they were all seated. 'In view of the fact that there appear to be possible connections between the deaths of Miss Bethany Mercier and Mr Patrick Grimhausen the decision has been taken to centralise investigations in the hands of the Metropolitan Police and I have been tasked with leading the enquiry. We have come to see you to listen to what you are able to tell us about the circumstances surrounding these two deaths and to hopefully clarify certain points for us.'

'I'll do all I can to help you but I have already told the police in Yorkshire all I know.'

'I am sure you have but you know Miss Mercier it is surprising how often some salient fact can emerge from a retelling of a story.'

'Where do you want me to start?'

'The very beginning is usually the best place.'

So, Louise outlined for them the story of her family, of her father's two marriages and his two daughters born some twenty years apart. She explained the close relationship she had had with her step mother and her affection for her much younger half-sister. They got along well enough, she said, given that Louise was an adult before Bethany was born. She explained how her father had arranged his financial affairs in his Will and how she had been appointed as a trustee of the fund to be paid to Bethany on her twenty fifth birthday. Everything had been going well until Bethany went to university where she seemed to get in with the wrong sort of people with the result that she left without taking her degree and started to live a nomadic life.

After that the only contact that she had with her half-sister was when she turned up at this house wanting to refresh her wardrobe, visit a hairdresser and have some of the income that had built up in the trust fund.

'Did your half-sister stay in this country or did she go overseas?' asked Thomasson.

'She did go abroad. Her first port of call was a kibbutz in Israel, then she went to Nepal and later to various European countries.'

'Tell us about Bethany's last visit here' said Buxton.

Louise explained how she had come home one evening in March of the previous year to find Bethany and Tod Grimhausen sitting in the garden. They had stayed for about a month and then had disappeared as suddenly as they had arrived.

'Didn't they tell you where they were going?' asked Thomasson.

'Not a word of explanation which was not unusual as far as Bethany was concerned. She appeared out of the blue and disappeared back into it when she saw fit. All I knew was that they had, before they arrived, spent some time at an archaeological dig on the Orkney Islands and at a craft centre in Yorkshire. I had told Bethany to make sure that she let me know where she was by the time of her twenty-fifth birthday. When that date came and passed, I began to get a bit worried. By cudgelling my brains, I recalled Bethany mentioning some place called The End of The Rainbow. That was when I asked Mr Lewis if he could help me find her.'

'Why Mr Lewis?' Buxton asked.

Louise explained how she had been secretary to Peter Lewis for over fifteen years. She added that he was a man determined to get to the top and had worked inordinately long hours without taking real holidays. He had, she said, one idea in mind, namely to get to the very top of the group of companies for whom they worked. This he had achieved in April of the previous year when he was appointed CEO but, no sooner had he reached his target than he was taken ill. He had suffered a stroke in the office and was off work for three months. When he returned he was retired on health grounds. The next she had heard of him was that, much to her surprise, he had bought an up-market bed and breakfast and holiday let property in North Yorkshire and moved there. When she was trying to find Bethany and getting no response to her letters or phone calls, she had written to him asking if he knew of The End of The Rainbow. He had very kindly agreed to visit the place to see if he could find her. He had not been able to do so as the people at the community refused to answer any questions. The next thing that happened was that she received a letter saying Bethany was dead, that she had died in a fatal fall some months previously and been cremated. They said they only knew about her when they found Bethany's Will naming her as executrix.'

'Did you know she had made a Will, Miss Mercier?' asked Buxton.

'No. We never discussed the subject.'

'Did you go to Yorkshire to try and find out what had happened?' asked Thomasson.

'No, I discussed the position with Mr Lewis and he suggested I appoint a solicitor to act for me.'

'Why did you go to Mr Lewis for advice?'

'He knew about Bethany and was the only person I could think of to help me.'

'Did he know Bethany?' asked Buxton.

'No, he had never heard of her until I asked for his help'

'I am not clear why you turned to Mr Lewis for help' said Thomasson. 'Was he a close friend as well as your boss?'

'No. As I say I was his secretary. It's true to say that he did not show the least interest in me personally or my family all the time I worked for him. He was a driven man to whom work came first and last. It was well known he had no family, he was divorced, and no close friends'

'Yet you turned to him for help?'

'I had no-one else I could turn to. I too have no close family nor friends. I have worked hard all my life and have led a quiet and private life.'

'Did you expect to be a beneficiary under Bethany's Will? After all you were her only relative.'

'I never gave the matter any thought. To my mind it was her money to do with as she pleased.'

'What was your reaction to your father leaving the greater part of his estate to your half- sister?' asked Thomasson.

'My father was a very moral man. He had inherited that money from my step mother. I had no moral claim to it. He left me all his own property.'

'Go on with your story please.'

Louise told how she had heard from Peter Lewis about a picture he had seen in a northern newspaper. She looked at it on the internet and was immediately struck by the likeness to Bethany. After discussing it with Peter Lewis it was agreed he would take the photo of Bethany that she had given him to the police to tell them she was dead in case other people had the same thought and it led to the police being sent on a false trail.

'Did the paper say why the picture was published?' asked Thomasson.

'Yes, they said it was an impression of someone whose body had been found in the Dales.'

'Was the likeness that close?' asked Buxton. 'After all it is not unusual for any of us to have other people who look like us.'

'It was almost uncanny' Louise replied. 'The police took the photo and the next thing I knew was that they asked me to go to

Yorkshire to discuss matters. It was then I was shown a picture of a reconstruction of the head of the person they had found. There was no doubt that it was Bethany added to which they had found a piece of jewellery that I recognised as belonging to Bethany. It was then they told me she had been murdered.'

'What was your reaction to that news Miss Mercier?' asked Buxton.

'I was shocked. How could this be Bethany when she had reportedly died in a fall months before? She may have been a virtual nomad but she was a nice and friendly young woman. Who could possibly want to kill her?'

'Did you contact the people at Netherton for an explanation?'

'No, it was for the police to find the answer to that question. I assume that is why you are here.'

'I believe you know a private enquiry agent call Gilbert Ravendale, Miss Mercier?'

'Yes, he approached me for information about Tod Grimhausen who was with Bethany when she was here the last time. It seemed that Tod's family had lost contact with him in the same way I had lost contact with Bethany. I told him what I knew which was not a great deal. I might add that before I spoke to him, I made some enquiries about the firm he said he worked for. I had never come across private detectives outside fiction. His firm seemed respectable so I agreed to meet him on neutral ground.'

'He's not your average Sam Spade is he' laughed Buxton.

'When I learned that Bethany was dead, I contacted him to tell him. He said he had been to Yorkshire but got nowhere. The next time I heard from him he told me that Tod was dead and that he had died in road accident in Cornwall. It all sounded a bit familiar. Then he contacted me to tell me about the body found in County Durham and how it had been identified as Tod by its dental records.'

'What was your reaction to that news?'

'I was at a complete loss. How could a supposed Bethany die in Yorkshire and a supposed Tod in Cornwall. When they were here, they were a couple. Why were they so far apart? Then the discoveries of their bodies seemed to be more luck than judgement. Added to which they had left considerable money to the same Foundation in Luxembourg.'

'All very valid questions Miss Mercier' agreed Buxton 'and ones we must try and answer.'

'What do you make of her Robert?' Buxton asked when they were on their way back to Scotland Yard.

'She seems an intelligent woman and, as far as I could see and hear, I think she answered our questions honestly.'

'I agree. However, here is a further thought. If it was found that Bethany Mercier's Will was invalid who would benefit from her estate of over three hundred thousand pounds given that she had only one close relative?'

'Louise Mercier?'

'Exactly, an interesting thought isn't it? I think we have done all we can for the moment here in London and it's time to go to where the crimes occurred. I will go north and I would like you to go south west

CHAPTER EIGHTEEN

AN INTERVIEW WITH PETER LEWIS

DECEMBER 1994

Having driven north Buxton had called at the police station in Barnard Castle and made himself known to Inspector Northcott. Here he heard at first hand the story of the discovery of Bethany Mercier's body and its subsequent identification from the skeleton. He heard also of the part played by Peter Lewis and asked the Inspector for his opinion of that gentleman.

'Outwardly he is very pleasant man and, I should guess, a very astute business man. That place he has bought must be one of the best in the whole area. Certainly, he is no-one's fool and what he has told us appears to make good sense. If he had not come to us in the first place I doubt if we would ever have identified the body.'

'Didn't you find it somewhat odd that he should be acting for a woman who lives down in London?'

'On the face of it I agree it seems out of the ordinary but the explanation he gave us stacks up.'

Buxton drove himself over to Peter Lewis's business address and found that it was a most delightful Georgian farmhouse set in an attractive location. Once admitted to the property he was struck by the style and quality of the furnishings. This was indeed a very up market bed and breakfast.

'Thank you for finding the time to see me Mr Lewis' Buxton said as he made himself comfortable in the small but well organised office that Peter Lewis showed him into. He had asked North-cott to accompany him so as to provide some sort of continuity.

'For my part I am pleased to learn that the police are centralising their investigations.' Lewis said. 'How can I help you?'

'It would be helpful' said Buxton 'if you could tell us in your own words how you came to be involved in this mystery.'

'I have become involved as you put it simply because Louise Mercier was my secretary for fifteen years.'

'Could you give us some information as to your background Mr Lewis?'

'I can't quite see how that will help you but if that is what you want. For twenty five years I worked for the Folkingham Group of investment and financial services companies. It's no secret that I had one objective in my life which was to get to the top of the tree. I was so determined that I would do anything that it required. I hadn't the usual entrée into senior management. I had not been to the right school or the right university, nor did I play golf nor was I a member of the right club. There was only one road open to me and that was hard work. I did exactly that, I worked about one hundred hours a week and took no real holidays. I was so dedicated that it cost me my marriage and my children but that was a price I willingly paid. Eventually, I achieved my goal and was named CEO. What I didn't realise was that there was a price to pay. My body decided that enough was enough and I had a stroke. I was forced to take three months off work and when I returned, I found that the American parent group which controlled the UK group had decided to retire me on the grounds of ill health. The consultant had told me that if I went back to me former way of life, he would give me just five years before I succeeded in killing myself. To cut the story short I decided that I had lost the taste for corporate life. While I was taking my enforced holiday, I visited this part of the world and actually stayed here. The result was I quit London and life in the

City and moved here to a completely new and, I thought, less stressful, life. That is how I was on the spot when Louise Mercier asked for my help.'

'I presume that you kept in touch with Miss Mercier after you left London.'

'No, I did not. Although she had worked for me for all those years, I neither knew nor cared about her personal life. She was a very good secretary who was willing to work long hours and accept all the burdens I placed on her. Heaven alone knows why she put up with me for all those years. I am not even certain how she managed to find my address in Yorkshire. Her letter seeking my help came out of the blue.'

'Yet you did agree to help?'

'Yes, it seemed the least I could do for her. Looking back, I could appreciate, for the first time, how hard she had worked for me and, quite frankly, what a rotten boss I had been'

'So, you decided to visit the place in Netherton?'

'Yes. I thought it was just a case of asking if she was there or not. Louise had sent me a photograph and I started to show it to various people who worked in the different parts of this Craft business. No-one admitted knowing her and before long a man, who appeared to be senior in the organisation, took me to an office and told me it was a closed community and they did not divulge information about their members past or present. I was then shown the door.'

'Tell me' said Buxton 'as a businessman yourself what did you make of this End of The Rainbow?'

'Actually, I was quite impressed by it. The first place I visited was the cafeteria and it served good coffee and quality refreshments. As I moved round from one department to another, I noticed how good was the organisation of the business. Not only that but the quality of the items offered for sale was higher than might be expected in a place like that. It certainly was not the usual tourist tat.'

'What was your reaction to their refusing to answer questions?'

"At first I was both surprised and annoyed. I couldn't see any harm in my asking if they knew or had known Bethany Mercier. On further reflection however I came to the conclusion that if a group of people wished to retain their anonymity that was their right.'

'I presume you thought that was an end of the matter?'

'I didn't see I could be of any further help. Then, I heard from Louise that she had received a lawyer's letter saying her sister was dead. She had died in a fatal fall at the community place. Not only that but she had been cremated because they had no knowledge of her next of kin.'

'What did you make of that Mr Lewis?'

'Naturally, I was sorry to hear what had happened. However, I was less than happy with the story about the Will remaining undiscovered for so long. Not only that but when Louise told me what had apparently been left to an unknown beneficiary, I became suspicious and said I thought she should consult a lawyer herself. It would show whoever was at the back of all this that Louise was not just some simple woman that they could pull the wool over her eyes.'

'Did you think the Will may be a forgery?'

'It wasn't that so much that, it was that the whole story was too glib. The only evidence that it was Bethany who had a fatal fall was the claim by the Community that it was her. There was no body that could prove that statement. It had been cremated.'

'What happened next?'

'Once again I thought that I had done all I could. It was then that I stumbled across a picture in the Northern Reporter. It was an artist's impression of someone whose body had been found in sinkhole up in the dales. I had the photo of Bethany that her half-sister had given me and I was struck by the likeness between it and what was in the newspaper. I contacted Louise and asked her to go to the Northern Reporter website and look at the drawing. She agreed with me that the likeness was uncanny. I offered to take the photo to the police and show them the likeness. I could tell them at the same time that Bethany Mercier was dead. If anyone came to them claiming that their picture was her, they could avoid some unnecessary investigations. After all we had no idea who else might see the drawing.'

'That's quite right' said Northcott. 'Mr Lewis did just as he said. After he had gone, I passed a copy of the photograph to the forensic laboratory for information. To my amazement the next thing I heard was that they had carried out some tests designed to compare a skull with a photograph and were satisfied that the skull did belong to Bethany Mercier.'

'It was then that Inspector Northcott asked to meet Louise and myself. I invited Louise to stay with me and we called at the police station. As the Inspector can confirm he showed us another picture. This time it was a physical reconstruction of the head from the skull. Louise said that she had no doubt that it was Bethany. Then the Inspector produced a piece of jewellery that had been found with the skeleton which Louise confirmed was the property of her half- sister. It was then he told us that the medical evidence indicated that Bethany had been killed and tied hand and foot before being dropped down that sinkhole. To say we were both flabbergasted is an understatement.'

'That is a correct summary of the position Commander' said Northcott.

'More than a bit unfortunate for you Mr Lewis to find that simply by offering to help trace Bethany Mercier you find yourself involved in a murder enquiry' Buxton said sympathetically. 'What do you make of it?'

'On the face of it there is a complete paradox. How can it be that a woman who was positively identified and who fell to her death from a third floor window and whose Will is found in a room she is said to have occupied, be the same person as a body of a murdered woman found down a hole in the hills. If it wasn't Bethany who fell to her death who was it and why did she call herself Bethany? Against that, how secure is the identification of the skeleton and how did it get put down that sinkhole? Then there is the problem of the young American where a similar set of circumstances appears to have occurred. One mystery is bad enough but two seems to be stretching credulity to breaking point.'

'Turning to Patrick Tod Grimhausen Mr Lewis' said Buxton 'what are you able to tell us about him?'

'Absolutely nothing. I had never heard of the young man until Louise told me that his people were searching for him.'

'Well thank you for your time Mr Lewis' said Buxton getting to his feet. 'If you see or hear anything that you think has a bearing on these cases or if anything unusual happens please let me know.'

'What do you make of our Mr Lewis, Inspector,' Buxton asked his colleague when they had returned to the police station.

'A man like that is nobody's fool, but I can't see any reason why he should have got himself mixed up in a double murder. He's more like a passer-by who is swept up in events that have nothing to do with him.'

At that point a police constable brought in some papers.

'These have come for Commander Buxton sir'

'Excuse me Inspector' said Buxton as he started to read them.

'These are reports I asked for before I left London, Northcott. They deal with Louise Mercier and Peter Lewis. As the summary says. "These seem to prove these people are exactly what they say they are." Here, read them for yourself.'

'I see what you mean' said Northcott when he returned the

papers. 'Louise is highly respectable single woman who worked for years as secretary to Mr Lewis. Since he retired, she has been made redundant and now does agency work. Lewis was a senior executive in a highly reputable, quoted finance company. It seems he had a pretty fearsome reputation as a slave driver among his former colleagues. As far as is known he was forcibly retired and has disappeared off the radar of the City.' There is nothing to suggest any relationship between Lewis and Mercier when they worked together.'

'Sometimes even negative evidence can be helpful' said Buxton. 'The next thing I need to do is to go and have a look at where the body was found.'

'You'll not find much there' said Northcott 'it's a pretty desolate spot up on those fells.'

'Even so I don't see how I can get a real grip on the story if I don't go.'

'Then I will take you.'

The last part of their journey was in a Land Rover over what was nothing but tracks made by the thousands of sheep that had called these hills home over the centuries. Having gone as far as they could the last part had to be done by foot. Standing at the edge of what looked no more than one of many gaps in the stony ground Buxton peered down into the blackness.

'I am glad I didn't have to try and get down there' Northcott said. 'Just think, if some silly sheep had not fallen down it, we should never have found that body in a million years. That was what they gambled on. They must have been gutted when they found out they had lost.'

'They must have had a nasty shock when that picture was posted in the press. The thing is how did they get the body up here without being seen. It's not the sort of place to be out in after dark.'

'If they chose the right night with a clear sky and a full moon it would be almost as bright as day up here' said Northcott. 'If they came from the west there isn't a farm or anything for miles.'

'Tell me' asked Buxton 'did you make any enquiries as to whether anyone had seen anything out of the ordinary in this area at about the time the body was probably deposited here?'

'There are not exactly that many people to ask' replied North-cott. 'If you look around there only a few very isolated farms. These people very much keep their eyes and their minds on their faming activities. The only kind of calendar they have is the one that relates to their beasts. They are naturally un-inquisitive and are not your chattering urban dweller or your gossipy villager. From that you will hardly be surprised to learn that we did not pick up anything useful.'

'The local mountain rescue people helped with the recovery of the sheep and the body, didn't they?'

'That's right. If it hadn't been for them, we would never have discovered the skeleton.'

'I am wondering if it might be worth asking their members if they had seen or heard anything out of the ordinary in these hills at the time in question?'

'I suppose there can be no harm in asking sir' replied Northcott doubtfully.

'I should be very grateful if you could and then let me know what they have to say.'

CHAPTER NINETEEN

NETHERTON

DECEMBER 1994

Having completed his enquiries at Barnard Castle, Buxton moved on to Richmond and called on Inspector Seagrave.

'Good morning sir' he greeted Buxton 'May I enquire what brings a senior officer from the Met to our rural parts?'

'You will have heard of the mystery surrounding the death of the young woman called Bethany Mercier. '

'Yes, I had a call from Inspector Northcott at Barnard Castle saying he had a body that had been identified as someone of the same name. An unusual event but not impossible.'

Well,' replied Buxton 'the picture has been complicated by another set of circumstances that are very similar. This time they refer to the death of a young American. Apparently, he died in a road accident in Cornwall yet a body fished out of a reservoir in County Durham has been identified as his. Not only that but the two deceased knew each other and both left not inconsiderable sums to the same foreign beneficiary. The general view is that all these things are too coincidental to be anything but connected. It's been decided to centralise an investigation at the Yard and I have been put in charge of the case. The reason for my being here is to look again at the death of the young woman who suffered a fatal fall at Netherton.'

'As I recall sir it was a pretty open and shut case.'

'I have no doubt it looked like that. Did you know, however, that a few weeks later a document was found taped under a drawer in the room occupied by the young woman that contained her Will?'

'No, I hadn't heard that. Not that there was any reason I should.'

'The signature on the Will is certainly that of Bethany Mercier. But the body found up above Barnard Castle has been medically identified as being that of Bethany Mercier. Added to which a piece of jewellery found with the body has been identified as belonging to her. As if that is not enough, she had been killed by a blow to the head and tied at her wrists and ankles before being deposited down a sinkhole in the rocks.'

'Are you saying the lass that had the fall wasn't the real Bethany Mercier?'

'That's what we have to find out.'

'It won't be easy sir. The body of the fall victim was cremated and the ashes scattered.'

'In that case we have to accept the challenge don't we' Buxton grinned. 'I would like to start by reading the report made by the original investigating officers and to see the photographs taken at the scene of the accident. Then I should like to see the pathologist's report and the inquest report. After that I should like to talk to the officers who were at the site. Depending on what I read I may ask also to have a word with the pathologist. First of all, I should like to chat with you about this The End of The Rainbow place. I have spoken to the half-sister of what I might call the real Bethany Mercier and to her friend who apart from instigating the identification of the skeleton had previously visited Netherton to try and find her.'

'On the face of it' replied Seagrave, 'the place is what it says it is. Originally a woollen mill it has been converted into a craft centre. They sell only things that are made on site and they are reckoned to be of a much higher standard than that usually found in these places. None of the usual "Made in China" sort of thing. There were stories going round that the people who lived and worked there were some kind of community which cut itself off from the outside world. However, there are some people who are only employees and although they work there, they do not live on site. They are paid a proper wage. The others, that is those who belong to this community are not paid but all their living expenses are met by the organisation. While most people thought the whole idea more than a bit odd, they adopted a live and let live attitude to the place. As far as could be ascertained it seemed to be quite a good commercial success. There had never been any trouble until there was this fatal accident.'

'I understand' said Buxton 'that they consider themselves a modern day secular version of a medieval monastery or convent.'

'That is what they told the investigating officers when there was the fatal accident.'

'How do they get business? Do they advertise or do they depend on passing trade?'

'They advertise in local magazines and tourist publications. There are also leaflets in libraries and supermarkets as well as tourist offices. I gather it's also a destination for certain coach companies as well as coach tours. It has a good class cafeteria and restaurant. There does not appear to be a shortage of customers.'

'Where do they get their members and their staff from? 'asked Buxton.

'I have seen adverts for paid staff in local papers. In addition, I suppose they use local job centres.'

'What about their members? How do they get them?

'A good question. To be honest I have no idea.'

'Then it's something we can ask them later. When they first opened, did they come with a readymade staff?'

'They must have done because they are highly skilled and not the sort of people you can pick up easily.'

'Does that mean there are other and related communities? Something else we need to find out. Perhaps I could now see the photographs and the pathologist and inquest reports please.'

These were produced and Buxton spent some time considering them and making an occasional note. When he had finished, he turned to Seagrave with a smile on his face.

'Some interesting evidence there.'

'Something we missed,' Seagrave looked worried.

'Not at all. It is only interesting in the light of what we know now compared to what you knew then. Most importantly we have a photograph of the young woman who fell to her death and I can tell you that it is not a photograph of Bethany Mercier. Secondly, the pathologist report says the deceased had had at least one child, which is another indicator that she was not Bethany Mercier.'

'Then who was she and why was she masquerading as Bethany Mercier?'

'Good questions. Could you please let me have half a dozen copies of the photo of the young woman and also a copy of the pathologist report. While you are arranging that perhaps I could speak to the two officers who were first on the scene'

Seagrave left the room to return with a police constable and a WPC.

'These are the two officers who were first on the scene sir. Constable Headlow and WPC Abbott.'

'Good morning' said Buxton. 'Take a seat. My name is Commander Buxton and I am from the Metropolitan Police. For reasons that need not bother you we are trying to find out more about the death of the young woman at The End of The Rainbow community centre in Netherton. I gather that you were the first officers at the scene.'

'Yes sir', replied Headlow. 'We were on patrol in that area when we had a call to go to The End of The Rainbow.'

'What did you find?'

'We arrived at the same time as the doctor sir' added WPC Abbott. 'We found the body of a young woman lying on the ground. We were told that she had fallen from the third floor. An open doorway was pointed out to us and we were told that it had been a place where, when the building as used as a woollen mill, sacks would be hoisted up to be taken into the works. You could still see the hoist over the open door

"When we asked who the young woman was no-one offered a name' said Headlow, 'then a middle aged gentleman appeared and said he was the manager. The young woman was a Bethany Mercier he believed. He went on to explain that the place was a closed community and that people gave up all their original identities and families when they joined and were given a community name. He would check their records to verify that the name he had given us was the right one. He confirmed later that it was the right name but that he had no information as to next of kin.'

'When asked what he thought the young woman had been doing at the open door, he said she had probably been taking photographs as she was a water colour artist' added Abbott. 'We found the remains of a camera under her body. She must have landed on it.'

'Did you go and look at the third floor from which she fell?'

'Yes sir, the door was fastened by a bar which had been undone. It opened out on the face of the building with no other handle or guard rail. If anyone had stood there and had lost their sense of balance or had suffered vertigo there was nothing to stop them falling'

'Was it windy that day?'

'No sir, it was quite calm.'

'Was there a good view from the door?'

'Yes sir, a very good view down the valley.'

'Detective Sergeant Barbour had arrived by then sir and he took over the investigation.'

'Thank you that has been very useful.'

As the constables left Seagrave returned with copies that Buxton had requested.

'Were they able to throw any light on what happened?' he asked.

'A little bit here and there' Buxton replied. 'Did you see the door that the young woman fell from?'

'I saw it from the outside and from the inside, although it was shut when I got there. It was clear that it was a health and safety hazard as there was only a simple bar across it that anyone might open even though you would have thought that common sense would tell you not to do it. I gave the manager a formal warning about it and sent someone back a week later to ensure that a padlock had been fitted so as to prevent easy opening. '

'It will be interesting to see if the padlock is still in place. So, let's go and pay a visit to The End of The Rainbow'

CHAPTER TWENTY

BUXTON REACHES THE END OF THE RAINBOW

DECEMBER 1994

When they parked the car outside the main building of the community centre Buxton stood and looked up at the doorway from which the young woman had fallen and noticed it was firmly closed. They went into the main entrance and instead of going to the ticket office rang the bell at a door marked 'Enquiries'. A hatch at the side of the door opened and a middle aged woman looked them up and down with a suspicious eye.

'Good morning' said Seagrave 'we should like to see Mr Martin Delaney please'

'Have you an appointment?'

'No.'

'Mr Delaney only sees people by appointment. Do you wish me to make one for you?'

'We are police officers madam and we want to see Mr Delaney in our official capacity. Please inform him that Commander Buxton of the Metropolitan Police and Inspector Seagrave of the North Yorkshire Police wish to see him.'

'This is most irregular; however, I will inform Mr Delaney of what you say.'

The hatch was closed and when it re-opened the woman said:

'Mr Delaney says it is not convenient to see you today. Please make an appointment in the usual manner.'

'Madam' said Buxton in a firm voice 'as my colleague has said we are police officers on official business. We are not casual commercial travellers. If Mr Delaney declines to see us here and now we shall have no alternative but to request him to accompany us to the police station and speak to him there. Please tell him that and ask him which of the alternatives he wishes to adopt.'

'And they call this a free country' she snapped and slammed the door shut.

'Not what you would call a friendly welcome' grinned Buxton. 'A real dragon.'

'They breed them like that in these parts' laughed Seagrave. 'Middle aged females of the species. Yorkshire's finest.'

The door next to the grill opened and they were ushered in by the dragon with a scowl. She led them along a corridor, opened a door and said through her teeth 'Here they are' and slammed the door behind her.

The room was panelled in dark oak with a green carpet and blinds over the window. A large desk was in the centre of the room and behind it was seated a man in his forties, going grey at the fringes of light red hair and wearing tweed jacket and twill trousers.

'What is all this?' he said without rising to his feet. 'I am a very busy man and don't have time for public relation exercises by public bodies.'

'Commander Buxton of the Metropolitan Police and this is Inspector Seagrave of the North Yorkshire Police. This is not a public relations exercise Mr Delaney, it is a criminal investigation.'

'What do you mean, a criminal investigation. I am not aware of any crime affecting this Community.'

'You will recall that some months ago there was a fatal accident on these premises.'

'I am hardly likely to forget it am I. There was a full enquiry and a coroner's inquest. The verdict was accidental death. That was an end to the unfortunate affair.'

'We met at that time Mr Delaney' said Seagrave 'and I drew your attention to what I thought were certain insufficient safety precautions.'

'You have not come to resurrect that technical breach of regulations which was in any event corrected when drawn to my attention. I fail why that should interest the Metropolitan Police.'

Buxton sat in one of the chairs facing the irate Mr Delaney without being invited and indicated to Seagrave to take the other.

'What has brought us here today Mr Delaney is a potential matter of identity theft.'

'And what is identity theft may I ask?' suddenly Mr Delaney seemed more relaxed as he assumed that they were not discussing the fatal accident.

'As the name applies 'said Buxton in a quiet voice,' it occurs when someone seeks to assume illegally the identity of another person. The name of the young lady who met a tragic death here was, as you know, Bethany Mercier. That name is being claimed by another person.'

For a moment a look of fear crossed Mr Delaney's face but he quickly recovered and said:

'I admit that Bethany Mercier is not as common a name as Mary Smith or Jane Jones but surely it is not impossible there are two people of the same name among the sixty odd million people in this country.'

'That is what we are trying to find out. Inspector Seagrave has very kindly explained to me the nature of your community here and how, when they join, people surrender their original identities and give up all contacts with the outside world. They are given, I believe, what I may be allowed to call a community name. Is that a fair description?'

'In very general terms, yes.'

'In that case Bethany Mercier would have used her community name?'

'Yes.'

'Presumably you keep records of the actual names of your members and their given community names otherwise you would not know who was who.'

'Correct.'

'Would it be possible for us to see the records for Bethany Mercier please?'

'No, it would not.

'May I ask why?'

'Because when a person leaves the community, we remove them from our computerised records.'

'Do people leave very often?'

'No, but we do not try to keep someone here if they wish to leave. There is nothing to be gained from keeping out of date records.'

' Tell me, how do you find new members of your community?'

'In various ways. Sometimes we are approached by people interested in joining us, sometimes it is in response to advertisements that we place in carefully selected publications'

'So, how did you manage when you opened this community?' enquired Buxton in a friendly tone.

'Obviously we did not recruit a completely new set of members Commander. No, we were able to bring in a core of experienced people from sister communities.'

'You have other communities?' Buxton feigned surprise. 'I rather assumed this was unique.

'Not at all' said Delaney becoming more confident in his replies.

'We have communities in various parts of Britain as well as in Europe and the United States where the movement started.'

'How interesting, I never realised that. Do you by any chance have any literature that shows where you have communities?'

'We do and I shall be delighted to provide one. It will demonstrate that we are a substantial organisation.'

'Oh yes, I almost forgot, can I ask' and Buxton threw in this new question out of the blue 'do you have Patrick Tod Grimhausen on your records?'

There was no doubt that this question disturbed Delaney.

'Now that is an unusual name. I should think I would remember it and I don't.'

'Can you check please?'

He turned in his seat and swivelled a computer screen so that Buxton and Seagrave could not see it. He entered certain details and then turned off the screen.

'As I thought there is no record of such a name. Is this another, what did you call it, an identity theft?'

Buxton did not answer the question.

'Thank you' he said getting to his feet 'I don't think we need to bother such a busy man any further. Although I should like to take a tour of your community if I may.'

'Delaney opened a desk drawer and took out a leaflet.

'This will give you a picture of the geographical spread of our communities' he smiled. 'We use them for marketing purposes. We may be a closed community but we are very business minded and orientated. Just like the monasteries and convents of former times.' He held out a hand. 'Pleased to have been of help Commander, Inspector'

He led them back to Reception and spoke to the dragon who Seagrave noticed wore a badge with the name of Cloda. With a nod of his head Delaney left them to the tender mercies of the dragon.

'You will need these' she held out two tickets. 'They are complimentary tickets which means you will not be charged if you do not spend the equivalent of the entrance fee. Lance, here, will take you round. He is one of our guides.'

A young man aged about twenty five rose to his feet.

'This way please' he said with a fixed smile.

There was no denying that the tour was interesting. The retail areas of the community were well organised, very professionally laid out and displayed a wide range of really quite high quality goods. They were not cheap but gave the impression of value for money. When they got to the third floor Seagrave spoke to their guide.

'We are police officers. I was here when that unfortunate young woman had her fatal fall. I should like to show my colleague where it happened.'

Lance led them to an area which was stocked with artist's materials, paintings and photographs. In one wall, about half way along the area, was a green door which was fastened by an iron bar which was held in place by a large padlock.'

'I am glad to see that proper precautions are in place' said Seagrave.

Having thanked Lance, they stopped off at the cafeteria for a coffee and a French pastry. They talked generally about what they had seen without mentioning the true reason for their presence. In the foyer Buxton tapped on the door to Reception. It was opened by the dragon, Cloda, who glowered at them.

'I don't want to trouble Mr Delaney again but I wonder if you could tell me whether his diary was full on the afternoon of the fatal accident?'

'Why do you need to know that?' she demanded.

'There is some doubt in the reports of the first police officers on the scene. It will help finalise our information.'

'Oh, very well' she sighed. 'Wait here.'

She returned holding a large desk diary. Flickering through the pages she said in a triumphant tone 'As you can see, he has a very full diary.' A fact confirmed by the many entries each day. 'Here we are' she said and then gave a deep breath. 'That day he has drawn a line through the afternoon which means he was taking some time off.'

Does he do that often?'

'Certainly not, but everyone is entitled to the occasional break.'

'Indeed, they are Cloda' smiled Buxton. 'Thank you for all your assistance.'

The irony was lost on her.

Back in their car Seagrave asked:

'What did you make of that?'

'Well, we certainly did not waste our time by coming here. Did you notice how he relaxed when we seemed to move on from Bethany Mercier?'

'I did and I noticed that he had a quite shock when you mentioned Tod Grimhausen. You didn't follow that up.'

'No, it's better to leave him to worry why we asked that question. Also, to leave him to worry why we didn't ask about the Will. The more he has cause to worry about unasked questions the more likely he is to make a mistake.'

'Do you think her death was an accident sir?'

'No, I do not. It's more a question of was she pushed or was she tripped up?'

Do you think Mercier and Grimhausen were ever there?'

'I have little doubt they were. The question is, Seagrave, when was that and how did they leave?'

CHAPTER
TWENTY ONE

BUXTON SEEKS INFORMATION

DECEMBER 1994

In order to get a better grip on understanding the workings of the Rainbow organisation Richard Buxton took a trip to West Sussex to see his old friend Donald Craigton who was curate at a village church. Buxton had met Craigton when they were both Inspectors in the Metropolitan Police. Craigton had taken early retirement and entered the church. A move that was made earlier than he had planned when, almost unexpectedly, he inherited the title of Baron Craigton of Acaster. A title he had expected to pass to his brother's family. It was a title that he did not use in carrying out his duties as a priest. Craigton lived in a lovely house that been designed by Edwin Lutyens which he had inherited with the title. A bachelor, he employed a housekeeper who was a reformed confidence trickster called Harold Whitehouse who carried out his role as if he were a latter-day Bunter or Jeeves.

'Commander Buxton, always a pleasure to see you sir' greeted the sober suited man with grey hair who opened the door.

'Hello Harold, and how are you keeping?'

'Very well thank you sir. His lordship is expecting you.' Harold insisted on giving his employer his full title.

'Richard, it's good to see you. How are things in the highest ranks of the Met?' the tall, thin man with hair rapidly turning white greeted his visitor. He was wearing tweed jacket and twill trousers over a light grey clerical vest and dog collar.

'Much the same as always Donald. There is no shortage of crime. How are you?'

'I am pretty fit thank you. Is this a social call or have you uncovered another murder in our village?'

'Nothing as unlikely as that' Buxton laughed. 'This is partly social. It's always good to see you but there is also something of an ulterior motive. I am hoping I can pick your brains.'

'You are welcome to anything I know apart, of course, from information that has come to me as a priest. So, what's your problem?'

At this point the door opened and Harold brought in a trolley containing tea things and a delicious looking fruit cake.

'You have not lost your culinary skills by the look of it Harold' Buxton grinned. 'This looks absolutely delicious.'

'I hope you will enjoy it Commander. It's a new recipe I am trying out.'

'Thank you, Harold,' said his employer 'I expect we can look after ourselves.'

'Very good my lord.'

'Still playing Bunter I see' smiled Richard as the door closed.

'Yes. He's as happy as a sandboy doing it so I don't interfere. It's far better that he should be playing the part of a butler rather than his previous roles as a senior churchman. Now then what is it you want from my addled brains?'

'It's about as odd a set of circumstances that I have ever come across.'

Buxton proceeded to give a brief but concise outline of the case that he was investigating.

'It's certainly an unusual set of circumstances Richard' Craigton said. 'How come it's landed on your desk?'

'The three chief constables agreed that a unified investigation was the best approach and asked the Home Office who should lead it. They, in their wisdom, chose the Met and the AC dumped it on my plate.'

'I'm not clear where you think I may be of help? I know little about the Yorkshire Dales or the far west of Cornwall'

'As I said both the victims, Bethany Mercier and Tod Grimhausen, were apparently members of some sort of commune called, in one case, The End of The Rainbow and in the other The Rainbow Craft Centre. Both these organisations are what can best be described as closed communities. When asked to define their organisations they say that the best they can do is to compare themselves with a medieval abbey or convent. By this they mean that anyone joining gives up all their worldly goods and cuts themselves off from all kith and kin. They then live totally community orientated lives. The individual owns nothing and has only very limited contact with the outside world. Not only that but they are given a completely new name when they join to underline the change in their lives.'

'Unusual' said Craigton 'but not totally unknown I should imagine. There are some quite large communities of that kind that exist today. In addition, there are, I suspect, even more smaller and independent ones.'

'That is as maybe Donald, but I have never come across any of them. The limit of my knowledge is that I have heard of the Amish people in the United States. Not only that but I have virtually no knowledge of the organisation of medieval monasteries or convents. That's where I hope you can help me. I need to understand what I am being told if I am to have a reasonable chance of spotting when the wool is being pulled over my eyes.'

'You have come to the wrong church to obtain detailed knowledge of medieval monastic orders Richard. They were all

Roman Catholic and owed ultimate allegiance to the Pope. Such knowledge of them as I have is more likely to be historical rather than theological.'

'You said just now there are some quite large communities today. Who are they?'

'You have already mentioned the Amish. Then there are the Bruderhof, the Hutterites and the Mennonites all of which, in one way or another, are descendants of the Anabaptists. Before you ask who they are or were, they preach adult baptism after a declaration of faith. They do not believe in infant baptism'

'But surely that doesn't mean that their members cannot live mainstream lives. As I understand it the Baptist church practices adult baptism, but their members do not live in closed communities.'

'That is quite correct. As far as the others I have mentioned are concerned, it would be difficult to give one hard and fast answer to that point. As far as I understand it members can and do leave or can even be expelled. It will all depend on the rules of the individual community. In most cases there are both single and married members. Children may go to outside schools in some cases and may be able to decide at a given age whether they wish to stay in the community. But in all cases the members live according to the rules and organisation of the community.'

'What about medieval monasteries and convents?'

'I suspect those are quoted as they are more likely to be understood than the rarer anabaptist orders. As you will know by the time of their dissolution under Henry VIII, they were very rich and powerful places. However, their origins were much simpler. What started out as simple places where men or women isolated themselves to devote their lives to God, by the time of the dissolution they had become major industrial and commercial enterprises. Take monasteries, for example, men decided to devote their lives to the service of God by joining one of the orders. That is when they gave up all their goods and, generally speaking, their contact with their kin. Over the years there was a practice for some men to make an endowment to an abbey who, in return, took in the youngest son of the benefactor who was still an infant, and that youngster spent their whole life in a closed order. There were different orders and they had differing rules so what I am saying is very generalised. They were usually known as Brother this or Brother that which may or may not have been their birth name. Monasteries used church law to govern their affairs and these could lead to the ultimate sanction of ex-communication.

'Which seems to be in general line with what these Rainbow places say.'

'Remember, as I said, that these monasteries were the big businesses of their day. They had to rely on people other than the brothers to be able to operate. Those additional workers were called lay brothers. They were not full members of the order and could lead the same lives as those outside the religious life.'

'That is interesting, because the larger Rainbow establishments do employ people who are not members of the community. It seems they keep their birth names and are treated as employees. Also, these places do trade and, I should imagine, make reasonable profits from the production of arts and crafts goods. What about the women in centuries past?'

'In very general terms they were similar to the monasteries. Women, sometimes widows or unmarried daughters were placed in a convent. They tended to be smaller and less business orientated than the monasteries. Also, they had to have a priest attached who could say the Mass. Women were not permitted, and indeed are still not permitted, to preside at the Mass. In the Church of England there have been women priests only from this year. In a medieval convent the priest would be unseen by the nuns when he led their Mass so that the sexes were fully separated.'

'Interesting; because these Rainbow communities seem to be

made up of both sexes. Were there no two sex monasteries or nunneries?'

'I believe that in the early days there may have been mixed sex communities. The nearest things got to that was one order called The Gilbertines who had mixed, though supposedly separated, communities for a while. Normally, if there were monks and nuns at the same location, they were kept totally separate, each having their own buildings. The modern-day communities that we have mentioned do not practice sexual division and indeed there are married couples among their members.'

'Thank you, Donald,' Richard said' that has been very helpful. Not only have you given me a clearer understanding of both religious and lay communities in the past and as they exist today but this will be a great help to me in trying to understand what I am told and what I find out. As you will know only too well it's not uncommon for witnesses to try and pull the wool over the eyes of the investigator and blind him with science or whatever.'

'I am glad to have been of help, but please do not over estimate the value of what I have said. I lay no claim to being an expert on these topics. Also, remember that there exist today all sorts and kinds of communities which, between them, will have a myriad of organisational rules. It would be a mistake to think they are all the same. They most certainly are not.'

'I will keep that warning in mind.'

Having dealt with the main reason for Richard's visit the two old friends moved on to talk about other things and mutual acquaintances.

Robert Thomasson was spending Christmas at home with his wife and two daughters. He had been playing scrabble with his elder daughter who was a student at Oxford University. When she was called away to help with the lunch preparations he sat at the board and idly played with the tiles, forming them into all kinds of unconnected words. His mind was ranging over his latest case, what he had learned so far and what needed to be done after the holidays? Which made him think of his senior officer. Buxton was a widower, his wife had died some years ago, and he had no children. He was spending his Christmas with his sister and her family. Seeing his own family round him made Thomasson appreciate that it could not be an easy time for Richard Buxton who was a man on his own. Had he known it he would have found that Buxton was not with his sister. Instead, he had chosen to work to allow married men to be at home for Christmas Day. On Boxing Day he had driven down to Sussex to share it with his friend Donald Craigton. There were just the two men, one a bachelor and the other a widower, so they were able to spend a relaxing day. The rush of services leading up to Christmas was over and Donald had to admit that he was more tired than he had realised. Harold Whitehouse had cooked an excellent lunch and, after some persuasion, he agreed to join the other two at the table. Once he had relaxed, they spent a very agreeable time reminiscing about years gone by.

Back at the Thomasson household on Christmas Day, his daughter, Jenny, released from culinary duties, had returned to the lounge and looked at what her father was doing. 'That's an odd word to make, Dad' she said looking at his latest creation. 'I didn't realise that you knew Latin.'

'I don't. Why do you think I do?'

'That word you have in front of you, Arcus, is Latin. In fact, it's Latin for an arch.

Are you sure?' he exclaimed.

'Of course, I am, silly; after all I am studying classics at uni.'

'Now that is what I call interesting' he grinned. 'I might almost say it makes the cost of your education worthwhile.'

'What are you on about?'

'Never you mind' he looked round 'but that piece of information is so useful that, if your mother isn't watching you can pour yourself another glass of sherry.'

CHAPTER TWENTY TWO

THOMASSON IN CORNWALL

JANUARY 1995

Chief Inspector Robert Thomasson stepped off the train at Penzance station to be greeted by a tall, broad shouldered man with brown eyes and ruddy cheeks. He looked like your traditional countryman and his handshake was like being crushed between the rollers of a mangle.

'Welcome to Kernow Chief Inspector' he smiled.

'To where?' asked Thomasson. 'I thought this was Penzance.'

'Kernow is Cornish for Cornwall.' His greeter laughed.' I am Inspector Christopher Vellacott. How well do you know this part of the world?'

'This is the furthest south west I have been' admitted Thomasson.

'We'll drop your luggage off at the hotel before we go on to our headquarters. I think you will find the hotel comfortable, a bit old fashioned may be but the rooms are well furnished and it has an excellent reputation for its food.'

Thomasson found his colleague's description of the King's Head accurate and soon deposited his luggage in his room which had a view of the sea over the rooftops. Once they arrived at the police headquarters, he was introduced to the uniformed Superintendent and then taken into a small but comfortable office which he was told he could use as his base whilst he was in town.

'I gather there is some question about this road death' Vellacott said 'although I must say it all seemed pretty routine to me.'

'Yes, the problem is that a body found tied to tree roots in a reservoir in County Durham has been medically identified as that of Patrick Tod Grimhausen who was said to be the man who was killed in your road accident.'

'I don't see how that is possible. Our man was cremated and his ashes scattered at sea in April.'

'And the other body was found in August. Interesting isn't it?'

'How sure are the medical people of their identification?'

'They are in no doubt. He was American and had some unusual dental work. They obtained his dental records from the States and got a complete match.'

'So, who was the man who died down here?'

'Exactly. Given that there is an almost identical case in Yorkshire the powers that be have decided that the Yard should investigate both cases. So, here I am. What I would like to do is to speak to the officers who were first on the spot, and with the pathologist. If possible, I should also like to see the man who discovered the body. Then I would like to see all the photographs that were taken at the time. Lastly, I shall need to visit the place called The Rainbow Craft Centre.'

Inspector Vellacott pressed a button on the internal phone and said:

'Please ask constables Trewella and Devoran to come to this room.'

The door opened to admit the two policemen who were both in their late forties or early fifties. They came smartly to attention.

'You wished to see us sir?'

'Yes. This is Chief Inspector Thomasson of the Metropolitan Police. He wishes to ask you some questions about the fatal road accident you attended on the St Gwennep road back in April. This is Constable Trewella' he pointed to the taller of the two 'and this is Constable Devoran.'

'Take a seat gentleman" Thomasson pointed to two wooden chairs. 'Sorry to have to rake up something that happened nine months ago but some later events in other parts of this island have made it necessary. Perhaps you could start by telling me how you came to be called to the scene.'

'We were on a routine patrol sir' said Trewella 'when we received a radio message telling us there had been an accident between St Gwennep and St Crowan. When we got there, we found that a tractor driver had set up a red triangle to slow down traffic. We stopped at the triangle and found that just on a tight left hand corner there was a body laying half up on the grass verge. It had been found by a chap on his way to work in Penzance. A passing tractor driver had put up two triangles and gone on into St Crowan to raise the alarm. The call centre had already alerted the ambulance and the local doctor.'

'There didn't seem any doubt that the man was dead sir 'added Devoran. 'we contacted base and asked for a diversion to be set up. It's a very narrow road with steep banks and would have to be closed to traffic for some time. Also, we asked for traffic people to attend the site as we realised there would be a need for photos etc.'

'You say that the man was laying half on the grass verge. Was there much blood about? Did he look as if he had been hit by a motor vehicle?'

'No there wasn't sir' said Trewella. 'it seemed as if he had been caught more of a glancing blow and knocked nearly into the hedge.'

'What happened next?'

'Well, after the doctor and the ambulance men arrived and they attended to the body. The doctor said he thought he had been dead some hours but it would be up to the pathologist to say precisely when. He left to go to his surgery and the pathologist arrived, examined the body and said it could be moved. Before that could be done there were photos to be taken and measurements made. Then the body was removed and the road reopened.'

'Had the body been identified?'

'I searched the pockets' said Devoran 'and found a business card for The Rainbow Craft Centre. Apart from that there was a name on a handkerchief. It was Tod Grimhausen, which sounded a sort of German name to me.'

'What was your reading of the accident Trewella?' asked Thomasson.'

'The man was on the right hand side of the road, facing oncoming traffic. It looked to me as if he had been hit a glancing blow in the back and thrown on to the verge.'

'Wouldn't he have seen a car coming? At that time of day, they should have been using lights."

'It's a very tight bend sir' said Trewella 'and he was only just round the corner. The high hedges there could make a car invisible till you were on it. If I was driving, I should have used my horn as a warning.'

'What was the state of his clothes Devoran? It was apparently a misty morning. How damp were they?'

'Not very damp sir.'

'How long had it been misty?'

'It came in the previous afternoon and stayed that way till mid-morning the next day.'

'So, if he had been there a long time you would have expected his clothes to be damp?'

'Probably sir.'

'How cold was the body?'

'Icy cold sir.'

'Thank you. Now what happened when you went to this craft centre?'

'Do you know the place sir?' asked Trewella.

'No, I don't'

'It's quite close to the St Just area on the site of what was once an old mine. When the mine was closed and the shafts closed off the place was abandoned for a long time. The old mine manager's house and some other buildings remained derelict until someone bought it about five years ago, restored the buildings and added some new ones and opened it as a craft centre. As far as can be seen it's quite profitable. They sell hand made goods of good quality not the usual tourist stuff. I hear that they send goods all over the south west.'

'Thank you, constable, that is helpful. Go on.'

'When we went to ask if they knew a Tod Grimhausen, they were very cagey. Then the man who said he was the manager came along and said that they did know someone of that name. When I asked if I could see him, they said he had gone into Penzance. It seemed he often walked it. I queried why they were uncertain about knowing him they said they were a closed community. People living there gave up everything from the past including their names and were given a community name. It seems this Tod chap was known as Hank. The manager agreed to go into Penzance to identify the body, which he did.'

'Thank you, gentlemen, that has been very useful. If I need to pick your brains again, I will ask to see you.'

When the two men had left Thomasson asked Vellacott for the photographs taken at the scene of the accident. Vellacott went and found these and handed over a file. Thomasson studied all the photos carefully, particularly those which showed the body in situ and the layout of the road.

'Do you know this road Inspector?'

'I have driven along it very occasionally. It's more of a lane than a road and has to be taken carefully because of the tight bends and high hedges. I take the point about not seeing an approaching vehicle round one of those bends.'

'Do you think I could have a word with the traffic people who checked the scene, please?'

A few minutes later a sergeant entered the room and was introduced as Sergeant Ashworth.'

'I have seen the photos taken at the scene sergeant' Thomasson said 'but I should be grateful for your personal opinion. I understand that the weather was very misty so presumably the road was wet.'

'Yes sir. It was wet without being flooded in any way.'

'You looked for skid marks I am sure.'

'Yes sir, we had a careful look for anything like that but found nothing.'

'Could that have been due to the weather?'

'Quite possibly sir.'

'How did you read what had happened?'

'It's a very sharp corner and the visibility was poor. The victim was just round the corner so it's quite possible he was hit by someone who did not see him until too late.'

'Would he have heard a vehicle coming do you think?'

'With the high hedges he might well not have done if the engine ran quietly. He was on the right hand side of the road and, in any event, may have thought he was safe.'

'What about car lights giving a warning,'

'Again, with such a tight bend this may not have happened. Further if the vehicle was only using dipped lights, he may have seen nothing coming up behind him.'

'How did you read the accident,'

'It looked to me as though he was hit in the back and catapulted on to the verge. He wouldn't have known what hit him.'

'How fast would the vehicle have been travelling do you reckon to get such a result?'

'It's a narrow road but there is hardly any traffic so anyone who knew the road could have been going faster than it was really safe to do so.'

'You were satisfied it was a hit and run?'

'Taking everything into account sir, yes I was.'

'Thank you that's very helpful.'

'How do we go about contacting the man who was first on the site Inspector?'

'He works in the town. The easiest thing would be to go and see him there.'

Inspector Vellacott was well known at the factory where Graham Whitton worked and they made no difficulty in arranging for the police officers to speak to their employee.

'Mr Whitton' said Vellacott when a man about thirty wearing blue working overalls entered the room. 'I am Inspector Vellacott of the Cornwall Police and this is Chief Inspector Thomasson of the Metropolitan Police. Please sit down. You will remember, I have no doubt, that some time ago you came across the body of a man who was subject to what seemed to be a hit and run accident.'

'Not something you are likely to forget in a hurry.'

'I would be grateful if you could tell us in your own words exactly what happened Mr Whitton' said Thomasson.

'I thought the whole thing was done and dusted. It was ruled to be a hit and run.'

'Yes, but the driver wasn't found was he or she?'

'That's true. Are you on to something new?'

'Let's just say that we are trying to get a clearer picture of what happened. That's why I should appreciate your recollection.'

'I was cycling from St Gwennep into Penzance like I do every morning. It was just about light but very misty and damp. A miserable sort of day. I turned a sharp right hand bend and almost hit something lying on the right hand grass verge. I stopped and looked. It was a man. I bent and touched his hand. It was ice cold so I knew he must be dead. A few minutes later I heard a tractor coming and stopped it. We didn't touch the body but put up red triangles while the tractor went on into St Crowan to call the police. I stayed put to slow down any traffic.'

'Was there any?'

'Just two cars, one in each direction. I signalled them not to stop but to continue on their way. It's a narrow road I didn't want to start a block up.'

'Tell me, had you been passed by any car going in the same direction as you?'

'No, but by the feel of the poor chap he had been dead some time.'

'How dangerous a road would you say that it is Mr Whitton?'

'It's not really dangerous if you take care. That's why I always make sure I have good lights and wear a fluorescent jacket. I stayed put till the police and ambulance arrived and I had made my statement then I came on to work. The police had phoned to explain why I was late.'

'That's all, I think. Thank you for your help Mr Whitton.'

Back at the police headquarters Thomasson asked if Vellacott had been able to contact the pathologist.

'Yes, he says he will be free until seven this evening.'

'Excellent. If I can make a couple of phone calls first, we will go and see him.'

They found Dr Conrad Finch in his office at the mortuary. He had just finished a post mortem and was dictating his report. He was a short man with wiry grey hair and piercing blue eyes.

'What's this all about Vellacott?' he demanded. 'Raking up PMs I did months ago on what was held to be a hard and fast case of a hit and run accident.'

'This is Chief Inspector Thomasson of the Metropolitan Police doctor.'

'What's brought the Yard into this Chief Inspector?'

'A question of disputed identity doctor.'

'Well, that's your pigeon not mine. What do you want from me?'

'Could we start with the time of death doctor?'

'That old chestnut!' snorted the doctor. 'You know as well as I do that it is impossible to be one hundred per cent accurate unless someone sees the death actually happen. However, I see no reason to change what I said. Death occurred ten to twelve hours before I saw the body.'

'Your report' Thomasson continued 'mentioned two other things. The deceased had suffered a broken leg at some stage and he had had his appendix removed.'

'That's correct but neither of them contributed to his death. Here, I will show you.' He opened an envelope and took out some x-ray prints, selecting one he put it up on a screen and turned on a light. 'There you are, you can see where there was a quite clean break which had healed nicely.'

'Could you estimate how long before death that happened doctor?'

'My estimate would be five to seven years given how well it had healed.'

'Do you, by any chance have a photograph of the head before you started your post mortem?'

'Of course, I do' the doctor snapped.

'Could I ask you to let us have a copy of that please as well as a copy of the x-ray. How about the appendicectomy, do you have a picture of that scar as well?'

'Very well, I will see they are sent round to you Vellacott. Is that all? Only I want to get this report finished.

'The cause of death doctor. Could you give me your opinion on that please?'

'It's all in my report why don't you read that?'

'I have read your very clear report doctor,' said Thomasson quietly. 'It's just that it would be very helpful if you could tell us in your own words what you think happened.'

'My view is the young man was walking along a narrow road and was hit square in the back by a motor vehicle that catapulted him forward so that he landed on his neck and shoulders and broke his neck which caused instant death.'

'I am very grateful for your help Doctor Finch and now we will leave you to finish your report.'

'Some interesting information there,' Chief Inspector Vellacott said when they got back to the police headquarters.

'Yes, very interesting. We are making some progress Inspector. But I think that will do for today. Tomorrow we will have look at your Rainbow.'

CHAPTER TWENTY THREE

THOMASSON SEES THE END OF THE RAINBOW

JANUARY 1995

When Thomasson arrived at the police headquarters the following morning Inspector Vellacott handed him an envelope that had been sent by express delivery overnight

'Ah' said Thomasson, 'replies to my phone calls, I hope. Have we heard from Dr Finch as well?'

'Yes, here is the information he promised.'

'Let's start with these photos. I asked if the Grimhausen's agent in London had a photo of Patrick Tod Grimhausen and here it is. Let's compare it with the photo taken just before the post mortem. Now, that's what I call interesting.'

He passed two photos across the desk to Vellacott who gave a long whistle.

'Well, I'll be damned' he said 'it's obviously two different people. So, the road accident victim wasn't the young American.'

'Which is confirmed by the fact that his family state that he had never broken his leg or had his appendix removed.'

'If it's not Grimhausen, who was it who was killed on that road?'

'That as they say is the six million dollar question. Added to which I am beginning to have my doubts as to whether he was killed where his body was found. Can you get someone to contact the mortuary attendant who prepared the body for autopsy to find out just how wet the clothes were when it arrived there?'

'I will get on to it straight away.'

'Good. When you have done that, I think we will take a look at this local Rainbow.'

Thomasson enjoyed his first views of the far south west of his country. They passed along narrow roads with field either side and through small villages and hamlets. Occasionally, he caught a glimpse of the sea. When they came to it, the road that led up to the craft centre was narrow and only clinker surfaced. As they drove slowly up it Vellacott said:

'Looking at this track and the grass verges I have doubts about our being able to find any evidence of a hit and run here.'

'It certainly does not look very promising' agreed Thomasson.

At the top of the track they were met by a high stone wall in the centre of which were a pair of heavy wooden gates that were open. Over the gateway was a painted sign that read 'The Rainbow Craft Centre' on each of the gateposts was a sign that said 'Private Property. They parked the car outside the wall and walked through the gateway to a stone building which bore the sign 'Entrance'. Entering through an automatic door they found themselves in a vestibule with a turnstile blocking the way. On the right hand side was a glass window over which was written Reception and on a shelf a button which Vellacott pressed. Their ring was answered by a middle aged woman dressed in a red blouse and green skirt. She pushed open the window.

'Good morning. You wish to enter the Craft Centre?' Then not waiting for a reply she went on 'There is an entry fee of five pounds per head which is refunded when goods to that value are purchased.' She slid two tickets across the shelf.

'We wish to see Mr Threlfall who is, I believe, the manager of this establishment.'

'Have you an appointment?'

'No.'

'In that case I must ask you submit your request in writing and you will be informed whether or not Mr Threlfall will see you.'

'We are police officers' replied Vellacott firmly and produced his identification. 'Please tell Mr Threlfall we wish to see him.'

'I have already told you that Mr Threlfall only sees people by prior appointment.'

'Let me make the position clear madam' said Vellacott pointedly 'either Mr Threlfall sees us immediately or we will arrange for uniformed police to come here, with a warrant, and take the gentleman to police headquarters in Penzance for formal questioning. Which is to be?'

The woman slammed the glass door shut and disappeared into the office. They saw her speaking on the phone and glaring at them. Then a party of four people entered and Vellacott and Thomasson stood aside and indicated they could go first. Another woman, similarly dressed, opened the sliding window, explained the entrance fee, took the money and handed over tickets, pressing a button which freed the turnstile. The first woman re-opened the sliding panel and said through gritted teeth:

'Mr Threlfall will see soon you as soon as it's convenient to him. Please wait.'

'Let me make myself clear' Vellacott said stopping her from closing the panel 'if Mr Threlfall is not here in four minutes, I will immediately call for police reinforcements and arrest him for obstructing the police in carrying out their duties.'

She returned to the phone and two minutes later a door opened and a man in his late forties came out.

'What is all this nonsense?' he demanded. 'Don't you realise that this is private property. There is a big enough sign at the gateway. This centre is a closed community and does not accept casual callers.'

'Has this lady told you that we are police officers?'

'She mentioned that fact.'

'Then, why may I ask does she refuse to let us talk with you when she has no idea as to the nature of our business?' asked Thomasson. 'In addition, I would respectfully remind you that no-one is above the law. Now may we come in and talk to you.'

'If you insist but it is under protest.'

He opened the door and they followed him down a corridor and into what was clearly a small interview room. They produced their identity documents and sat down.

'I am Inspector Vellacott of the Cornish police and this gentleman is Chief Inspector Thomasson of the Metropolitan Police based at Scotland Yard.'

Threlfall blinked and swallowed hard.

'I have no wish to be difficult but it is a firm rule of this community that we do not see unauthorised callers. As I said we are a closed community. By that I mean that our members having joined us have cut themselves off completely from their past lives and from any contact with life outside. It may help clarify the position if I say that we are a lay organisation but, in some respects, are similar to a religious monastery or abbey. It is not unknown for us to have all kinds of unsolicited callers who use a whole variety of excuses to try and obtain entrance. That is why we have a firm rule that we see people only by prior appointment. That allows us to sort the sheep from the goats as it were. I don't think we have ever had anyone from the forces of law and order calling and this caused the difficulties. Now, how can I assist you?'

'If I may correct you Mr Threlfall 'said Thomasson with a smile

'I think you did have a visit from the police some months ago on the occasion of a fatal accident befalling one of your community.'

'When I made my previous remark, I admit that I did not count that as a similar visit. It was a most unfortunate occurrence.'

'It is about that earlier occurrence that we wish to talk to you.'

'But that is all completed surely. There was an inquest and a verdict of accidental death. What else can there be that requires additional questions?'

'We have information that there may be a case of identity theft.'

'Identity theft? I don't understand what you mean.'

'Identity theft happens when someone steals the identity of another person, who may or may not be dead, and assumes that identity' explained Vellacott.

'Are you suggesting that someone has stolen our member's identity?'

'I am not suggesting, I am simply investigating' said Thomasson. 'Could you tell me who was his closest work contact? If so, I would like to talk to him or her.'

'I am afraid that is not possible.'

'Why not?'

'Because the person who most fits that description is no longer here.'

'What exactly do you mean by no longer here?'

'The person concerned left the community about four weeks after the accident. I think he found it hard to come to terms with what had happened. You see Hank, as we knew him, was going into Penzance specially to buy a tool that this other person requested. He seemed to think he was responsible for the accident.'

'Was he the same person who had the envelope?'

Envelope?' Threlfall tried to look mystified.

'The envelope that led to the discovery of the Will?'

'Oh, that envelope, yes, it was the same person.'

Thomasson thought that answer a bit too glib and doubted its honesty.

'When you say the man left, does that mean that members of the community can leave if they so wish?'

'We do not keep people here against their will.'

'Do you know where he went?'

'I have no idea. You see he left unannounced in the middle of the night.'

'What was his name?'

'I cannot tell you that.'

'Why not?' demanded Thomasson. 'Is it against the rules of the community?'

'The reason is, Chief Inspector, quite simple. When a person joins the community, we note their name and any next of kin they wish to have recorded. They are then allocated a community name which is a simple forename. If a member leaves then his or her record is deleted from our system. The young man in question left and he has been deleted from our records.'

'Are you able to tell us if there is anyone else who might be able to help us with information about Hank?'

'It would be impossible for me to know who knows who in the community.'

'Is everyone here a member of the community?' asked Vella-cott.

'Not at all' sighed Threlfall. 'Tell me is all the questioning necessary?'

'We need to understand your organisation Mr Threlfall.'

'As well as full members we have a number of lay members. They are employees of the community and work in places like the kitchens, the cafeteria, the members dining rooms and on maintenance of the buildings and grounds.'

'Do you have both single and married members?'

'We do. Now, I trust I have answered all your questions.'

'One more' said Thomasson. 'You said that your members cut themselves off from the outside world. If that is the case why was that young man going into Penzance?'

'If one of our members has a particular craft need that requires a personal search of suppliers then it is logical that they may have to visit somewhere like Penzance.'

Threlfall got to his feet to signal the end of the meeting.

You will have no objection I hope' said Thomasson 'if we have a look round your public areas. Just to get a clearer understanding of what you do here.'

'You are free to do that if you wish. I will ask someone to act as your guide.'

'There is no need to put you to that trouble. Just let us be given the same access as any other customers.'

'I will see that you are given the appropriate pass otherwise you will be asked to pay £10 when you leave' smiled Threlfall. 'Unless, of course, you spend that amount on goods.'

He took them back to the entrance and arranged for them to have complimentary passes. After which he simply nodded to them and returned through the door. Once through the turnstile they parted company. Vellacott took one part of the units and Thomasson the other. The goods on offer were well displayed and were of undoubted quality, a fact that was reflected in their prices. The staff in each unit wore a shirt or blouse of a single rainbow colour and they noticed that virtually all the items on sale, other than clothes or textiles, bore a stamp in the form of a rainbow. The marketing of the goods was extremely professional. The two officers took the opportunity at each unit's cash desk to identify themselves as police officers and to show a photo of the accident victim and ask if he was recognised. Some of the people did look at the photo for a moment while others simply glanced at it. The responses were always the same. Either it was "sorry never seen him" or a simple "no". The tones of the responses left the questioner in no doubt that it was final.

Thomasson and Vellacott met up again in the cafeteria. The staff there wore white shirts or blouses and a rainbow coloured apron. They too said they had never seen the person in the photo. They drank their coffee and ate their danish pastries in silence. Fortunately, their passes allowed them through the turnstile and they left the buildings.

'Did you have any luck?' Thomasson asked when they were back in the car.

'No. It was the same thing no matter who I asked. They either glanced at the photos or simply looked in their direction before denying any knowledge.'

'I have the clear impression that the community members have been well schooled into see no evil, hear no evil and speak no evil. In other words, know nothing and say nothing.'

'Exactly' agreed Vellacott. 'Incidentally, I noticed that you didn't tell Threlfall that we know the person killed was not Grimhausen.'

'No, let them go on thinking they have pulled the wool over our eyes. We will fire that gun at a later date.'

Back at police headquarters they reviewed their meeting with Nigel Threlfall.

'Was it only me or did you get the impression that he was relieved when he found that we wanted to talk about the fatal accident?' Thomasson asked.

'Yes, I thought the same. I wonder what it was he didn't want to talk about?'

'It would be useful to keep an eye on the place to see what, if anything, happens there.'

'It is not the easiest of places to keep under observation, being at the end of the track with a high wall round it.'

'I agree. I think all we can do is to have a police car drive up the road to the gateway and make it seem as if they are checking on cars parked there. If we do that every day, they will either complain or they may try to do something out of the ordinary and give the game away. So, let's play a bit of cat and mouse with them.'

It was at that point that the door opened and a constable entered.

'Sorry to interrupt sir' he said to Vellacott 'but this was found when the boot of the car you used earlier was opened.' He held out a piece of paper.

Vellacott took it, opened it out and read it.

'Well I'll be a monkey's uncle' he grinned and passed the paper over to Thomasson. 'Read this.'

The piece of paper was part of a till roll from the Rainbow Craft Centre shop. On the back was written the words "Julian or Alan Vickery".

'How did that get in the boot of the car?' asked Vellacott

'Someone wanted to answer our question but didn't want anyone to know they had. Not that it does us that much good. What we have to do now is to see if we can find an Alan Vickery who is missing and who fits our photograph.'

'I think I might be able to narrow the list down a bit' smiled Vellacott. 'One of the units I looked at sold wooden goods from small decorative items to hand made chairs and tables. I picked up a very nice carved model of a seal and noticed on its base were carved the initials AV. We know the deceased was based in the woodworking unit. It could be we need to find an Alan Vickery who is a more than competent wood carver. It should limit the field when we find anyone called Alan Vickery.'

'Well spotted' congratulated Thomasson. 'Look, can you send someone in plain clothes to the craft centre to buy that carved model? How much was it?'

'Forty pounds'

'Not cheap but still' Thomasson pulled out his wallet and extracted two twenty pound notes. 'If it is not used in the case, I will give it to my wife. In the meanwhile, I will set the ball rolling in trying to trace an Alan Vickery who is missing and who was a skilled wood sculptor.'

'What about Tod Grimhausen? We don't seem to have got anywhere trying to find if he was ever in Cornwall and, if so, what happened to him.'

'My gut feeling is that he was never down here. They used of Cornwall was a smoke screen. Commander Buxton is up in Yorkshire. Let's hope he can find the answer to that question.'

CHAPTER TWENTY FOUR

HOW SAFE ARE WE?

JANUARY 1995

'Is that you Threlfall?'

'Yes, it's me speaking'

'Are you alone? Is it clear to talk? It's Delaney here.'

'It is all clear. I am at home and my wife is out at a bridge evening.'

'Have you had a visit from the police?'

'Yes, there was an Inspector from Penzance and a Chief Inspector from the Met.'

'What did they want?'

'They asked some questions about the American. When I queried why they were doing that seeing he had been dead for months, they said they were investigating identity theft.'

'The same tale as they told me. I had a visit from a local Inspector and a Commander from the Met. They wanted to know about the American's girlfriend.'

'Do you think they suspect anything?' asked Threlfall.

'What can they suspect? Both of them, as far as they are concerned, are dead and buried, well not actually buried, which is a good thing, because they can't dig them up. Not only that but, there were proper inquests, so everything was legal. I reckon they were just fishing. Did they ask about the Will?'

'Yes, and they wanted to speak to the man who had the envelope.'

'What did you say?'

'That had left here and his details had been removed from the system.'

'Good. That closes that line.'

'Yes, after that they seemed to lose interest.'

'Did they want to go round the site?' asked Delaney.

'Yes. I didn't think I could refuse their request without it seeming suspicious. I found out later that they had been showing a photo of the American and asking if anyone knew him. Of course, they all denied any knowledge.'

'Which was true seeing that he was never there.'

'Why all this interest all of a sudden?' asked Threlfall.

'I have been wondering about that. The only answer I have come up with is that the girl had a half-sister. Some months ago, we had a man asking about this young woman. We managed to fob him off with the usual story about privacy and then we showed him the door. The half-sister is named in the Will and is, as I say, the only person who may be asking questions. Have you had anyone asking about the American?'

'Not that I know of' replied Threlfall. 'Did he have any family?'

'Only in the United States. It can't be them because they would stick out like a sore thumb. If it is anyone, it must be the half-sister.'

'What are you going to do?'

'The most important thing for both of us is to do nothing that could raise any questions about the accidents. In other words, we must make sure nothing is said in your place or here. Proceed as if the whole thing is done and dusted. That way they have no hope of questioning what happened.'

'But why this question of identity theft?' asked Threlfall.

'There is no doubt that sort of thing does happen' replied Delaney. 'There has been quite a bit of publicity about it. Both these people lived like vagrants before they appeared on our radar. Given the sort of people they mixed with it's quite possible someone stole a credit card or some other identity document, even a passport, and have been trying to use it. If the police got on to that it would be quite natural to try and find the true owner of the document. Their searches probably led them to the fact that they had died in accidents, hence their visit to us.'

'So, you think we are safe?'

'We are if we do nothing to rock the boat Just remember what you will get when we have pulled this off.'

'But, what about the half-sister?'

'Leave that with me. Just remember to let me know if anything else happens regarding the road accident.'

Before Threlfall could reply the phone went dead.

The next morning Delaney arranged to meet his Head of Security Kenneth Walby in a coffee bar in Richmond.

'I have a job that needs to be done' said Delaney.

'By me?' asked Walby.

'No, by someone who has no connection with our organisation and where there will be no way it can ever be shown that there was such a connection. I think you are the man who might be able to help me.'

'How can I help if I am not to be involved?'

'You can assist by identifying someone who will do a job for me in London. Can you do that?'

'I don't see why not?' replied Walby. 'What sort of job have you in mind?'

'I want someone who can arrange for a person to meet an accident.'

'What kind of accident?'

'The ideal would be a fatal road accident. I can't use you Walby because of your trip to Cornwall. I need someone from outside. Do you know anyone?'

'I know someone who might know someone. What you want is some person who can be persuaded to do the job because he will be in even greater trouble if he refuses. Not only that but they must realise that if they talk out of turn they will be in even bigger trouble.'

'You mean the person making the arrangements has to have a hold on the man being used? If so, what kind of hold had you in mind?' asked Delaney.

'A man who owes money to his dealer and cannot pay his debt. That way no money has to pass to him.'

'But, what about the dealer?'

'Well, he is not going to get paid as things are so anything on offer will be a bonus.'

'I can't give you a fixed price. Just tell me how much you are prepared to pay, then give me the details of who is going to be hit and leave the rest to me.'

'OK. You go ahead and fix it. I want the job done as quickly as possible.'

'What's in it for me?' asked Welby

'Let's put it this way Welby, if you don't get this job done you could very well lose what we have already agreed. Treat it as an insurance against losing your fee.'

'And if I won't do it for free?'

'You might meet an accident yourself. We are not playing games Welby. This is for real. This evening an envelope will be put through your door with details of the person concerned. Get it fixed and let me know what, if anything, your contact needs. Only, don't try to be clever and cut yourself in for a slice.'

With this Delaney got to his feet and walked out.

Three days later Walby met up with Delaney at the Community.

'We need to talk' he said.

'I'll come to your workshop later this morning.'

'I have it fixed' Walby said. 'My contact gets rid of a client who is holding back his payments plus he wants £500. The other chap will probably be high on drugs so if he gets caught they will think it is a simple hit and run.'

'Pay him the £500' said Delaney 'and submit an invoice for £500 of electrical goods and you will be paid by the Community.'

'Will do.'

'Make it soon' said Delaney

CHAPTER
TWENTY FIVE

WHY ME?

JANUARY 1995

It was a cold and very misty morning as Louise Mercier left her house at about nine thirty to go to an appointment with a professor at London University who wanted her to type up a paper he was writing for a learned journal. She had taken the first turning on the right which would lead her to the nearest tube station. Suddenly a voice yelled out:

'Look out!!'

She hesitated in her steps and then she felt a hand grab her arm and pull her off the pavement and through a gateway until she found herself laying on wet grass. There was the loud roar of a motor engine close by her which changed in tempo as the vehicle, or whatever it was, sped off down the road. Breathless from her fall and with her head spinning she looked round her. A man, obviously a postman from the bag that was round his neck was kneeling by her side.

'Are you OK?' he asked.

'I think so' she gasped 'what happened?'

'I saw a white van drive up on to the footpath and head straight for you. I thought he was going to hit you. As you stepped by the gateway of this house, I was just able to grab you and pull you inside the garden. He can only have missed you by inches.'

At this point there was the sound of running feet crossing the road and a middle-aged man entered the garden.

'Is she alright?' he panted. 'I saw the van go up on the path and drive at her. I thought he must get her. I closed my eyes. When I opened them again, she wasn't there and the van was scorching up the road.'

'I am alright I think' said Louise 'just a bit battered and bruised. It seems as though I owe my life to you' she turned towards the postman. 'Thank you so much.'

'I had just put a small parcel on the doorstep and rung the bell. I turned to go back to the road when I heard the noise of a car and when I looked, I could see it was a van driving at a rate of knots right along the footpath and heading at the lady. It was right on her heels as she passed the gateway and I just made an automatic grab at her.'

'What on earth is going on here' claimed an angry female voice as an elderly woman came out of the front door. 'I heard the doorbell ring but by the time I managed to get downstairs and open the door all I could see was people on my front lawn.'

'The postman' replied the man from across the road 'has saved this lady from being run down by a van being driven along the pavement.'

'What happened to the van?' the woman demanded.

'It drove off like a rocket' said the postman.

'What about you dear? Are you hurt?'

'Not very much thanks to this quick thinking man.'

'Has anyone called the police and the ambulance?' the woman asked.

'I don't need an ambulance' Louise protested.'

'Oh yes you do dear. You have had a very nasty shock and you should be seen to by a doctor. I know because I used to be a nurse. And, if what you say is right, someone tried to kill you and that has to be reported.'

Louise was escorted into the house, sat down and given a cup of hot sweet tea while the postman telephoned for the police and ambulance. The ambulance men checked Louise over but could find no broken bones or other damage but they still insisted that she be taken to the Accident and Emergency Department to be seen by a doctor. Before she was carried off in the ambulance Louise did manage to thank the postman.

'You saved my life' she said 'just to say thank you seems so inadequate. But I really do thank you for your quick thinking.'

'It was lucky that we were both in the right place at the right time' he grinned. 'You look after yourself and look where you are walking in future.'

While Louise was being taken to the hospital the police took statements from the postman, the man from across the road and the lady in whose garden she had ended up. Although their stories tallied there was absolutely no information about the white van other than the fact that it had driven off like a rocket. No-one had been able to read a number plate. The only physical evidence was some white paint marks on the front hedge where the van must have brushed against the bushes.

'Though how we are supposed to find one white van in the hundreds of the thousands there must be in London I am damned if I know' muttered one of the policemen.

They caught up with Louise at the hospital where a doctor, after a full examination, had declared that she had suffered nothing worse than a stiff shoulder joint from where it had been jerked by the postman and a few bruises. However, they insisted that she remain in the hospital for the rest of the day to make sure there was no delayed shock. Having taking details of her name, date of birth and address the police constable asked her:

'Is there anyone we should notify about what has happened?'

'Only Professor Gideon Standish at London University. I was due to meet him at ten o'clock about a typing job. He will be wondering why I haven't turned up. His phone number is on this piece of paper.'

'OK, we will give him a ring. But what about family?'

'I have no family apart from a couple of cousins who live in Herefordshire and with whom I have practically no contact. I live on my own and am technically self-employed.'

'Can you think of anyone who would wish to harm you Miss Mercier?'

'I can't. As far as I know I have no real enemies. I am sure that, like most people, there are those who don't like me too much but I can't imagine that anyone would deliberately try to run me down. All I can think is that the driver must have lost control of the van and swerved off the road on to the path. Perhaps he fell asleep or was taken ill or something like that. Or, perhaps he was drunk or had been taking drugs. They are the only reasons I can think of.'

'Well, if you do remember anything at all that could throw light on what took place please contact the police station.'

'Yes, of course and thank you for your help.'

When she was released Louise took a taxi home. Sitting in her lounge she felt cold and shivery and realised that the narrow escape had been more traumatic than she first thought. Luckily there was some brandy in the house and she had a stiff drink, took a couple of paracetamol tablets, made a hot water bottle and went to bed. To her surprise and relief, she slept well and next morning, apart from a stiff shoulder joint and some bruises, felt none the worse for wear. It wasn't until after lunch that she decided to tell Peter Lewis what had happened and to see what he advised her to do.

'Peter, it's Louise. Something very odd has happened and I am wondering what, if anything I should do.'

'What's the problem Louise?'

She told him succinctly what had happened the previous morning and how lucky she had been there was a quick thinking postman on hand.

'The police have been told I suppose?'

'Oh yes, and an ambulance was called and I was carted off to the local hospital but they didn't find anything seriously wrong, just some bruises and a stiff shoulder joint. The local police questioned me and wanted to know if I knew of anyone who wanted to harm me which, of course, I don't. I think it's more likely the driver was drunk or on drugs and simply lost control of the van.'

'Did you tell them about Bethany,'

'No, I didn't mention that at all. I mean it can't be related to what happened to her can it?'

'I don't know but it does seem a bit too coincidental to my suspicious mind. Have you told Commander Buxton?'

'No.'

'Well, I think you should. If there were to be any connection with what happened to Bethany you could be in danger down there in London. I appreciate that you are working but couldn't you do your work from somewhere else?'

'I suppose I could. But where could I go? I have a couple of cousins in Herefordshire but I can hardly wish myself on either of them.'

'Then come up here. There would be no problem in finding space for you and you would be very welcome.'

'I can't keep taking advantage of your kindness.'

'Oh, I dare say we could agree suitable terms' he laughed. 'Think about it and, in the meantime, contact Commander Buxton and see what he thinks.'

Richard Buxton was immersed in the mass of information that was being gathered.

'There is lady asking for you sir,' said his secretary.

'Did she give a name?'

'Yes, it is Louise Mercier.'

'Put her through, please. Good afternoon Miss Mercier, what can I do for you?'

Louise once again went through the events of the previous day and the fact that Peter Lewis had told her to tell him.

'How are you? Were you badly hurt?'

'No, I was very lucky and suffered nothing more than a stiff shoulder and some bruises. Mr Lewis asked me if I had told the police about Bethany when they questioned me about what had happened. I didn't as I couldn't and don't see any connection between the two things. I thought it was probably someone who was drunk or had been using drugs. That was when he suggested I tell you. Do you think the two things are connected?'

'The answer to that question Miss Mercier is that I don't know. This is a very complex affair and, to be honest, we have not yet worked out all the ramifications. I will contact the local police to see what they have discovered although, like you, I think it unlikely they have found the van or the driver.'

'One other thing Commander, Mr Lewis has suggested that as a precautionary measure I should go and stay with him in Yorkshire, in case there is a second attempt on me. Do you think that would be a good idea?'

'It sounds sensible to me. You live on your own and it would be quite impossible to provide you with twenty four hour protection in London. If someone is planning a second attempt, they very well might give themselves away if they hang around your house. If you do decide to go please let me know.'

When he had finished his telephone conversation Richard Buxton contacted the police station in Louise's neighbourhood. The Inspector at the station, who had read the reports prepared by his constables, said that all the evidence pointed towards it being a drunk or drugged driver who lost control of the van.

'I don't suppose you have had any luck in tracing the van?'

No, sir. It's like looking for a needle in a haystack.'

'Have you tried the Traffic people to see if they have any abandoned vehicles?'

'We put through a general enquiry but have heard nothing.'

Well, if anything does crop up would you please make a note to let me know.'

'Very well sir'

Buxton decided to pull some rank and contacted the Traffic Section. Prompted by an enquiry from a very senior officer at the Yard, they carried out a thorough search of their records.

'Commander Buxton? Phillips from Traffic here sir, about your enquiry concerning a white van. As you can imagine, quite a lot of these go missing. They are easy to steal and there are so many of them about no-one takes any notice of them. But we have had a bit of luck. A van was found abandoned in the car park of a supermarket. A check revealed it was stolen in Watford three days ago. What caught the attention of our chaps was that there were scratches along the offside of the vehicle that looked like they could have been caused by it scraping against a hedge of some sort. Luckily the owner is in no haste to collect the van which is in a pretty poor condition. I have asked the forensic people to check on the paint and to check the hedge of the house where the attempted hit and run took place.'

'Well done Inspector. Whilst you are at it could you make sure the van is tested for finger prints. If there are any please send them on to me. Oh, and if the owner appears you might get his prints as well.

Two days later Buxton received news that the forensic people had confirmed that the van had been scraped against the hedge. Small items of paint taken from the hedge matched the paint on the van. The finger prints collected from the vehicle did not match any on the files.

The same day he heard from Louise Mercier that she had decided to go and stay with Peter Lewis.

CHAPTER TWENTY SIX

FURTHER AND BETTER PARTICULARS

JANUARY 1995

With their visits to Cornwall and Yorkshire over Buxton and Thomasson regrouped in the former's room at Scotland Yard. Each had had an opportunity to review the detailed report the other had produced on their trips.

'How would you summarise the situation Robert?' asked Buxton

'Well, it seems, sir, that we have good evidence that the people said to have died in accidents in Cornwall and Yorkshire were not the people it was claimed they were. Added to that we know that both Bethany and Tod were killed and their bodies disposed of with the intention of concealing their identity. The main questions remain where were they killed and by whom. On balance I would say that they were both in Yorkshire and that they were killed in that county. I do not think Tod was ever in Cornwall. There can be little or no doubt that the Rainbow organisation is involved in some way or another.'

'A fair summary but what was their motive?'

'I have discovered one more interesting fact' smiled Thomasson 'thanks to my elder daughter who is studying classics at Oxford. The word 'Arcus', the name of the beneficiary in both Wills is Latin for Arc which describes the shape of a rainbow.'

Is it indeed!' exclaimed Buxton with a wide grin. 'That proves the benefit of a classical education.'

Buxton's phone rang whilst he was setting out what he saw as their next steps.

'Inspector Seagrave of the North Yorkshire Police would like to speak to you sir.'

'Put him through. Good morning Seagrave, what can I do for you today?'

'We have a hit sir'

'A hit?'

'Yes, on the photograph of the victim who fell to her death at Netherton.'

Buxton signalled to Thomasson to listen in on the extension.

'Well done Seagrave! That was quick. What have you found out?'

'I put up one of the photos to remind everyone here that we were trying to identify the woman. This morning, one of the cleaners employed by the firm who are contracted to do the cleaning here told the desk sergeant that she knew the woman. Her name is, or was, Julie Cranston, she was reported missing at the end of 1993. It seems there was domestic trouble with the boyfriend and she walked out and has not been seen by anyone who knew her since then. Not only that but our informant says she had a child who died shortly after its birth.'

'Was this Julie Cranston local to Richmond?'

No, she came from Darlington. The woman who has identified her only moved to Netherton a month ago. I am getting out the missing person file and also checking to see if we have any other information about the woman Cranston. If we have her finger prints on file, we should be able to check them against those taken at the autopsy.'

'Keep me in the picture please Inspector and copy me in on all the information you are able to gather.'

'Very good sir. Do you want us to say anything to the people at Netherton?'

'Not at the moment. I prefer to keep that shot in my locker.'

Further enquiries by the police in Yorkshire revealed that Julie Cranston was a graduate of Newcastle University and had a degree in art history. She was an accomplished artist but got involved with a man who was already married. He refused to leave his wife so that when Julie had her child, she became a single mother living on benefits. Sadly, the child died at only three months old. Afterwards, Julie resumed her relationship with the father of the child, who proved to be physically violent. She told friends she was going to leave him, so when she disappeared, they all thought she had simply run away. It looked as if she had used her artistic skills to hide in the Rainbow community.

The leaflet given to Buxton at Netherton showed that there were no less than a dozen Rainbow Communities in Great Britain, ranging from Cornwall to Inverness and from Ramsgate to the Isle of Mull. He initiated enquiries with all the relevant police forces to obtain information about each of these communities. The information gathered showed that they were all run on similar lines to those in Cornwall and North Yorkshire.

In addition to details of the communities in Great Britain the leaflet told that the Rainbow movement had been founded in California in the early 1940s, a direct tribute to the classic film The Wizard of Oz and the hit song 'Somewhere Over The Rainbow'. It had moved into Europe after the end of World War II, initially in the American Zone of West Germany, and had then spread to most other western European countries including Britain. Each country organised its communities independently and there was no overarching world headquarters, not only that but each country granted apparent autonomy to the individual communities within its borders. Thus, there was nothing to stop all the communities in one country being the subsidiaries of a principal community.

Enquiries made of the local police did not bring to light any incidents at the other ten Rainbow communities. Selecting three of the locations Buxton contacted the local police to inform them that an undercover police officer would be operating in their area in the guise of someone writing a guide book to secular communities in the British Isles. He would not identify himself to the local force but Scotland Yard would be grateful, if the need should arise, for him to seek assistance that they would do all within their power to be of help.

'We have good reason to believe that there have been illegal activities carried on at some of these communities. There is a dozen of them scattered over the British Isles. Apart from two none of the others have reported anything out of the ordinary. What we need to try and ascertain is the degree to which these places are connected. 'he concluded.

The undercover officer selected was a member of the Special Branch and was able to achieve his objective of visiting each of the selected three Rainbow communities. His report underlined the information gained by Buxton and Thomasson. In addition, he was able to discover that the structure of the communities was such that the one at Netherton was the head office for all of them.

Thomasson had set in place enquiries about the Arcus Foundation in Luxembourg. With the assistance of the European Affairs Ministry and Interpol he uncovered what little information was available on the organisation. It had been formed only about eighteen months previously and was registered as an investment vehicle with the objectives of capital and income growth. As far as was known it was a private investment fund. The local office of a well-known insurance group provided investment and custody services. The officers of the Foundation were Luxembourgers about whom there was no negative information. Apparently. It was not an unusual kind of arrangement in that country which actively encouraged foreign investment and offered an advantageous tax regime. If, as was likely, the local officers were simply acting as nominees for the real owners the latter's' details were not in the public domain.

Thomasson was completing his report on his findings when his intercom buzzed. It was Buxton.

'Robert, could you spare a moment please.'

'On my way, sir'

'Take a seat Robert' Buxton pointed to a chair. 'I have had a phone call from Louise Mercier.'

'Has she come up with anything new?'

'You could say that. She has been the victim of an attempted hit and run accident.'

'Was she hurt?'

'It seems she was remarkably lucky. A very alert postman saw a white van careering along the pavement and pulled her into a garden. The van simply drove off at a rate of knots. She was badly shaken but suffered only very minor injuries. She seems to think it must have been a driver who was drunk or under the influence of drugs.'

'What time of day was this?'

'Quite early, just after nine in the morning.'

'Drugs are a possibility but I shouldn't think there was a drunk driver around at that time of day. What do you think sir?'

'I share your scepticism. So incidentally, does Peter Lewis who is trying to persuade her to go and stay at his place in the Dales.'

'If it wasn't an accident, sir, then the likelihood is that it was an attempt to silence her. But if that was the case, why was it done and who did it? '

'At the minute it's easier to suggest an answer the first of those questions. The identification of the skeleton in the Dales is almost entirely dependent on her confirming the hypotheses of the forensic people. With her out of the way it might be impossible to produce enough proof of identity which, in its turn, would mean that the young woman who fell to her death at Netherton could be said to be Bethany Mercier. What the perpetrator or organiser of the hit and run does not know is that we know who that young lady really was. All they have succeeded in doing is increasing our suspicion of The End of The Rainbow.

As a follow up to his visit to Cornwall, Thomasson had contacted the Missing Persons Unit to see if they were able to offer any help in tracking Alan Vickery. Although the Unit confirmed that there were over 150,000 persons who went missing each year it did not mean that every person who did so was reported. When provided with the information gained about Alan Vickery, they were not able to identify anyone on their books who seemed to fill the case.

Then, in another of those strange twists of fate that seemed to litter these cases, Thomasson had a call from the police in Worcester. A man had called at their headquarters to ask if they had any information about an Alan Vickery. The man was Richard Vickery who was trying to trace his younger brother. Worcester police had no record of an Alan Vickery and took details from his brother although they pointed out that as it was over a year ago since the younger Vickery had last been heard from it was unlikely there was very much they could do. It was after Richard Vickery had left that the name Alan Vickery rang a bell as one that had been circulated to all police stations in the country.

They contacted Thomasson who asked that they invite Richard

Vickery back for another interview. In particular they were to try and obtain a photograph of the young man and ascertain what trade or profession he had followed together with any physical attributes that might assist in an identification. Having obtained that information, they were to send it on to Thomasson at Scotland Yard. When the information arrived from Worcester, Thomasson took out the photograph he had obtained of the victim of the road accident and compared it to this new print. There could be no doubt that they were a match. The identification was underlined by the fact that Richard Vickery had said that his brother had broken a leg in a motor cycle accident and also that he had had his appendix removed. Not only that but Alan Vickery had trained as a furniture restorer and was also an amateur wood sculptor who marked his products with his initials. There was no doubt. They had identified the man killed in Cornwall.

It was left to Thomasson to contact Richard Vickery and pass on the sad news of his brother's death

'First of all, Mr Vickery, thank you very much for the helpful information that you have given to Worcester Police. This has allowed us to trace your brother in our files.'

'Do you know where he is?' the anxious voice demanded.

'Can you tell me why you are looking for him so long after his disappearance?' asked Thomasson

'It's our mother. She is terminally ill and keeps asking to see Alan.'

'I am sorry to hear about your mother Mr Vickery but I am afraid that it will not be possible to fulfil her request.'

'What do you mean? Why isn't it possible?'

'I very much regret that your brother died in a road accident in Cornwall some months ago. The local people had no information as to next of kin and so were unable to inform you of what had happened.'

'Poor mother! This news would have killed her if the cancer is not already doing it. Now, I have to work out what I can say to her. You are totally sure of what you say? Where is he buried for instance, that information may comfort her.'

'He is not buried anywhere, Mr Vickery. In the absence of information, he was cremated and his ashes scattered at sea.'

'It's not exactly the news I was hoping to receive, but thank you for letting me know.'

'Just one further thing Mr Vickery. Would you very kindly go back to the Police Station in Worcester and make a formal statement about your brother. This will allow us to close his file.'

When his mother asked, yet again, why Alan had not been to see her all that Richard could think to say was that she should not worry about Alan, because he was waiting for her. Mrs Vickery died that same night.

CHAPTER TWENTY SEVEN

BUXTON AND THOMASSON ATTACK

JANUARY 1995

'That's one more piece of the jigsaw in its place 'said Commander Richard Buxton when Chief Inspector Thomasson relayed the result of the search for Alan Vickery.

'What do you plan to do next sir?'

'The first thing is to prepare a case for the DPP. His approval is necessary before we can take any action. I would like you to make a start on that straight away. We have now obtained all the evidence we need to prove that the young woman who died at Netherton was not Bethany Mercier and that any claim that she was is completely false. Instead, we have legal proof that the skeleton recovered in the Yorkshire Dales was that of the real Bethany Mercier. Secondly, we have proof that the person killed in a road accident in Cornwall was not Patrick Tod Grimhausen and that claims that it was him are false. The body of the real Tod Grimhausen was that that was fished out of a reservoir in County Durham. It is time to use that information to attack the stories given to us by the two Rainbow centres. What I propose to do is this. We will mount simultaneous raids on the Cornish and the North Yorkshire premises. The idea being to prevent them from communicating with each other. We will carry out a complete search of the premises and interview everyone who lives or works there. At the same time, we will confiscate all the computers on the premises so that the data recorded on them can be searched by our IT people. Unless I am right off target, I believe that this will set us on the road to proving that these two young people were not only known at Netherton but also that it was the last place they were seen alive. It is that kind of information that we need to be able to build a case for bringing capital charges against the people who caused their deaths.'

'We have sufficient already to charge both Threlfall and Delaney with falsifying death records and for committing perjury at a Coroner's Inquest.'

'Agreed. But we don't have enough to bring the more serious charges. What we have to convince the DPP about is the fact that unless we put pressure on Threlfall and Delaney we are unlikely to be able to prove who killed the real Bethany Mercier and Tod Grimhausen and when and where. Don't forget to include information about the Wills and that foundation in Luxembourg.'

'Then, I will get on with drafting a paper for the DPP.'

As he got to the door Buxton called out:

'There is one other point I think we need to include.'

'What's that sir?'

'The attempt on the life of Louise Mercier. We should underline the fact that she is the one person who could upset the killer's plans. So it would be as well to say that we are planning to check the validity of both the wills.'

Whilst Thomasson was getting on with his task Buxton made a series of telephone calls. His first was to Gilbert Ravendale.

'I thought that I should bring you up to date with our investigations about what happened in Cornwall.'

'I was wondering how you were getting on Commander. I am conscious that I should try and keep the family in the States as up to date as possible. If you had not rung I should in all probabilities contacted you.'

'The main progress is that we have been able to formally identify the body that it was claimed was that of Tod Grimhausen. In actual fact it was that of a young Englishman called Alan Vickery.'

'Well done! How did you manage that?'

'A mixture of routine police work and a slice of luck' chuckled Buxton. 'In addition, we have found out that the Arcus Foundation which is the body in Luxembourg who is due to get all the money left by those two young people is, in an Latin translation, the Arch Foundation and that word describes a rainbow. It is claimed to be an investment fund. The named controllers are local Luxembourgers although the odds are that they are nominees for someone else.'

'Very interesting' said Ravendale 'I suspect that you will not be surprised if I say that I shall be advising the family that any transfer of funds to that body should be delayed until we have been able to discover exactly what happened to their son. Can you tell me what you propose to do next?'

'We are discussing with the Director of Public Prosecutions with the idea of bringing to justice those responsible for false identification. That is for your ears only, by the way, at least for the moment. I will let you know when you can inform the American family. Incidentally, how are things in that area?'

'Obviously they are very shocked at what has happened. Once the formal inquest on Tod is completed, they will want to take his remains back for burial in the United States. Tell me, what is the police view on that point?'

'For the moment we do not know when or where Tod was killed. You will understand this may delay other formalities. Also, the defence of those accused in the other deaths may want to have access to the real Tod's remains to formulate their defence. All

I can do is say that we will not delay matters any longer than necessary.'

'Thank you for letting me know how things stand Commander. I hope that we can stay in touch as things develop.'

Buxton's next call was to Louise Mercier. He assumed that, by this time, she would be in Yorkshire and so rang Peter Lewis' number.

'May I speak to Miss Mercier please?' he said when someone answered the phone.

'Who shall I say is calling?'

'Commander Buxton.'

After a short silence a man's voice came on the line.

'Commander Buxton, this is Peter Lewis. Louise will be here in a minute. How are you?'

'I am fine thanks and you?'

'We are fit and well here. Ah, here is Louise.'

'Commander Buxton, good morning. How can I help you? Do you mind if Peter listen's in on the extension?'

'Not at all. I am ringing, in part, to check that everything is alright with you. There have been no further attempts on your life?'

'No, nothing like that.'

'No odd or unexpected enquiries about you?'

'No, it's all quiet here at the moment.'

'Good. Don't forget to let me know at once if anything suspicious occurs.'

'You don't think someone will try, again do you?'

'I hope not but we cannot simply assume that as you are not in London, they have not traced you to Yorkshire. That is why you should take particular care at the moment.'

'Are we allowed to ask what progress you are making Commander?' asked Peter Lewis.

'We have been able to identify the young woman who fell to her death in Netherton. Her name was Julie Cranston. I don't suppose that means anything to you does it Miss Mercier?'

'Nothing at all. I don't think I have ever known anyone called that.'

'How did you manage to do that?' asked Peter Lewis. 'From what I saw of them I can't think the people at the Rainbow would have told you.'

'Like most cases it was a mixture of solid police work and luck. We were able to compare the information we were given with the autopsy information and there was an undoubted match.'

'What happens next?'

'We are discussing this with the DPP. We may well proceed against someone for false registration of death and perjury at the inquest. That, plus other routine work, will give us the leads we need to find out when and where Miss Bethany Mercier met her death. Oh, and we have discovered quite a bit more about the Arcus Foundation in Luxembourg. Did you know, for instance, that Arcus is Latin for arch which is the shape of a rainbow'

'How very interesting' laughed Peter Lewis.

'I presume Miss Mercier that you are not processing the distribution of the trust fund?'

'No, my solicitor has advised that we stall things until they become clearer.'

'One other thing 'Buxton said 'if things start to hot up for these people it is going to be very important that you make no contact with them and take all the care you are able to prevent another attempt on your life. We can't tell how desperate they might become if things start to go against them. I will keep you informed of any major developments and I would like you to let me know of any untoward happenings at your end.'

Buxton's next step was to initiate a conference call to Inspector Vellacott in Cornwall and Inspector Seagrave in Yorkshire.

'Good morning, gentlemen' he said when the connections had been established. 'I am contacting you today to bring you up to date on what is happening with the investigation. As you know we have obtained confirmed identities for the young people who died at the Rainbow centres in your areas. There can be no doubt that false statements were made when their deaths were registered and at the inquests. Therefore, we are seeking DPP approval to bring charges against Messrs Threlfall and Delaney. What I want to do is discuss with you how we are to proceed when the warrants have been issued.

My plan is to carry out a raid on both premises on the same day and at the same time. The two men will be arrested and taken into custody. At the same time, we will have a warrant to confiscate all computers that are located at those premises. They will be brought to the Met's IT specialists to see what secrets they hide. Personally, I have no doubt that the records have been tampered with and we need to be able to demonstrate that. Additionally, we shall carry out a thorough and detailed search of the two sets of premises and everyone who lives or works there should be questioned as to what they know about events at the centres. The object being, of course, to get someone to talk or for there to be conflicting stories told. In particular we need to identify and talk to the person who found the Bethany Mercier's Will under a drawer and to the man who had the envelope that led to Tod Grimhausen's Will. Would each of you prepare a list of the questions that you think should be put to those who live or work at your local Rainbow centre. When we have these, we can compare notes and agree that as far as is possible we are asking the same questions of everyone. Use your local knowledge in formulating the suggested questions.

'What we need, above all else, is some information about what happened to the real Bethany Mercier and Tod Grimhausen. To date we do not know when or where they were killed. If you have not already done so, Inspector Seagrave, could you initiate enquiries to see if anyone saw anything unusual in the area where the skeleton was found at about the time it was deposited in the sinkhole. As far as Grimhausen is concerned Inspector Vellacott, I know that Chief Inspector Thomasson has doubts as to whether he was ever in Cornwall. Also, we are not completely sure that Alan Vickery, the actual victim of the road accident, was killed where his body was found. Thomasson will lead the raid and he will instigate a thorough search of the road or track leading to the centre to see if that throws any light on this question.

I shall come to Yorkshire, Inspector Seagrave, to lead the raid at Netherton.

I am well aware that these raids and their follow ups are going to require a great deal of work for you gentlemen and put pressure on your resources. That is why I am giving you this information now, to enable you to start planning. When we have the green light from the DPP I have no doubt that our AC will contact your CC to confirm the position. Do you have any immediate questions?

'Presumably we shall have to close the site to the public while the searches and questioning is in progress' commented Vellacott.

'Luckily, at this time of year there are not likely to be many groups planning to visit the site' added Seagrave.

'What about the media? As soon as they get wind of this, they will be buzzing around like wasps round a honey pot' said Vellacott. 'We shall need to agree what we say to them so that we are all singing from the same hymn sheet.'

'A good point' agreed Buxton. 'I will ask our PR people to prepare a draft statement. At this stage we don't want anything said about the bodies in the Dales and the County Durham reservoir. One thing that is vital is that nothing is allowed to leak out to anyone before the event. Make sure that your people are made aware that if anyone talks out of turn it will be considered a serious breach of discipline. We don't want this whole operation going off half cock. We will keep in close touch as things progress.'

Later that day Thomasson brought in his draft of a paper to the DPP. The two men worked through it and made the necessary amendments to finalise it. Buxton took it to the Assistant Commissioner and, having obtained his agreement to its terms took it personally to the Director.

'Well Commander' said Sir Harold Lowther, who, as a Queen's Counsel, had had a vast experience in criminal cases before assuming his current position, 'you appear to have a most interesting enquiry on your hands. Taking the steps you propose will not, in itself, guarantee that you will be able to formulate a case against anyone with regard to the deaths of the two young people.'

'I agree entirely Sir Harold 'said Buxton 'but I believe that the steps we are proposing will prove to be the key that unlocks the secrets of the two murders.'

'I shall of course need to see a further case on that aspect of matters before I could give approval to additional action.'

'I quite understand Sir Harold.'

'

CHAPTER TWENTY EIGHT

IF AT FIRST YOU DON'T SUCCEED

FEBRUARY 1995

'Listen Walby' said Delaney into his phone 'I need to see you urgently. Find an excuse to be at the workshop at eight this evening. Got that?'

'Got it.'

At a few minutes past eight a car drew up outside the workshop used by the Community. Delaney got out of the vehicle and, looking round to ensure that he was not seen, typed a number into the keyboard by the door of one of the units and pulled it up and over. The interior was lit by a fluorescent tube and sitting by a bench reading a newspaper was Kenneth Walby the Head of Security.

'What's the panic boss?' he asked.

'There isn't a panic yet, but things haven't been helped by the fact that the bloody fool who was supposed to do the job made a complete pig's ear of it. He missed the target who escaped into a garden.'

'Did he get away?'

'More by luck than judgement. That's the only positive thing about the whole fiasco. All he managed to do was to make sure the police have got themselves involved. It seems he used a stolen van which he has ditched. There is nothing to tie him to the van or to us. At least I hope there isn't. How reliable is your contact?'

'He won't talk. He'll be too busy arranging to settle with the fool of a driver who won't talk either for the simple reason he will not be talking to anyone.'

'Have you paid your contact the £500?'

'No, it was payment on completion of the job.'

'Well, make sure he doesn't get paid now.'

'What are you going to do?'

'Screwing up this job makes it all the more important we get rid of the woman and quick.'

'How?'

'See this' Delaney reached into his coat pocket and produced a document. 'Its title tells you all you need to know.'

'Where did you get that?'

'Off the internet of course you idiot. Where else would you find that sort of information. Now listen carefully. Terry Shebdon is a good electrician, isn't he?'

'Yes, he can fix just about anything.'

'Give him this and tell him to make up one of these things' Delaney pointed to the document. 'Then, put it in a parcel and leave it here. When he has done that you are to tell me and I will deal with it. If Shebdon needs to buy anything then he has my approval to do so and the bills can be paid by the Community.'

'How are you going to square Terry?'

'That's your problem. I will increase your cut to thirty grand but you must pay Shebdon out of that. How much does he think he is going to get for what he has done to date?'

'Five'

'You can offer him up to another five, but make it absolutely clear to him that if he talks he will not live long enough to regret it. His pay-out comes from yours. That will still leave you with plenty of cash. Just one other thing. I want this job done in two days at the most. So, get on with it.'

Sure enough, two days later Walby phoned Delaney to say his parcel was ready. Delaney told his secretary to cancel all his appointments for the following day as he had to attend a British Tourist Board meeting in London. He drove to the lock-up and carefully wrapped the parcel in thick brown paper and attached a typed label to it. In addition, he added a second label which simply said United Kingdom Delivery Service to make it look as it if had been delivered by a courier. He put the parcel carefully into a brief case and drove to Darlington Station where he took a train to London. He stayed the night at an hotel in a quiet street off the Euston Road and, early the next morning he took the tube to his destination. He walked along the road and turned into the first turning on the left, down a tree lined street, until he found the house he wanted. Making sure there was no-one about, he opened the front gate and walked up the path to put his parcel carefully on the front step. He then retraced his steps back to his hotel, collected his overnight case and took the train back to Darlington. This time he was making quite sure there were no mistakes. If you want something done, he told himself, the best way is to do it yourself.

The plan was fool proof. No woman could resist opening a parcel she found on her doorstep. When she did, the result would put an end to her and leave insufficient evidence to trace the device back to him. Nothing could go wrong this time.

CHAPTER TWENTY NINE

BETHANY'S WILL

February 1995

Louise Mercier had settled in to the guest suite which was part of the owner's apartment at the Culver Hill Farm in North Yorkshire. Initially, she had been hoping that she would be able to continue to work for the agency from a distance. However, as her solicitor pointed out to her, she could not do that without her address becoming known which, in itself, defeated the objective of her whereabouts being kept secret. She had managed to find a neighbour to keep an eye on her house for her and had arranged for her mail to be redirected to Yorkshire. The inability to earn a salary posed a problem for her. She could not go on indefinitely without any income, nor could she depend on Peter Lewis' hospitality for longer than essential. When she raised this point with him, he was adamant that she should not go back to London until the police had been able to make more progress in their investigation as to what had happened to Bethany. After some thought he came up with a solution. He would employ her as Administrator for the business, a job which involved managing the bookings, keeping the accounting records and dealing with the guests on arrival or departure. This applied to the main guest house and to the holiday cottages. He offered her a salary which, taking into account that she was receiving full board and lodging was, she felt, more than reasonable. Not only that but he suggested that he drive her down to her house in London to allow her to clear any personal property which would allow her to let the house furnished on a short term basis. This would provide her with enough to be able to keep the house going. Louise accepted both these suggestions with delight and no little relief. If truth be told she was enjoying her life in Yorkshire and it was a pleasure to be working with the new Peter Lewis who treated her more as a colleague than a minion. The trip to London was carried out without any problems and she was soon settled in to her new job and way of life.

With Spring approaching the business in Yorkshire was picking up not only with guests but also with enquiries for the holiday cottages. She was enjoying the fresh challenges the job brought to her. Then, one morning, she received a phone call from Commander Buxton saying that he was in the area and asking if he could come and see her.

'Good morning Miss Mercier. How are things? No more alarms about your safety I trust.' He greeted her on his arrival.

'Good morning Commander. Things are as good as they can be in all the circumstances and I am quite safe here. Come this way will you please.'

She led him into an office where he found Peter Lewis seated behind the desk.

'I thought it best to ask Peter to sit in on this meeting Commander' explained Louise. 'I hope that is alright.'

'Of course. How are you Mr Lewis?'

'I am fine thanks. Have a seat and a cup of coffee.'

'Thank you.'

'How are you progressing?' asked Peter as he handed over a cup.

'We are moving ahead and have sufficient evidence for us to

identify the young woman who died at Netherton as one Julie Cranston and the young man who died in Cornwall as Alan Vickery. Do either of those names mean anything to you?'

'Nothing at all' said Louise and Peter nodded his agreement.

'As a result,' continued Buxton 'we plan to arrest the two men who identified the bodies and charge them with obtaining a false death certificate and of committing perjury at an Inquest. The charges are pretty solid but they will get bail until the trial.'

'But what about Bethany and Tod?' asked Louise.

'At the moment we have two people killed in supposed accidents as well as your half- sister and the young American. We believe that we are well on the trail of the person who killed Alan Vickery in Cornwall and we have a good deal of circumstantial evidence about the death of Julie Cranston. If we can find who killed those two, I believe that we shall be in a strong position to find who committed the other crimes.'

'But you have no real evidence at the moment?' asked Peter.

'We are hoping that someone might have seen something near to the point where the body was discovered in the dales at about the time that we suspect that Bethany disappeared. It is a pretty remote place and whoever deposited the body there would have needed transport. Vehicles   re pretty rare in such a location which actually makes it all the more likely that is would be noticed. We have a pretty good idea of what vehicle was involved in the accident in Cornwall. We know who drove it so what we need to do now is to prove it was the one which was involved

'Are we allowed to ask whose it is?' said Louise.

'All I can say at the moment is that it is another thread in the pattern that is appearing. We plan to seize all the computer equipment at both the Cornwall and the Yorkshire sites and are hopeful that we shall find some interesting corroborative facts when we make a thorough search of the data stored on them.

But I have to admit that in cases like this we often have to rely on a confession or on someone willing to talk about what they know in an effort to reduce their guilt.'

'You mention computers' Peter said 'what do you hope to find from them?'

'People assume that if they delete or alter records the earlier data is lost. That is not the case and our experts will track such events if they have taken place. But my main reason for coming to see you Miss Mercier is another point that has arisen. Can you tell me, has probate been granted to your half-sister's Will?'

'Not at the moment. My solicitor has advised that we delay matters whilst your enquiry is ongoing.'

'So, he will have the original of her Will in his possession?'

'Yes. Do you think that is important?'

'It could be. Tell me Miss Mercier are you completely satisfied that the signature on that document is the signature of Miss Bethany Mercier?'

'I have never seen the original document only a photocopy. When the solicitors said they had been asked to act in the estate Peter advised me to seek my own advice. As a result, I appointed my lawyer to act for me and the first firm had to hand over the Will to him.'

'Do you think the Will is phoney?' asked Peter.

'I don't have enough information to answer that Mr Lewis. Can I ask you to authorise your solicitor to let the Yard at least see the Will and, if need be, carry out certain tests on it? Do you have any examples of your half-sister's handwriting that could be used for comparison purposes?

'Bethany was not much of a letter writer Commander. The only one I can think of was when she decided to leave university before she took her degree. I think she thought it easier for her to let me know in writing rather than by word of mouth. Do you want to see that letter?'

'If possible, I should like to borrow it.

'One other thing Miss Mercier, it is quite probable that we shall have to use the media to try get to people who knew Bethany and Tod and who may have information that can help us trace what happened to them. I will keep you posted as to if and when we are going public. Needless to say, if you hear anything as a result of such publicity please do let us know. And, finally, a warning to remain vigilant for your own safety. We have poked a stick into their wasps' nests and they may try to bite back.'

'I will get that letter for you and contact my solicitor and tell him he can expect to hear from you.'

When Buxton had gone Louise asked Peter:

'What would be the position if the Will was found to be false?'

'Presumably the same as if Bethany had never made a Will, in other words she would have died intestate. Although I am not an expert on these things, I assume her estate would pass to her nearest relative which would be you. Equally, if I am right and it was found that the person responsible for her death would have benefited from the Will that person will not be allowed to inherit which would bring us back to intestacy. I remember once reading that such a situation is covered by a ruling following the Crippen case.'

'I had better get on to Roger Branton.'

Following a conversation with the solicitor, Buxton arrange for the Will to be collected and taken to the Yard's document experts.

A couple of weeks later Buxton had a phone call from Peter Lewis.

'How can I help you Mr Lewis?'

'You said to let you know if anything out of the ordinary occurred. I don't know if what I am going to say comes under that heading or if I am becoming neurotic but something tells me I should at least mention it to you.'

'What has happened Mr Lewis?'

'The letting agents in London have phoned Louise to say that a parcel has been delivered to her house addressed to her. The thing is that she cannot think of any reason why anyone would send her a parcel. The tenant dropped it off at the agent's office this morning and that is where it is now. They are planning to post it on to Louise today.'

'Have you the name of the agents?'

'Better than that I have their phone number as well as their name and address.'

Peter read this out to Buxton who said.

'I am going to ring off now Mr Lewis. I will get back to you when I have some news.'

He rang the agents and spoke to the senior partner.

'My name is Buxton and I am with the Metropolitan Police. I understand that a parcel has been handed into your office addressed to a Miss Louise Mercier. Is that right?'

'Quite correct. I spoke to Miss Mercier a short while ago to tell her we would post it on tonight.'

'Where is the parcel at this moment?'

'It's on top of a filing cabinet in my room.'

'Now listen carefully. It is just possible that parcel is not safe. Do not touch it or move it. Then, leave your room and close your premises and let no-one in until the police tell you that it is safe to do so.'

'You're not suggesting it's a bomb are you?'

'I am not suggesting anything. Just please do what I say.'

'But how do I know you are the police? This could be a hoax.'

'Ring the number I am going to give you and please do what I say.'

Having told the estate agent the number to call, Buxton got on to the nearest bomb squad and alerted them, then he contacted the local police and arranged that they send officers to cordon off the area. Having done that, he called for a car and drove to the location. When he got there the local police had cordoned off not only the agent's premises but those two doors either side. A small crowd of people were gathered on the far pavement.

'Move those people on and close off this road at either end.' He told the local Sergeant.

He crossed to speak to the uniformed Inspector who was standing at the agent's door.

'Any news from the bomb squad?' he asked.

'A call three minutes ago sir. They should be here any time now.' He had no sooner spoken than two vehicles with sirens blaring tore down the road and stopped. Buxton went to speak to the officer in charge.

'Potential parcel bomb inside on top of a fling cabinet.'

'Very good sir. Leave it to us.'

They donned heavily padded suits and put on hamlets and visors and entered the building. They had constant radio contact with their colleagues outside. After several minutes Buxton heard them say:

'It looks as if it could be a bomb. We are going to bring it out and take it to be made safe. Keep everyone back'

The parcel was brought out and put in a special box and placed in one vehicle. It then drove off and Buxton gave orders for the road to be reopened and for people to return to work. An hour later he had a call at his office. It was the chief bomb disposal officer.

'It was a homemade bomb alright. If anyone had opened that parcel the result would have been very unpleasant for them.'

'Were you able to open it without an explosion?' asked Buxton.

'Yes, it was of a fairly standard pipe bomb construction with a trigger connected to the opening of the box in which the bomb was placed. The pipe was filled with nails and other bits of metal so you can imagine the kind of result it would have created.'

'Did you make a note of to whom the package was addressed? asked Buxton.

'Yes, we did. The parcel was addressed to 'The Property Owner' at the address given and was additionally marked 'Strictly Private and Personal'. It was a typed label probably produced by a computer. There was also a label from a courier firm but there is no such organisation as far as we have been able to find. Have you any idea as to may have sent it?'

'We have no specific evidence but the indications are that it is connected with a case we are investigating. I doubt if it's part of a series of parcel bombs. What we have to do now is make sure that no other such items are delivered to that house. You will, of course check for any finger prints or other identifications.'

'Of course, Commander and we will keep you posted on that. Also, we will arrange with the Post Office that all mail addressed that house is to be x-rayed before delivery. That should pick up any further nasties. Fortunately, it will mean the people at the house never need to know what is happening. I will get a detailed report off to you as soon as possible.'

Buxton buzzed Thomasson and asked him to join him. He explained what had happened.

'This is getting nasty' Thomasson said through gritted teeth. 'I suppose there can be no doubt that it was intended for Louise Mercier. But why? How can she be seen as a danger to whoever sent it?'

'It must be the Will. If they are afraid that she could spot it as a fake document they would stand to lose out on some three hundred plus thousand pounds. That's a motive by anyone's standard. Remove her and you remove that risk.'

'What are you going to tell her?'

'I think I will say that, to be on the safe side, the parcel was opened under strictly controlled safety rules. It was found to contain a mail order catalogue that was destroyed in the opening. That way there is no need for her to worry. We will also assure her that all mail to the house is to be examined before delivery.'

'What about the media sir? We can't hope to get away with no comment when a street was closed and the bomb squad was called.'

'I am in touch with the Press Department and have agreed that we will simply tell them it was a hoax and of no news value. With any luck the sender will think the thing t failed to go off. I doubt that they will have a second try.'

Buxton telephoned Peter Lewis and assured him that the parcel was harmless publicity material and there had been no danger to anyone but to be on the safe side steps were being taken to monitor post to that address. He thanked him for alerting the police and asked that they continued to keep a very careful watch out for any odd or unexplained events.

A few days later he asked Thomasson to come to his room again.

'We have got the document people's report on the Will. Have a read of this' and he handed out a couple of foolscap sheets. Thomasson sat down and began to read.

"The Will of Bethany Laura Mercier

Having carried out a close comparison of the handwriting in the letter written by Bethany Louise Mercier with the handwriting in the Will provided to us we have come to the conclusion that the two documents were not written by the same person. The Will is, in our opinion, a very clever forgery.

The reason for our reaching this conclusion are the differences in the writing of certain letters, e.g. *f* and *k* and *m* and *r* and *t* and *w*. A detailed analysis of the evidence that supports that conclusion is set out in Appendix 1 to this report. In summary, those conclusions clearly indicate that the stress and strokes used in certain letters are not consistent with the two documents being written by the same hand.

Furthermore, an examination of the signature of the testatrix assisted by chemical analysis shows that the signature on the Will is written over what was a carbon copy of the original signature of Bethany Louise Mercier. A detailed report and the reasons for arriving at this conclusion are set out in Appendix 2 to this report.

A careful examination of the Will has failed to find any finger print of the testatrix on the document. The extent and full description of the tests carried are detailed in Appendix 3 to this report.

Careful examination of the signatures of the two witnesses shows that they are original signatures although it is not possible to say when they were added to the document."

'So, you were right sir' grinned Thomasson handing back the report. 'The Will is phoney. Do you think the same applies to Tod Grimhausen's Will? '

'The first thing is to contact the two witnesses to see what they have to tell us. At the same time, I think we need to speak to Mr. Ravendale and see if there are any doubts about Tod Grimhausen's Will.

Enquiries quickly showed that there were no such addresses as those used by the so called witnesses and there was no evidence to prove that either person ever existed. There were no finger print records in police files of the persons who had handled the

Will. The only people who had done so were members of staff in the two firms of lawyers. Whoever had written the Will had used gloves.

These facts were passed on to Louise Mercier and to her solicitors.

CHAPTER THIRTY

THE END OF THE RAINBOW IS RAIDED

FEBRUARY 1995

Commander Richard Buxton, accompanied by Inspector Seagrave from Richmond, led the police raid on The End of The Rainbow. The police vehicles swept into the main courtyard at exactly nine o'clock in the morning and, at once, officers secured all the exits from the site. The other members of the search party entered the main building. Apart from Buxton and Seagrave and six other officers they swept into the other parts of the buildings to move all the personnel to the cafeteria and dining room. When these were filled, they took over the community hall. Women police officers visited all the living accommodation parts of the site and moved all those in the houses or apartments into the community hall. When this had been done some of the officers started a detailed search of every part of the buildings and others began to question those herded into the halls.

Meanwhile, Buxton hammered on the door leading to the office rooms and announced in a loud voice:

'Open this door. This is a police raid.'

When there was no immediate reply one of the officers used a piece of plastic to open the yale lock and they entered the corridor.

'This is a police raid' Buxton repeated in a loud voice and when the same middle aged lady appeared from the reception area he repeated what he had said and told her to go with the officers to where she was directed. The woman opened her mouth to object but was hustled aside and led to the cafeteria.

'Secure all computers that you can find' ordered Buxton as he and Seagrave walked down the corridor and straight into the office of Mr Delaney who pushed back his seat and got to his feet.

'What is the meaning of this?' he demanded.

'Martin Delaney' said Buxton 'I have here a warrant for your arrest.'

'Arrest? On what possible grounds?'

'You are charged that you knowingly falsely identified a body of a young woman as that of Bethany Mercier and that, in addition, you committed perjury by confirming that identification under oath at a Coroner's Inquest.' Buxton then read the full warning and statement of rights to Delaney who collapsed back into his chair.

'What are you talking about? The body that I identified was that of Bethany Mercier as our records will prove.'

'I do not doubt that your records will state that, but computer records can be altered to show what you want them to show. That is why all computer equipment found on these premises is being seized for technical examination. You see when someone changes a computer record the original entry does not get wiped out. It is set aside of future use and is still recorded in the system. Equally a computer will maintain an audit trail which will show which records were made on what date.'

'That may be so but it does not mean that I gave false information.'

At that point there was a tap at the door and a police constable entered.

'Excuse me sir' he said 'is it convenient to collect the computer equipment in this room?'

'Go ahead by all means' replied Seagrave.

'What are you doing' yelled Delaney as the police constable turned off his computer screen and started to unplug it. 'I need that to do my work.'

'As I said' pointed out Buxton producing a piece of paper and showing it to Delaney.' We have a warrant to seize all computer equipment on these premises.'

When the officer and a colleague who had followed him into the room had taken the equipment away Buxton said:

"The person you said was Bethany Mercier Mr Delaney, has been formally identified both medically and from photographs as Julie Cranston.'

'That may be her name but the one she gave us was Bethany Mercier.'

'You may be interested to know Delaney' snapped Seagrave 'that we have reason to believe that the real Bethany Mercier is dead and her body was disposed of in the dales. Not only that but we believe that Bethany Mercier was murdered.'

'Now just a minute' shouted Delaney. 'You can't come here and accuse me of murder without a shred of evidence.'

'No-one is accusing you' Buxton replied quietly. 'Though, of course, if you wish to make a statement.'

'Get lost' snarled Delaney.

'Can you please tell us where you were the afternoon of the day the young woman fell to her death?' asked Seagrave.

'How the hell should I know. I am a busy man who has a full diary of meetings and appointments. You can't expect me to remember where I was on one day all that time ago.'

'Then let's see if your diary helps us' said Buxton and leaning across the desk took hold of a desk diary. He opened it and found the page he was seeking. 'According to your diary Mr Delaney you had no appointments that afternoon.'

'I am entitled to the same holidays as other members of the Community. I can only assume that I had taken a half day off.'

'Yet you appeared on site very quickly after the young woman fell from the third floor. Where were you that afternoon?'

'How should I know.'

'Were you in the main building?'

'I might have been. Sometimes I keep a morning or an afternoon clear to do an unannounced tour of our operations. You can learn a lot more if people are not expecting you.'

'Would your tour have taken you to the third floor?'

'It might have done but on the other had it might not have done. I have no set itinerary on such occasions.'

At this point, the door opened and a police constable entered and handed Buxton a note that he read and handed to Thomasson. Then, turning to Delaney he asked in a quiet voice, 'What about Patrick Tod Grimhausen, Mr Delaney?'

'I don't know what you are talking about.'

'But you know the name?'

'I do not. I have never heard of anyone of that name.'

'Think again Mr Delaney because your colleague Mr Threlfall in Trescowen Cove says that you instructed him to identify the body of a young man killed in a motor accident at Patrick Tod Grimhausen.'

'Threlfall is lying. I never told him any such thing.'

'Why should he lie?'

'You must ask him that. You have no evidence to prove what he says is true. It is simply his word against mine.'

'Just like the false Bethany Mercier Mr Delaney, the man who died in Cornwall was a false Patrick Tod Grimhausen. In both cases, shortly after their so called deaths Wills were discovered, apparently by accident. Wills that left their entire estates to the Arcus Foundation in Luxembourg. In case you didn't know Mr Delaney the word "Arcus" is Latin for arch which is the shape of a rainbow.'

'How very uninteresting' smirked Delaney.

Buxton looked across at Seagrave and nodded.

'Maybe you will find this interesting Mr Delaney' the Inspector said in a cold voice. 'The body of the real Patrick Tod Grimhausen was recovered in a reservoir in County Durham. It had been placed in black plastic sacks and tied to tree roots. Those remains have been medically and legally identified as belonging to Patrick Grimhausen. Patrick Tod Grimhausen had been murdered before his body was put in the water. We now have four suspicious deaths on our hands every one of which has or had a connection with this Community.'

'I do not propose to comment on such wild and unfounded allegations.'

'Martin Delaney' Buxton said rising to his feet 'Inspector Seagrave will now take you to the police headquarters in Richmond where you will be formally charged with giving false information and committing perjury. I must warn you that, depending on our ongoing enquiries, further and more serious charges may follow.'

When Seagrave and Delaney, accompanied by two officers, had left to go to Richmond, Buxton made his way to the control point that had been set up to monitor the searches and the interviews. Here, he learned that all the computer equipment seized was on its way to London for processing by the experts of the Metropolitan Police. He asked that Delaney's and the receptionist's diaries be obtained for further examination. In addition, he said he was anxious to know if the person who had found the Will of Bethany Mercier had been identified and, if so, he wanted to see his or her statement and to interview them. In the meantime, he went up to the third floor to see for himself where the fatal accident had happened. The area was used partly as an art workshop and there were easels and tables spread out that were covered with paintings and drawings in process of completion. He noted the door which was now barred and secured by a padlock. It seemed that the room was originally used for looms. The wall the other side of the room from the door was largely glass and, as this faced north, it provided an excellent site for an artist studio.

'Have you found anything interesting?' he asked the officers carrying out the search.

'Not especially sir' one replied. 'Just the kind of things you would expect to find in an art studio.'

'There was just one thing sir' said another 'that I thought rather out of place.'

'What was that?'

'It was a pole with a sort of hook at one hand. The type of thing you use to open some kinds of windows that are out of hand's reach or to pull down a sun blind. The thing is none of the windows in this room need that kind of gadget.'

'Where did you find it?' asked Buxton.

'There's a sort of beam at the far end of the room and its laying on top of that beam.'

'Did you touch it?'

'Well, no sir, I just saw it when I climbed up to see if anything was on the beam.'

'Good. I see you are wearing gloves. Now can you get that pole down and then make sure it is tested for finger prints. It seems to me that if anyone wanted to hide the thing, they chose the hiding place quite carefully. That was a good spot, Constable, well done!'

'What would they have wanted it for sir?' asked the first officer.

'A young woman apparently fell to her death out of that door' Buxton pointed to it. 'It's just possible she didn't simply fall but was pushed using that pole. That's why I want it tested for finger prints.'

'Flipping heck! 'breathed the first constable after Buxton had left. 'I wouldn't have thought of that in a hundred years.'

'That's why you are a constable and he is a Commander at Scotland Yard' the other replied.

Back on the ground floor Buxton phoned Seagrave.

'Do you think you could contact the pathologist who did the autopsy on Julie Cranston and ask if there was any sign of her having been hit in the back by a quite small round metal object?'

'Found something interesting sir?'

'Just an idea.'

'I will get on to it straight away.'

Buxton next went to see if the person who had found the Will had been questioned. Although, by now, virtually everyone who had apparently lived in that accommodation had been identified, no-one had been found who admitted to finding the Will. Buxton asked to be taken to see the room where it was said to have been found. It was a single bedroom with a bed, an armchair, a small desk and a chest of drawers. He took out all the drawers in the room and studied the bottoms of them carefully. There was no indication that any of them ever had an envelope taped to the bottom. To have done that would have required probably four separate pieces of tape and it was highly unlikely that these could have been removed without leaving some trace, but there was nothing. Indeed, all the furniture appeared to be made of flat pack items and all of them looked completely new. The next step was to find who had occupied the room at the time of the "discovery'. It turned out to be a young woman who worked in the needlework department. Her name was Melanie Crowthorpe. Buxton asked to see her. She was in her late twenties he guessed, slim with dark hair and brown eyes.

'Good morning' Buxton greeted her with a smile. 'My name is Commander Buxton and I am with the Metropolitan Police. I am hoping you may be able to help me.'

'How?'

'I believe you occupy room numbered 279?'

'That's right.'

'How long have you lived there?'

'About a year. Is there a problem?'

'Not at all Miss Crowthorpe. There is nothing to worry about. All I need to ask you is whether you have ever found any papers hidden in your room?

'What do you mean papers hidden in my room?'

'Have you ever found an envelope taped to the bottom of one of the drawers in your room?'

'Never.'

'And has any of the furniture in your room been changed while you have lived there?'

'No, it's exactly as it was when I moved in.'

'Thank you very much Miss Crowthorpe. Whilst I am sorry to have bothered you I should be grateful if you would make a formal statement confirming what you have told me.'

When the young woman had gone to make her statement, Buxton sat back in his chair and said quietly:

'Interesting.'

As he sat in Delaney's seat behind his desk, he tried to get some order into the diverse pieces of information that made up this complicated saga. It was clear that Delaney was the brains behind what had happened. Having disposed of two innocent young people to try and hide the truth about the fate of the other couple, how had he contrived to arrange their deaths and the disposal of their bodies?

The door to the room opened and Inspector Seagrave entered.

'You have Delaney safely in your cells?' he asked.

'Yes. He is asking to see his solicitor.'

'He'll be wanting bail. He needs to try and see if he has left any lose ends. You will bring up tomorrow morning?'

'Yes, do you want me to object to bail?'

'No, I don't think so. The terms should be the surrender of his passport and his driving licence and a daily report to the police station.'

'There's something else I think you will want to know sir.'

'What's that?'

'I have only just heard it myself. One of the sergeants here told me as I came into the building. It seems that one of the WPCs doing the questioning found that she knew the young woman she was interviewing, they were neighbours when the young woman, who is now a lay member here, was a child. The WPC played on that past friendship to get her to speak freely. What she has told us is worth hearing.'

'Where is she at present?'

'She has gone back to her work in the cafeteria.'

'Does she live here?'

'No, she lives at home.'

'Good. Then, I suggest that we call to see her this evening. She may be even more forthcoming if she thinks that no-one here knows she is being interviewed a second time.'

'Right sir, I will fix it.'

So it was that Buxton and Seagrave called at the semi-detached house where Glenda Vernon lived with her widowed mother and a brother. They were accompanied by the WPC who knew the family in the hope that this would help Glenda feel more relaxed.

'Thank you very much for finding the time to see us' Buxton said as they were seated in the lounge of the house. 'Please do not be worried as to why we are here. It is simply that we think you may be able to help us better understand The End of The Rainbow and will find it easier to talk to us here rather than at the site.'

'I don't know that I can be of much help' replied Glenda, a young woman not much older than twenty with short fair hair and blue eyes.' I am not a member of the Community; I just work in the cafeteria.'

'You haven't thought of becoming a full member?'

'No, I am only working there until I can apply to join the Navy. You see I promised my Mum that I wouldn't leave home until I was at least twenty two. By then my brother will have finished his apprenticeship as a motor mechanic. I am working on an Open University degree in IT but have to have a daytime job as well.'

"Do you recognise either of these two people Glenda?' asked WPC Helen Yardley holding out some photographs.

'Yes I do. They used to be at the Community but left some time ago.'

'About how long ago?' asked Seagrave

'It must be about a year.'

'Do you know where they went after they left Netherton?'

'Not really, but I do know they were talking about going to

Devon or Cornwall to open a craft studio of their own.'

'Did they tell you that?' asked Buxton 'or did someone else mention it?'

'I heard them speaking about it when I was serving tables and tidying up those that had been used. I just assumed that was where they had gone to. People do leave from time to time but no-one ever says where they go afterwards. It's as if they never existed.'

'Do you think other people knew what these two were planning?'

'It's quite possible. Not only that but it is possible that someone reported them to the Security Department.'

'Why should they do that?'

'It is the way the place is run. Everyone is encouraged to spy on everyone else. If they hear anyone complaining or criticising the Community or they learn something about the private affairs of another person they are told they must report it. By doing that they hope to protect their own position.'

'What happens if someone is reported?' asked Seagrave.

'It depends. They may be moved to another and less nice job or they may lose the right to one or other of the privileges that can be earned. The whole place is run like some dictatorship. That's why I would never join it. In fact, I can't wait to get away.'

'Is telling tales the only way those in charge keep tabs on people?' asked Buxton.

'No. I have heard that if someone is reported to the Security Section they, that is the Security people, may bug their living accommodation to listen in to what they talk about privately.'

'Thank you for speaking so frankly, Glenda' smiled Buxton. I am going to ask WPC to write down what you have told us and to pop round and see you another evening and ask you to sign that statement if you are happy with what it says. That way no-one from the Community should know that you have spoken to us.'

'What do you make of that sir?' Seagrave asked when they were outside.

'It was very interesting and, I think, helpful. If Bethany and Tod's room was bugged the people in charge would have known what they were planning. It is quite possible that they talked money so that Delaney and his crew knew what was at stake. Thank you for your help Constable. I needn't tell you to keep all this to yourself. It could be just the sort of information we are going to need.'

CHAPTER THIRTY ONE

THE RAINBOW CRAFT CENTRE IS RAIDED

FEBRUARY 1955

It was a crisp and clear morning in the far south west of England. Already there was a hint of spring in the air. The group of police cars were parked in a field waiting for the signal to start the raid on the premises of The Rainbow Craft Centre. Chief Inspector Thomasson and Inspector Vellacott were in the lead vehicle monitoring the clock. It was essential that the raid passed off smoothly and without any violence. Every person involved had been given a specific role and knew exactly what they had to do as soon as entry into the premises had been secured. At precisely eight forty five Thomasson gave the instruction for the raid to proceed. A line of police cars drove up the lane to the craft centre, the last vehicle stopped just inside and erected a barrier closing the site to anyone other than authorised personnel. At the end of the road the cars spread out to form a barrier round the site and some of the police officers hurried round its boundaries erecting the usual tape barrier and securing any possible exit. Thomasson and Vellacott, with the remaining officers entered the main doors of the building. At the reception desk Thomasson rapped on the door and when it was opened, he spoke to the woman he had seen previously.

'This is a police raid. I have here' he said holding out some papers 'warrants for the search of these premises and the questioning of everyone in them. The warrants also give us power to remove all computer equipment that is found on the premises. Everyone should go immediately to the cafeteria and wait there for further instructions. Please open the door and the entrance to the showroom and other parts at once.'

The woman who had opened the sliding door moved as if to reach for the phone.

'If you try to use that phone you will be arrested for impeding the police 'barked Vellacott. 'Now do as you are told.'

When the main door was opened Thomasson and Vellacott went immediately to Nigel Threlfall's office. At the same time officers entered the showrooms and escorted everyone on the premises to the cafeteria and restaurant. Others went to the residential parts of the community and shepherded all the people in those places into the same areas.

When Thomasson and Vellacott entered Nigel Threlfall's office without knocking he got to his feet and glared at them.

'What is the meaning of this intrusion?' he demanded.

'Nigel Threlfall' Thomasson said going up to the desk 'I have here a warrant for your arrest.'

'Arrest? What are you talking about man? On what charges are you proposing to arrest me.'

'You are charged that you knowingly gave false information in order to obtain a death certificate for one Patrick Tod Grimhausen and you are further charged that you committed perjury at a Coroner's Inquest on the body in that you illegally identified who it was.' Thomasson then gave him the formal warning.

'This is ridiculous' protested Threlfall. 'The body I identified was a man I knew as Tod Grimhausen. I cannot be blamed if that was not his name.'

'His name was actually Alan Vickery and that fact that has been established medically and by identification by a close relative.'

'How can he be identified? He was cremated.'

'He was identified from medical evidence and photographs taken at the post mortem.'

'So, Vickery pretended to be Grimhausen. You cannot blame me for that.'

'Oh, I think we shall find that Alan Vickery was known here.'

'You will not find him in our records I tell you.'

'I disagree. That is why we are seizing all the computers on this property for detailed examination. You may not be aware of it, Mr Threlfall, but computers do not wipe out data they just put it aside as possible usable space. They also create audit trails. If Alan Vickery has been here, we shall find him in your records.'

Threlfall looked as if had been hit by a rock. His shoulders sagged and his face turned white.

Deciding to keep the pressure on Threlfall, Vellacott added:

'You might also be interested to know Mr Threlfall that we have reason to believe that the real Tod Grimhausen was killed. That means that someone is going to be faced with a murder charge.'

'Not only that,' Thomasson said 'but we believe that Alan Vickery was deliberately killed to make it look like a motor accident. What we need from you Mr Threlfall is the truth about what happened here last April.'

'The only thing I did that might be seen as wrong was that I obeyed instructions. I was not the instigator of any criminal activity.'

'What instructions and who gave them to you?' demanded Thomasson.

'If I tell you exactly what happened does that mean that you will not take action against me?'

'We can make no promises Mr Threlfall but if you co-operate with us that fact will be taken into consideration.'

'What you have to understand is that when you become a member of the Rainbow Community you are required to sign a document that sets out a number of rules and regulations by which you freely undertake to be bound. These include that you will treat all information about the Community that comes into your possession as being strictly private and confidential and you that you will not divulge any such information to any third party. Another says that you will agree to accept without questioning all the orders and instructions given to you by those who hold authorised positions in the Community. I have done nothing that was not within the scope of those undertakings. In normal events I should have treated those undertakings the same as if I had signed the Official Secrets Act.'

'Go on Mr Threlfall' said Thomasson.

'The organisation of the Rainbow Communities in this country means that each unit is not fully independent of the others. There is a central management body which is in overall control. Instructions by that body or by its members have to be followed without questioning.'

'Where is that body located and by whom is it constituted?'

'Our head office, if I can put it that way, is situated at the Community at Netherton in North Yorkshire. The central committee is made up of the elected chairman and his deputy, the secretary and treasurer and the nominated chief executives of the regional Communities'

'Who is the chairman sir?'

'Martin Delaney who is also the chief executive at Netherton.'

'Was it this Mr Delaney who gave you the instructions to which you are referring?'

'Yes. He told me to replace the name of Alan Vickery in our records with that of Patrick Tod Grimhausen. In addition, if anyone was to ask who was the person I knew as Alan Vickery I was to say it was this Patrick Tod Grimhausen. Once I had done that, I had no alternative but to follow through the consequences and identify Vickery's body as that of Grimhausen'

'Did he say why you were to do this?'

'No. He simply gave me the order.'

'That was the only order he gave you Mr Threlfall?'

'No. He also ordered me to tell Vickery on a specified date to leave these premises at a specified time to pick up from a vehicle on the main road some valuable items that were to be put on sale here. The next thing I knew was that the police were here saying that the man Grimhausen was dead as a result of a road accident.'

'That was all that happened?'

'Apart from the fact that he mentioned that the post of vice chairman of the central committee would be falling vacant soon and he proposed to recommend me for that role. As you can see Chief Inspector, I have done nothing wrong except obey orders.'

Surely you are aware Mr Threlfall' pointed out Vellacott 'that ever since the International War Crimes Tribunal of 1945 the obeying of an order is not an acceptable defence.'

'Nigel Threlfall' said Thomasson getting to his feet 'you will be taken to the police headquarters in Penzance where you will be required to make a full statement and where you will be formally charged with the offences of falsifying a death record and of committing perjury at a Coroner's Inquest.'

The next thing that Thomasson did was send a message to Commander Buxton at Netherton telling what Threlfall had said about obeying orders..

While Vellacott accompanied Nigel Threlfall to Penzance to process his formal arrest, Thomasson made sure that all the computers on the site had been collected and were on their way to the IT experts at the Metropolitan Police. In addition, he checked that the questioning of everyone on the site was proceeding according to plan and that the search of the whole of the premises was being carried out. One interesting fact that was reported to him was that the officers delegated to carry out a fingertip search of the driveway from the road to the centre had found not only a lot of extraneous rubbish but also some pieces of a red coloured plastic. One of the searchers who was an expert in road accident investigations identified them as being part of the lighting system of a motor vehicle. They were carefully separated and sent to the forensic laboratory for detailed examination. This confirmed that they were what the officer had claimed. The question now was from what vehicle had they come. This called for comparison of the pieces with the lighting systems of known vehicles. The result was that it was likely that they came from a four by four such as Land Rover. There were no records of any Land Rovers belonging to any community members or employees. Nor did enquiries at the centre bring to light any records of vehicle collisions in the driveway. The weather had obliterated any tyre tracks that may have been left at the point where the plastic was found. Fortunately, the clothes worn by Alan Vickery at the time of his death were still held at the mortuary. A careful examination of these revealed tiny slivers of red plastic in the back of his coat. When they were matched with the pieces found by the driveway, they were declared to be a match. It was increasingly likely that Alan Vickery had been killed on the driveway and his body deposited on the road where it was discovered. A probability that was underlined by the fact that no pieces of red plastic had been found at the supposed site of the fatal accident.

The questioning of the members of the community brought to light information about the discovery of Tod Grimhausen's Will. The young man who had said he had been given an envelope that he was not to open until Tod had been missing for two months admitted that his story was not true. He had been handed an envelope and had been instructed by Nigel Threlfall to say he had held it in his possession for two months when, in fact, he only had it for two hours. The local Catholic priest who had also held an envelope that was said to have come from Tod was shown a photograph of him but said he did not recognise it as the person who had handed him the envelope. He did, however, recall the name of that person which was checked against the Community records and proved to be Nigel Threlfall.

When photographs of both Alan Vickery and Tod Grimhausen were shown to people at the Craft Centre none of them recognised Tod but several recognised Alan. Asked what had happened to him they said they were told that he had left to take, up a senior position at the Rainbow site on the Island of Mull.

One other interesting fact came to light when the police questioned the man who was in charge of health and safety and security at the Craft Centre. He mentioned that, at the time that Alan Vickery had left they had had a visit from the Head of Security at what he termed headquarters, in other words from Netherton. That visitor had left the same night as Alan Vickery. When asked how the security manager had travelled to the site, they were told he used a Land Rover. His name was Walby.

CHAPTER THIRTY TWO

THE INVESTIGATION CONTINUES AND EXPANDS

FEBRUARY 1995

Following the raids on the Rainbow premises Buxton and Thomasson carried out a detailed review of the current situation.

As a matter of urgency, the computer experts at the Metropolitan Police had examined the computerised records maintained by the centres in Cornwall and Yorkshire. They had found that, in general terms, what had been said was accurate. When someone joined a Rainbow community as either a lay person or as a full member a record was created showing their date of birth, their birth name and any name change. Against each name was a second one which was the Community name allocated to them. The name and address of any next of kin was also recorded in the case of full members, but not everyone supplied that information. The department to which they were allocated was additionally shown together with the date of any transfer to another department. If anyone left the community then their records were cancelled and deleted from the system. In addition to personal information records there were accounting and tax records for each individual. The community seemed fully compliant with tax and national insurance rules for lay members who received a salary. Full members continued to have their records kept but their notional pay was always at a level that did not incur a tax liability. That notional pay was used towards the cost of their accommodation, food and clothing and other costs which were all met by the community.

Having ascertained the general systems being applied the investigators turned to the records of the individuals of concern. On the face of it those records reported the facts as explained by the communities. However, when the computer experts started to look behind those records, they uncovered some interesting information. There was a computer audit record for each and every entry which reported the date on which the entry was made. This brought to light that for Bethany Mercier and for Tod Grimhausen the records as at the dates of their "deaths" had been changed some days before their "death". The previous entries that had been replaced by their names were those of Julie Cranston and Alan Vickery. At the same date the original entries for them had been removed from the system. Anyone looking for them on the system would see from the original records for Alan and Julie that they had left the community. Those looking at the original entries for Bethany and Tod would have seen that Bethany had died and that Tod had gone to Trescowen Cove in Cornwall. Those for Trescowen Cove showed that Tod's name had been interposed over the record for Alan Vickery. Here was clear proof that the records had been falsified. The cases against Delaney and Threlfall were conclusively proved as to falsifying death records but there was still a need to prove that the two deaths were not accidental but premeditated. In addition, there was the question as to what had happened to Bethany and Tod.

'How are we getting on with processing the statements taken from the other people at those two places?' asked Buxton.

Thomasson reported the evidence they had recovered in Cornwall showed that Alan Vickery had been there. His record showed he had left the community but people still there said they had been told he had moved to the Island of Mull, a fact denied by the Rainbow Centre in that location who had never heard of an Alan Vickery. The search in Cornwall had addition-ally recovered evidence that pointed to Alan having been killed on the trackway up to the Craft Centre and that the Community national head of security had been in Cornwall at the time of the "accident". Buxton added the information from Netherton in so far as it mirrored that from Cornwall. Both Bethany and Tod had been recognised but everyone thought they had simply left the community. No-one had been allowed to view the body that fell from the third floor. The clothes the victim wore were recognised as similar to those worn by Julie Cranston. However, everyone who knew her was told she had left the community the day after the accident because of a family bereavement. Yet her records on the system did not show any information as to next of kin.

At this point their discussion was interrupted by a phone call from Inspector Northcott in Barnard Castle. At Buxton's sugges-tion Thomasson joined the call on the extension phone.

'You will remember sir' said Northcott 'that you asked if I could get any information about unusual activity in the area where the skeleton was found. Something has come to light that I thought might be of interest to you. One of the people I con-tacted was the chap who is the leader of the mountain rescue group who discovered the skeleton. He told me of an odd hap-pening. It seems that some time just after Easter last year he was talking to a local farmer who happened to say that he had seen the rescue group doing a training session up on the dales. The odd thing was that the group had not been in that area for at least two years before they went to rescue that sheep. He told the farmer that whoever he had seen it wasn't the rescue group.'

'Interesting' said Buxton 'what did you do about it?'

'I got the name of the farmer from him and went to see the man. Said we were looking into some sheep stealing and asked if he had been out and about on the dales at Easter time last year. He repeated the same story he had told the mountain rescue leader. I said that the rescue team denied being there and asked him what he could tell me about what he had seen. He told me it was a dark coloured Land Rover or similar vehicle and it was parked near to where they found the skeleton later. There had been three men round the vehicle and what appeared to be a stretcher on the ground. He assumed they were practising a rescue and gave it no more thought. When he was told it was not the usual team, he supposed it must have been one from another area.'

'Is that possible?' asked Thomasson.

'Not really the nearest other team is based about forty miles away. Just to be sure I contacted them and they said they had never been to that area.'

'How near was this farmer to the vehicle?' asked Buxton?'

'He was across the dale about half a mile away so he couldn't see faces or recognise anyone. However, he was accompanied that day by his son who is studying at Lancaster University and who had with him a pair of high powered binoculars as he was hoping to see an eagle that had been reported in the locality. He was not with his father at the time having moved down into the valley so that he was nearer to the vehicle. The young man had looked at it through his binoculars and was able to read the licence plate on the vehicle. Not only did he see it he could remember it. It was ELV15P. It happens he is a great Elvis Pressley fan and the plate reminded him of his favourite singer. If you read the 5 for an S you have   Elvis P! It struck so much of a cord with him that he still remembers the number today.'

'That's a bit of luck' laughed Buxton. 'Have you been able to trace the number?'

'We have. It is a Land Rover and it is registered to – wait for it – Kenneth George Walby and the address given is The End of The Rainbow Community at Netherton.'

'Well done Inspector!' Buxton cried 'Very well done! We need to get a warrant to seize that vehicle and have it thoroughly searched to see if we can find anything that links it to Bethany Mercier.'

'I can tell you who Kenneth Walby is 'said Thomasson. 'He visited the Rainbow Centre in Cornwall at the time of the road accident and was described as the Head of Security based at Netherton. He left Trescowen Cove the night that Alan Vickery was killed. Also' continued Thomasson 'I would like the front of that land Rover studied to see if there is any sign that the vehicle has been in a collision, with particular reference to its indicator lights that may have been replaced. I think there is every chance it was used to kill that young man in Cornwall. If those lights have been replaced can you find out who did the repair and when. It's a very long shot but we might be able to tie it in with the pieces of red plastic recovered in Cornwall.'

'Can you tell me Chief Inspector do you think both the indicator lights were broken?'

'I am not sure but I think it's likely it was only one of them. Why do you ask?'

'Because' said Northcott,' if it was only one then it may be possible to compare the unrepaired one with the pieces you mention.'

'An excellent point' agreed Thomasson.

'I will arrange for Inspector Seagrave to get a warrant to seize the vehicle and send it to the traffic people for a detailed check. In addition, I will ask him to get this chap Walby in for questioning' Buxton said.

'The one area we do not seem to be making any progress with 'Thomasson said after Buxton had spoken to Inspector Seagrave and given him his instructions 'is what happened to Tod and how did his body ended up in the reservoir in County Durham.'

'Added to that is how were the two of them removed from Netherton' added Buxton 'did they leave The Rainbow's End of their own free will only to be kidnapped and then murdered or were they, like young Vickery, sent off on some wild goose chase and then caught and killed. Also, we need to see if the Netherton interviews give us any clue as to whether the people there knew that Bethany and Tod were worth a lot of money. Somehow or another the Rainbow management must have found out.'

As the results of the questioning of the staff and others living at the Rainbow sites were analysed Buxton and Thomasson found confirmation of what Glenda Vernon had told them. The publicity about the search of the site and the arrest of Delaney had resulted in a number of people who had been lay members but who had left their employment or had been full members and had abandoned their membership coming forward with their own stories. They all confirmed that everyone, either a lay member or a full member, were required to sign a declaration that they would not reveal anything they learned about the Community to a third party. Those who had left said they were required to sign a form confirming that they would not disclose anything they had heard or learned while they were a member of the Community. Not only was there this rule of silence but it was confirmed that people were encouraged to report any comment or remark that was a criticism of the Community to the management. Anyone found guilty of doing such a thing would be subject to disciplinary procedures if they were a full member or would lose any bonus if they were a lay member. In other words, the Community at Netherton was run like a police state.

The questionnaires completed during the raid on The End of The Rainbow identified three people who admitted that they had known Bethany Mercier and Tod Grimhausen. They were all lay workers and the police arranged to see them at their homes out of working hours.

Fiona Ingham was a married woman with two teenage children and in her late thirties. An expert at knitting and crochet she had worked for the Community as a lay member ever since it opened. Having been shown the photographs of Bethany Mercier, Tod Grimhausen and Julie Cranston she said that she had known the first two, although she referred to them as Claudia and Kirk which were the names given to them by the Community. She had met Debbie when working in the craft workshop at the Community. According to her Debbie had been a water colour artist of some considerable skill who produced paintings for sale in the shop. They had often shared coffee and tea breaks and had got to know each other quite well. According to Fiona, Claudia and Kirk were a couple. They shared accommodation and were treated like any married couple. Two things of particular interest that came out of her interview were that Claudia had told her that she was due to inherit a lot of money from her late mother's estate and that she didn't think that Kirk and herself would stay much longer in the Community. She had gathered from comments made by Claudia that she was used to leading a wandering kind of life and she supposed that the young woman was going to move on again.

Douglas Satterthwaite was a married man in his early forties. He worked for the Community in their furniture workshop where they built small items of handmade furniture and did wood carving. That was where he had got to know 'Kirk' the alias for Tod Grimhausen. Kirk, he said was a highly skilled wood carver and created a series of carved animals and figures which he thought were true works of art. Kirk had told him about his family in New York and how he had revolted against the idea of joining the family investment firm and had come to Europe to lead what he thought was a life in which he was free to do what he liked when he liked. He was able to do this because of the quite considerable funds that were held for him by the family firm. Douglas got the impression that Kirk saw his stay at the Community as only a temporary one.

Jacqueline Birdwood, or Jackie s she preferred to call herself, worked as a waitress in the Cafeteria and Restaurant at the Community. She was doing so as her boyfriend was in the army and stationed in York. If he was transferred somewhere else, she would follow him. She recognised all three photographs as people she had served in the cafeteria. Claudia and Kirk, she knew as a couple and had heard them talking about a plan they were forming to set up their own studio in South Devon. She had not been surprised, therefore, to learn that they had left the Community and had assumed that was where they were heading. It seemed from what they said that they had money that would allow them to do what they planned. Julie Cranston was a nice girl who worked in the art and craft section and Jackie had been very sorry to learn of her fatal accident. When asked about life in the Community, Jackie said that if it were not for wanting to be near her boyfriend she would not stay there. The reason she gave was that the full members of the Community were encouraged to report what they learned about other members and what they said to the Security Department. In fact, it was felt by many people that it was the only way to protect themselves from gossip of other members. It was, she said, a bit like a police state. When asked if she thought the fact that Claudia and Kirk had money would have been reported she said she knew it had been and gave the name of a full member of the Community as the informant because she had seen this woman talking to the Head of Security.

CHAPTER THIRTY THREE

TOD'S ESTATE

FEBRUARY 1995

'Good Morning gentlemen' Gilbert Ravendale welcomed Richard Buxton and Robert Thomasson to his office. 'I was hoping to hear from you soon.'

Thomasson brought the private investigator up to date with the investigation, reporting on the raid at The Rainbow Centre in Cornwall and the arrest of Threlfall. Buxton then took over and reported on the raid in Yorkshire and the arrest of Delaney. He then went on to explain the results of the checks carried out on the various computers.

'So, as you can see, the records have been deliberately altered in an attempt to make the facts tie in with the stories we have been told.'

'But have you any proof that the young man and the young woman who died in those places did or did not suffer accidental deaths?' asked Ravendale.

'Their deaths were not accidental' replied Buxton. 'Both of them were murdered. We have strong circumstantial evidence that the young woman was pushed out of the third floor doorway by Delaney. He pushed her in the back with one of those poles that are used to open shop blinds. We found the pole, which has his finger prints on it, hidden away on a rafter and the pathologist has confirmed that the body had a bruise on her back between her shoulder blades.'

'The young man was indeed hit by a motor vehicle but not on a country road' said Thomasson. 'He was run down on the lane that leads from the road to the Craft Centre. We found shards of red plastic that came from a broken traffic indicator light. Not only that but we know the Head of Security from Netherton was at the Cornish site at the time and he drove a large black Land Rover. Examination of that vehicle shows the offside front indicator has been replaced and the plastic of the nearside indicator matches the fragments found in Cornwall. All of which points to the young man having been killed there and his body placed where it was found'

'Threlfall, the man in charge in Cornwall has admitted he was instructed by Delaney, who seems to be the Chief Executive of all the Rainbow sites, to alter his records to show that it was Tod who was killed. Yet, he denies he had any involvement in the death of Alan Vickery. No-one at that site recognised a photograph of Tod. It is our case that he was never there.' added Buxton. 'Not only that but the vehicle driven by the Head of Security was seen in the dales near where the body of Bethany was found at about the time the body was dumped down that sinkhole.'

'You seem to have made a lot of progress' said Ravendale. 'Are you saying this Head of Security killed Bethany Mercier as well as the young man in Cornwall?'

'He may have disposed of the body but whether or not he killed the young woman is still unclear. However, there are a couple of other things we need to talk to you about Mr Ravendale and they are the main reasons for this visit.'

'What are they?'

'First, there have been two attempts on the life of Bethany Mercier's half-sister.' Buxton outlined what had happened.

'But why try kill her?'

'Because they believe that she is the only person who might query the validity of Bethany's Will. They are obviously nervous that if she is able to do that they could lose out on a large sum of money. All they have managed to do is to highlight the question of the validity of the Will which has been examined by a hand writing expert and held to be a very clever forgery. Not only that but neither the two witnesses or their addresses are valid. Bethany's Will is a fake which raises the obvious question.'

'You mean is Tod's Will a phoney as well?'

'Exactly. We have not seen the Will so cannot comment on that point. However, we have established that the young man who said he had been given an envelope by Tod denies he ever said he had done anything of the sort. Not only that but the priest who had a second envelope has identified Threlfall as the man who deposited it with him. What we need to do now is find out how the bank came to be in possession of it. Banks, as you may know, can be sticky when it comes to giving information about customers to the police. They probably will not be so restrictive to you as you are the family's legal attorney. Could you contact them and ask how they got the Will?'

'Of course,' said Ravendale and picked up his phone. 'Can you please get me Mr Malvern, the manager of the Anglo American bank in Threadneedle Street and tell him it is in connection with the late Patrick Tod Grimhausen. Thank you.'

Whilst they were waiting Ravendale turned to Buxton and asked:

'Would you agree that I should tell the New York family about Bethany Mercier's Will and suggest that they have Tod's testament subjected to specialised document analysis?'

'Yes, I would' replied Buxton. 'If one document was a forgery there must be a more than even chance the same applies to the other Will.'

At this point Ravendale's phone rang and he held a brief conversation with the bank Manager.

'From what Malvern says the envelope that contained the Will turned up in the bank's letter box one morning. The envelope was simply addressed to the Manager and when it was opened it was found to contain a smaller envelope on which was printed "Patrick Tod Grimhausen" and underneath the name the words "My Will" and below that "Please keep in safe custody". The matter was referred to Malvern as the circumstances were unusual, also the bank no longer accepts documents like wills from customers. However, given that the Grimhausen family are important customers of the bank, Malvern told his staff to accept the envelope and lock it in their strong room after recording its details as a miscellaneous document. There it stayed until they received the lawyer's letter enclosing a death certificate and asking for the Will. I will get on to the family right away and ask them to get the Will checked by a recognised document examiner. You said just now that you think there have been attempts on Louise Mercier's life. I don't want to start unnecessary hares but I am concerned that the same thing is not tried with the Grimhausen family.'

'In your position' said Buxton 'I think I should recommend that they keep an eye open for any out of the ordinary events. Although, on balance I have to say that I think it unlikely there will be any action taken all the while they think the Will has been accepted.'

Two weeks later Buxton received a telephone call from Gilbert Ravendale. An examination of Tod Grimhausen's Will had shown it was a very sophisticated forgery.

'The family are asking what progress you are making in finding out who did kill Tod' Ravendale said.

'It's like peeling back an onion' Buxton replied. 'We are making progress in several directions but we still have a lot of work to do.

CHAPTER THIRTY FOUR

HOW SECURE IS SECURITY

FEBRUARY 1995

Following Buxton's conversation with Inspector Northcott arrangements were made to obtain a warrant to search the black Land Rover driven by the Head of Security at The End of The Rainbow. The Vehicle Examination Department of the North Yorkshire Police carried out a detailed check of the vehicle which, on the face of it, was in excellent condition and was well cleaned and polished. One point that did become clear was that the front traffic indicator lights were not of a similar age. The offside one was clearly the newer of the two. When the nearside light was dismantled it was possible to obtain a very small sample of the red plastic cover. This fragment was sent to the crime laboratory and compared with the pieces found on the trackway at Trescowen Cove as well as the fragments found in Alan Vickery's coat and the three samples were an exact match. To provide a full comparison a similar sample was taken from the offside light and this was compared to the newer light and to the fragments from Cornwall. There were small but significant differences between the samples. Consultation with the manufacturer of the lights showed that they had been manufactured at different dates. The offside light was only introduced in March of 1994.

Apart from this the vehicle seemed clean and the searchers were unable to find any incriminating evidence.

Before taking any further action, Buxton asked for a search to be made in the name of Kenneth George Walby. This showed that he had been found guilty of assault on a police officer in 1983 for which he was sentenced to two years in prison. In addition, he had had been convicted of grievous bodily harm on the manager of a petrol station that he had tried to rob in 1987 for which he was jailed for five years.

'It seems our man is no stranger to violence' Buxton said to Thomasson.

'I don't see him carrying out the killing of Bethany and Tod on his own' replied Thomasson.

'Nor do I' agreed Buxton. 'He is described as Head of Security. Presumably there is a deputy. Do we know who that is? If so, it might be worth looking him up to see if he has any prior record.'

'I will get on to that.'

Thomasson found that there was a deputy at Netherton who went by the name of Luke but whose real name was Terrance Paul Shebdon. A search of the criminal records showed Terence Paul Shebdon had been jailed for robbery with violence in 1985 and again for armed robbery this time in 1989. Further enquiry revealed that Walby and Shebdon had shared a cell in the prison in Birmingham in 1991.

At that point Buxton received a call from the Finance experts whom he had asked to examine the financial records of the two sites.

'Generally speaking' the Inspector in charge of the investigation said 'the accounts appear to be pretty straight forward. However, one point that has come to light that may be of interest to you is that the Community in Yorkshire is renting a storage unit in Darlington. Apart from the payment of the rental there is no other information on the system. If you like I can send you the information we have uncovered.'

'A storage unit eh?' replied Buxton. 'Yes, I should be grateful for a fax detailing the information you have uncovered. Thank you very much for drawing it to my attention. I think it might prove interesting.'

'Robert, I think the time has come for us to go north again. Arrange tickets for the afternoon train, will you?' Buxton said when he had updated the Chief Inspector. 'I want a warrant to search that place as soon as is possible' The longer we wait the more the chance that anything of interest will be removed and disposed of. The best thing in our favour is that I doubt if they will have twigged that we have unearthed the fact that they are renting the place. Tell me, what level of watch is being kept on the Netherton?'

'I will get on to the Darlington police to obtain a warrant. As to the level of observation on Netherton, I know there are unmarked cars on twenty four hour survey with particular reference to Delaney, now he has been granted bail, and the two security men. Delaney has had to hand in his passport and the other two don't appear to have one.'

'Tell Darlington that I will brief their best SOCOs before we carry out the search of that rental unit. They need to be on the lookout for anything that may be connected with the disappearance of Bethany and Tod. And anything that may be connected to that Land Rover. Oh, and any indication of bomb making equipment.'

'Do you plan that we should be there when the warrant is served, sir?' asked Thomasson.

'I do, because I feel we have a better idea of the sort of thing they should be looking for than anyone else. Make sure that we have all the information from the bomb people about what was used to make that thing. Also check with the pathologist reports on Bethany and Tod to see if they give us any indication of the sort of thing that was used to hit them over the head.'

Buxton spoke to the suitably dressed and equipped SOCO team

at six thirty the next morning. He explained the involvement of the Yard and outlined, in broad terms, the four deaths that were being investigated as well as the attempts on Louise Mercier's life. He then went on to tell them the kind of clues that they were hoping might be found in the lock up.

'If my ideas are correct, it is quite probable that this unit has been used by those who carried out at least some of the crimes, not only that but it is possible that, believing that no-one knew of the rental unit, they have been less than careful in covering up their tracks. What we need to uncover, if it is there, is evidence to tie these crimes to known perpetrators. Chief Inspector Thomasson and myself will not take part in the search. We will leave that to you experts. However, we shall be on site to help with any questions you may have and to get an idea of what you are finding. We have brought with us a range of photographs that will possibly assist you in identifying what we think may be of help to us. If you are all ready then, we will get on with the job.'

Chief Inspector Lennox of the Durham County force had arranged for the manager of the facility to be available for their arrival. Having produced his search warrant he asked the manager, a woman in her early forties, to take them to the unit and to use her pass key to open it. At first sight the interior looked like many another garage or storage area. There were metal shelves across the back of the unit and down one side which had a wide variety of items stored on them. One half of the other side was taken up with a workbench with racks of tools above it. The remaining space was filled with boxes and plastic sacks. It was clear that it was going to take a long time to go through everything in the place.

While the search was underway Buxton asked the manager how access to the site was controlled. She explained that when someone rented a unit, they were given a code which they could key into the pad at the entrance thus allowing them full and free access twenty four hours a day. Once on the site they could use the key to their rented unit they had been given to gain access to it. Looking around Buxton noticed that there were a number of CCTV cameras fixed to the various buildings which the manager told him were lit up by lights during the hours of darkness to avoid the risk of accidents and to help provide evidence of who had been to the site. This was necessary as it was not unknown for some people to claim that they had not visited the site as part of their argument as to the period for which they should pay rent.

'How long do you keep the tapes?' asked Thomasson.

'There are four cameras 'she replied 'that is one at the gate and one on each of the three blocks of units. We replace the tapes every week but, to be on the safe side in case any dispute arises, we keep each tape for twelve months.'

'I think it's going to be necessary for us to view the tapes for the entrance and for the block where the unit we are interested in is located for a full twelve months' said Buxton. 'If need be, we will supply you with replacement tapes for any we wish to keep.'

Buxton and Thomasson made their way back to where the SOCO team were working.

'How is it going?' he asked the Police Sergeant in charge.

'We are making progress sir' replied Sergeant Heather Temple.

'How long do you expect your search to take?' asked Thomasson

'With any luck, we should be through here today and be able to let you have our report by tomorrow afternoon sir.'

'Have you found anything of interest?' asked Buxton.

'There is this sir,' she went to their vehicle and produced a plastic envelope inside which was a small booklet. When she showed the title to Buxton, he read the title - How to Make a Bomb in Your Garden Shed'

'Very interesting' he said. 'You have information about the ingredients of the London bomb. I don't have to tell you that anything you can find that might be linked to that device would be very useful.'

'We are keeping that very much in mind sir'

'Then, we will leave you to get on with your work. Is there anything you want to ask us before we go?'

'I don't think so sir.'

Back at police headquarters Buxton set in place arrangements for the CCTV footage from the two cameras at the storage site to be screened. In particular he asked for all and any information there was regarding the use of the unit and who were the people who went there. Any loading or unloading of goods was to be noted. All this would take some considerable time and he had no alternative but to be patient and await results.

'The news about the search of the rental unit is going to get out before long' he said to Thomasson. 'Although it's going to be some time before we get all the results from what we find I don't think it's a very good idea to let Delaney, Walby and Shebdon have more time to get their act together. So, I think we will ask Seagrave to invite the latter two in for an interview and we will go down to Richmond to take part in the questioning.'

'You're not going to question Delaney about Julie Cranston?'

'Not today. I want to have another look at the statements made by the staff and residents to see if there is anything we may have missed first time around. He's not going anywhere, so let him think he has got away with it for a bit longer. Will you give Seagrave a ring and ask him to be good enough to bring in the two security people by telling them we just want to verify certain information that came to us from our searches. I want to alert the bomb people in London to be ready for anything we find in the rental unit.'

'It looks as if things could be warming up sir' said Thomasson.

'Yes, we may have found the end of some threads and if we have, then the whole thing could well start to unravel like grandma's knitting.'

CHAPTER THIRTY FIVE

THE TRAVELS OF A LAND ROVER

FEBRUARY 1995

Inspector Seagrave had arranged for Walby to be the first who was asked to visit the police headquarters. When he was shown into the interview room, he proved to be a short stocky man with broad shoulders, thick blonde hair and steel blue eyes. He was wearing a donkey jacket and jeans and on his feet were heavy work boots. Buxton was already seated in the room.

'Good afternoon Mr Walby' he said rising to his feet. 'Take a seat will you?'

'Walby looked round the room and could see that as well as Buxton there was a second police officer who he recognised as Inspector Seagrave and a constable who was ready to control a tape recorder. His body stiffened. This was not the first time he had undergone a police investigation and he was immediately on the defensive.

'Who are you?' he demanded. 'You're not local. I know the local police well enough.'

'My name is Buxton and I am with the Metropolitan Police.'

'What's this got to do with the Met? I was told the local people wanted to talk about the security arrangements at Netherton.'

'Mr Welby we are going to record this conversation starting now.'

'I know what you have charged Delaney with, but that was nothing to do with me. I was not involved in any way with the death of that girl.'

'You are, I believe, the Head of Security at The End of The Rainbow at Netherton?'

'Yes.'

'What exactly does that role involve Mr Walby?'

'Like any organisation the size of Netherton you need to have a proper security system in place. We make sure that the premises are secure, that there is adequate control of the goods that are for sale in the shop and that there are proper safety rules in place for everyone. That means, for example, running regular fire drills and making sure all that necessary signs and notices are in place.'

'Yet a young woman managed to fall to her death from a third floor doorway. How do you account for that?'

'That was nothing to do with me. If I had been there, I would have told her that door was to stay shut.'

'Did she have access to the key?'

'She must have got hold of one mustn't she because she opened it then came over giddy or something and fell out. I have a full set of keys but all the spares are kept in a locked cupboard in the office. Someone must have borrowed one of the spares.'

'Don't you control those keys?''

'Of course, we do. There is a key book in which every key that is removed has to be recorded and its return noted. After the accident I looked at the book and it just said Julie Cranston had taken the key.'

'Does that mean anyone could get hold of one of those keys?'

'Course not. They need an authorisation signed by one of the managers.'

'Who signed the one used by Julie Cranston?'

'I don't know. You'll have to ask the office for the slip.'

'You didn't check up on it afterwards?'

'It wasn't any of my business.'

'Where were you that afternoon Mr Walby?'

'Me? I was out on business.'

'What business would that be?'

'I was in town to buy some new Fire Exit signs.'

'Do you have any responsibility for other Rainbow sites?'

'What do you mean?'

'The question is quite simple.'

'Only in a support kind of way. Netherton is the main place but sometimes I am asked to go and give advice to one of the other sites.'

'To the Centre at Trescowen Cove in Cornwall for example?'

'Could be.'

'Were you there in April?'

'Could be.'

'Only the people there say that you were.'

'Then I must have been, mustn't I?'

'Can you tell me the reason for that visit?'

'Just a routine call. I try to get to all our places each year.'

'How did you travel to Cornwall?'

'By road'

'What vehicle do you drive Mr Walby?'

'You know I drive a Land Rover. The local people called it in to search it. Not that they found anything.'

'Who owns it?'

'The Community of course, although it's registered in my name for convenience.'

'Have you had any accidents or collisions with that vehicle?'

'No.'

'None at all?'

'The only thing I can think of was when I was on my way back from Cornwall. Some foreign lorry threw up a stone and when I got back here, I found it had broken the offside traffic indicator.'

'Was that the only damage?'

'Apart from a small dent.'

'So, it had to go into the garage to be repaired?'

'No. My assistant is a good mechanic and he fixed the new light and sorted out the dent.'

'Whereabouts did this happen?'

'How should I know there are dozens of those lorries on the motorway. I didn't find out till I got back.'

'What time did you get back here?'

'I can't remember exactly. Probably early afternoon.'

'So, you would have left Cornwall when?'

'What's this all about?'

'Just answer the question please.'

'Well, if it does you any good, I reckon it would have been four o'clock. I wanted to get an early start.'

'Did you see anyone as you left the Trescowen Cove site?'

'I was hardly likely to at the hour of the morning, was I?'

'Then you would be surprised to learn that the body of a young man, who was the victim of a hit and run accident, was found on a road near to Trescowen Cove? And even more surprised to find that he did not die there but his body had been placed to make it look as if the accident took place on the road where he was found.'

'What are you on about? I have told you I left about four and drove back here. Some lorry threw up a stone and broke my off-side traffic indicator. End of story.'

'I don't think so Walby. You see we found shards of the glass that comes from a traffic indicator in the long grass beside the track leading out of the Craft Centre. We also found very small shards of the same glass embedded in the coat being worn by the man who died. Not only that, but we know, from what you have told us, that your offside front indicator was broken. We have proved that a new one was fitted and we have also proved that the glass in the nearside indicator is scientifically similar to that found at Trescowen Cove and in the dead man's coat.'

'You can't fix that on me' yelled Walby jumping to his feet. 'I am not staying here to be framed for something I never did.'

'Sit down Walby' Buxton snapped. 'This interview is pausing at this point.'

Buxton got to his feet.

'We will give you some space to think over what we have said and to see if you wish to amend anything you have said.'

The police officers left the room. At this point Chief Inspector Thomasson led Terrance Shebdon into another interview room. On their way they passed the room in which Kenneth Walby was sitting. Both men now knew that the other was in custody and that what they said would be compared with what the other said.

Having given Walby fifteen minutes on his own Buxton and Sea-grave returned to the room and restarted the interview.

'What was your vehicle doing on a remote part of the dales in early April?' asked Buxton completely changing the subject.

'It wasn't' replied Walby. 'Why should it be up in the hills?'

'We have a witness who saw it parked there.'

'Then you had better get his eyes tested.'

'He saw you alright and he saw your number plate through his binoculars. It''s ELV 15 P isn't it. Well the witness remembers it because he is an Elvis fan.'

'What are you on about?'

'Quite simply that ELV 15 P looks quite like ELVISP. What were you doing there Walby?'

'Who said I was there. If I was there I was minding my own business.'

'Or were you minding someone else's business?'

'What are you on about?'

'Just where you were parked there is a sinkhole in the rocks. A sheep fell down it one day and when they went down to rescue it, they found the skeleton of a young woman who had been hit over the head, tied at her hands and feet and dropped down the hole.'

'Coincidence' snorted Walby 'where's your evidence?'

''The skeleton has been scientifically identified as being that of a Bethany Laura Mercier who was, at one time, a member of The End of The Rainbow in Netherton.'

'You can't pin that on me' shouted Walby. 'I never killed her.'

'Who is insured to drive the Land Rover?' Buxton asked switching the subject once again.

'Only me and my assistant.'

'Do you both have keys to the vehicle?'

They could see Walby thinking that here was a possible way out. If there was more than one driver, he could argue it wasn't him who had been driving that day.

'Of course, we do.'

'Are there any other keys to the vehicle?'

'A set is kept in the office for security reasons. Anyone might have borrowed the vehicle. I don't sit and watch it all day I have other things to do. Sometimes I don't use it for a week or more.'

'Are you a member of the Community at Netherton.'

'That's not a crime is it? But I don't live there. I have my own place in Richmond.'

'The Community rents a storage unit in Darlington doesn't it?'

'What if it does?'

'You may be interested to know that the police in Darlington obtained a warrant to search that unit and started to do so this morning.'

'So?'

'So, stop and think Walby. You were in Cornwall and the day you left a young man named Alan Vickery was killed in a hit and run. Your vehicle suffered damage to its offside front traffic indicator. We have proof that it was that vehicle that hit and killed Vickery. Not only that but your vehicle is seen on the dales close to a spot where the body of a young woman, who has lived and worked at the very place where you work, and who had been murdered was dumped down a sinkhole. Unfortunately, some silly sheep fell down the same hole and her body was recovered. Whichever way you look at it Walby you are likely to be facing two charges of murder.'

For five minutes, Walby said nothing. He sat with his head in his hands and breathed heavily.

'Alright' he said at last. 'I admit that it was my vehicle that hit the young chap. He stepped right out in front of me. I couldn't miss him. It wasn't my fault. I panicked and put him in the vehicle and dropped him off by the side of the road so people would think he had been hit there. The worst you have me for is dangerous driving and not stopping after an accident. As far as the other thing you are talking about, I never killed the girl and you will never prove I did.'

'You will be charged with the killing of Alan Vickery, Walby. But don't think you have got away with the death of Bethany Mercier. Because you haven't. Take him away.'

CHAPTER THIRTY SIX

SHEBDON'S STORY

FEBRUARY 1995

As Chief Inspector Thomasson led Terrance Shebdon towards the interview room, they passed Commander Buxton in the corridor but neither man acknowledged or spoke to the other. Thomasson was careful to ensure that, as they passed the room where Walby was being questioned, Shebdon could see him sitting in the chair looking downcast. Once they were settled in the interview room allotted to them Thomasson opened the meeting.

He looked at the other man who was in his late thirties, was above average height and of slim build with dark brown hair, brown eyes and a thin mouth.

'I am Chief Inspector Thomasson of the Metropolitan Police and this is Detective Sergeant Yeoman of the North Yorkshire Police. We shall be recording this interview which starts now. You are Terrance Paul Shebdon. Is that right?'

'What if it is? Why am I here? You have nothing against me.'

'We want to talk to you Mr Shebdon because we are hoping that you may be able to help us with our enquiries. You are based at The End of The Rainbow in Netherton. Are you a full member of the Community or are you a lay member?

'I work for them and am paid a salary.'

'Do you live on site?'

'No, I have a flat in Darlington.'

'In what capacity are you employed?'

'I am on the security staff.'

'How many of you are on that staff?'

'Just two of us, there's the Head of Security Ken Walby and my-self.'

'How would you describe your duties?'

'I do whatever I am told to do by my boss.'

'And what does that entail?'

'Generally, I am on security patrol around the premises, in particular the shop and places where there are customers. Other than it could be anything that needs to be done.'

'Does the Security Department have a motor vehicle?'

'Yes, we have a Land Rover. The boss sometimes has to visit other sites.'

'Do you drive that vehicle sometimes?'

'Sometimes'

'A good solid motor a Land Rover, isn't it? Can go over rough ground quite easily.'

'If it needs to it can.'

'Do you have anything to do with the maintenance of the vehicle?'

'As a matter of fact, I do. I am an experienced motor mechanic; I have worked in garages in the past. I can handle most repairs and servicing.'

'Do you have many repairs?'

'Not a lot.'

Did you, for example, repair a broken traffic indicator on the vehicle some months ago?'

'What if I did? Are you suggesting I didn't do it properly?'

'Not at all. I simply wanted to get the facts straight. How come the indicator needed repair?'

'Because it got broken.'

How?'

'I wasn't there when it happened. The boss said a big lorry had thrown up a stone that broke the light.'

'Where did that happen?'

'I don't know. The boss had been to Cornwall and it must have been down there or on the way to or from there.'

'You only repaired one of the indicators?'

'The other wasn't broken was it.'

'Do you know that a young man was killed in a hit and run accident at the place in Cornwall that your boss was visiting?'

'No'

'He was run over by a Land Rover which left traces of its traffic indicator at the site and in his clothing. Those traces match the near side indicator in your Land Rover. We have scientific evidence to prove it.

'You can't pin anything on me copper. I was nowhere near Cornwall and I can prove it.'

'I am sure you can' nodded Thomasson before adding;

'Did you know the young woman who had a fatal accident at Netherton?'

'Can't say I did. Can't expect anyone to know everyone in a place like that.'

'Does the name Bethany Mercier ring any bells?'

'Only that the boss said she was the woman who had the accident.'

'What about Julie Cranston, did you know her?'

'No.'

'Where were you on the day of the fall?'

'I was at our lock up unit in Darlington doing some work on a warning light that had broken down.'

'Are you an electrician as well as a car mechanic?'

'I reckon I can put my hand to any DIY job.'

'Do you often work off site?'

'Only when I am told to do so.'

'If you were in Darlington that day does that mean that your boss was on site?'

'You'll have to ask him. I am not his keeper.'

'Surely one or the other of you should be on site all the time it is open to the public.'

'That's the general rule. The big white chief doesn't like both of us to be away without his say so.'

'But it does happen sometimes?'

'Sometimes'

'Who looks after security then?'

'The Managing Director is in charge if we are both off site.'

'So, 'Thomasson said in an even tone 'when you and Walby were in the Land Rover up on the dales near Barnard Castle it would have been Mr Delaney who was in charge?'

'Yes' Shebdon replied and then added quickly' What are you getting at? Who said we were up on the dales?'

'You were seen. We have a witness who recognised the licence number of the Land Rover.'

'Try another one! I am not falling for a tale like that.'

'Aren't you Shebdon? Well you may be interested to learn that it is true. Also, you might be interested to know that the body of a young woman was recovered from a sinkhole in the rocks very near to where you were seen. All that was left of her was a skeleton but we have identified her as Bethany Mercier. The name familiar Shebdon? That was who was said to have had a fatal fall at Netherton. Not only that but the real Bethany Mercier was murdered.

'Hang on a moment! 'yelled Shebdon. 'You can't pin a murder on me. I never killed anyone. Anyhow there must be dozens if not hundreds of people who use those dales. Why pick on me? You haven't got any evidence and you're' not going to trick me into admitting something I never did.'

'What were you doing up there?'

'There's no law against having a break up in the dales is there. Even if there was a body there you've no evidence I was involved.'

'I am going to pause this interview Shebdon to give you a chance to consider what you have told me and to say if you want to alter anything you have said.'

Leaving the interview Thomasson went to meet up with Buxton and Seagrave so that each of them could bring the others up to date with what had happened in their interviews and to plan their next steps.

'While we have got Walby on a charge of the manslaughter of Alan Vickery and we know their vehicle was up on the dales where the body of Bethany was dumped, we don't yet have enough to charge anyone for the two murders' Said Buxton. 'Somehow we are going to have to get one or the other of them to talk.'

'What are we going to do with Shebdon?' asked Thomasson.

'I think we will let him go tonight and tell him to report back here tomorrow morning. By then we should have the SOCO report and we can see what else they have uncovered. We can then return to the attack and try to see if one of them breaks rank.

Seagrave, can you arrange for Shebdon to be kept under constant review tonight. Don't forget to cover all exits to the place where he lives. There is no need for your men to try and conceal themselves. Let him see them. That will keep the pressure on him.'

'Do you think we could hold him on the grounds that we have found bomb making details in the lock up?' asked Thomasson.

'We could, but on balance, I prefer to let him have a night to sleep on what he has said. We can explode the other bombs under him later. My guess is that he's the sort who won't want to take the rap for someone else.'

'What instructions do you want given to the men if he leaves the place where he lives. Are they to follow him or bring him back here?' asked Seagrave.

'Follow him and make sure they don't lose him.'

'I'll go and fix that up.' Seagrave said leaving the room.

'I will go back to Shebdon' said Thomasson. 'I think I will arrange for one of our cars to take him home. Just to make sure he does get there.'

'A good idea and tell him we will pick him up tomorrow morning. Use unmarked cars to give him a sense of security.'

Back in the interview room Thomasson switched on the recorder.

'Well, Shebdon, have you had any second thoughts about what you have told us? Do you want to alter or clarify your statement?'

'I never killed anyone. All I have ever done is do my job and obey the orders I was given.'

'Very well. You are free to go this afternoon, but I want you back here at nine o'clock tomorrow morning. Is that clear?'

'I have job to do I can't keep coming here to answer your stupid questions.'

'We will tell your employer that you are helping us' Thomasson said. 'Not only that but we will give you a lift home now and we will pick you up in the morning. And don't worry, we will use unmarked cars so your neighbours won't think you are in trouble with the police.'

'Having sent Shebdon on his way Thomasson re-joined Buxton.

'Did he say anything new?'

'Only that all he had done was to obey orders. I thought I would leave asking what orders till next time.'

'The SOCO team are back and I have asked the Sergeant to give us a summary of what they have found. She should be here in the next few minutes.'

There was a knock at the door and Sergeant Heather Temple entered.

'Take a seat Sergeant, 'Buxton said with a smile. 'What have you got for us?'

'We have had an interesting day sir' said the Sergeant who was a woman in her mid-thirties with short blonde hair and steel blue eyes. 'I will put it all in my report.'

'Just give us a broad outline for the moment, will you?'

'Well sir, you remember we found that leaflet about bomb making? That put us on the alert and we spotted some metal tubing, some blue and yellow wires and a box full of nails and other bits of metal. They seem to tie in with the things that booklet tells you are needed to make a bomb. They also tie in with the details given by the Bomb Squad so we have sent what we have found down to London to be checked with the items they found in that parcel bomb.'

'Good work Sergeant! What else did you find?'

'We have found some rope that looks as if it is the same as was used to tie up the murder victims. That will have to go to the crime laboratory for checking. Also, we found some black plastic sacks and sticky tape that look similar to that used to bundle up the body in the reservoir. That too will need confirmation by the crime lab. And finally, we found in a black sack a set of car seat covers. There were stains on them which show a preliminary positive as blood. These are on their way to the crime lab as well.'

'Did they fit a Land Rover,' asked Thomasson.

'We are checking up on that sir.'

'An excellent result Sergeant' said Buxton. 'We will leave you to write your official report while we digest what you have told us.'

'Lucky for us these villains seem to have been almost unbelievably careless' said Thomasson.

'I don't suppose they ever thought we would search that lock up so there was no need to clear up behind themselves.'

'I wonder what inducement was offered to those two to get them to follow orders?'

'Money' said Buxton. 'it's pounds to pennies they were to be paid for their services and well paid I have no doubt. What we need to do now is plan how we're are going to use this information. Messrs Shebdon and Walby are going to find some very nasty depth charges are about to explode right under them.'

CHAPTER THIRTY SEVEN

PRESSURE IS APPLIED

FEBRUARY 1995

Buxton and Thomasson had agreed that the time had come to move the interrogations to London so as to centralise their enquiries. They arranged with Inspector Seagrave that Walby would be brought before the City of London Magistrate's court in London and, after he had been remanded in custody, he would be taken to Holborn Police Station for further questioning. Shebdon would be charged with possession of bomb making information and, after a remand in Darlington, would be taken to Holborn Police Station for questioning. Inspector Vellacott of the Devon and Cornwall Police was asked to conduct Threlfall to London, telling him he was wanted for further questioning regarding the death of Alan Vickery. For the moment they would leave Delaney in Netherton under close observation. If he made any effort to leave The End of The Rainbow he was to be detained and brought to London to be charged with being an accessory to the death of Julie Cranston.

These arrangements would take the best part of a day and would allow the police time to liaise with the Crime Laboratories and the Bomb Squad regarding the evidence that had been found in the storage unit in Darlington and to prepare for the further questioning of the four potential criminals. By applying persistent pressure Buxton hoped that one or another of them would crack and either confess or try to do a deal with the police.

With the help of the various experts, it was possible to establish some interesting information on the items found during the search of the rental unit in Darlington. The Bomb Unit confirmed that the lead piping and the electric wiring were exact copies of those used in the bomb delivered to Louise Mercier's house. Not only that but the instructions in the leaflet found at the unit provided proof that the defused bomb had been manufactured in the unit. Finger prints from the bomb and the items found matched those of Terrance Shebdon.

The Crime Laboratories were able to demonstrate that the black plastic sacks at the unit were of the same manufacture as those found wrapped round Tod Grimhausen's body. Not only that but samples of ropes discovered were of the same type as that used to tie up Tod's body and were also the same as those used to tie round Bethany's ankles and wrists. Final confirmation would depend on detailed tests. The car seat covers had large blood stains on them. However, it was felt that they were too degraded for the capabilities of the new DNA testing. The best that could be established was that there were two blood types, one was type AB and the other was type B.

The results of the survey of the security cameras at Darlington had shown that a car identified as belonging to Delaney had arrived at the site in the early evening of fifth April to be followed a short while later by the Land Rover. The car had been driven into the storage unit and shortly after their arrival Walby and Sheldon were seen to leave the area on foot and to return about an hour later. Both vehicles left the site forty five minutes later. The tape for the next day showed the Land Rover arriving at nine fourteen. It backed into the unit and left again half an hour later. The film at the gate showed there were three men in the vehicle, one of whom was Walby who was driving.

Buxton held a council of war before the interrogations resumed so that the tactics to be employed could be agreed.

'We have four killings that need to be brought home to the offender' he began. 'As far as Alan Vickery is concerned Walby has admitted causing death by dangerous driving. In the case of Julie Cranston, we have evidence that she was pushed out of the third floor doorway by a thrust of a window pole. The clear perpetrator here is Delaney because the others were nowhere near the site at the time of the so called accident. In the case of the attempted hit and run in London we have the van which was used but not the driver. At the moment all the suspects have an alibi for that day and time. This indicates that whoever drove the van was hired to do that job. Unless one of our suspects talks we may never know who this man was. Turning to the bomb attempt on the life of Louise Mercier we have enough evidence to charge both Walby and Shebdon but I doubt if it was their idea. Not only that but we know that Delaney claimed his was in London to attend a Tourism conference. There was no such conference on that date. In addition, we have traced that he stayed at a hotel off the Euston Road the night before the so called conference, left that building early and returned to collect his luggage before returning to Darlington by train. The odds are that he was the one who planted the bomb on Louise Mercier's doorstep.

This brings us to Bethany and Tod. We now have evidence that ties their deaths to the rental unit in Darlington. The criminals have been remarkably careless and provided us with plenty of items that we can trace to Walby and Shebdon and, through them, to Delaney. That leaves Threlfall, who claims he was acting on instructions in falsifying the computer records and claiming the victim was Tod Grimhausen. Shebdon and Walby also maintain they were only obeying orders. All this points to all three of these being hired to do what they were told. We need to get either Walby or Shebdon to admit this. I think we can get the information we need out of Threlfall, not only that, but to let on what was the exact part played by Delaney. Vellacott will you deal with Threlfall and put pressure on him to say what he was to be paid. Seagrave will you take Shebdon. You can let on about the sort of data we have found in that lock up unit and leave him in no doubt he faces a very long term in jail. It's quite possible he will try to cut a deal. Thomasson will you take Walby and, again, put pressure on him as to the charges he is likely to face. Try and get him to say how much he was to be paid. I will deal with Delaney and start with Julie Cranston. I will also let him know that we have discovered that the Wills are fakes. If we can add to that the fact that one or more of the others have ratted on him, we might get some interesting responses. Finally, I suggest that we break off our interviews after an hour unless the person being questioned is giving us the information we want. This will allow us to compare notes and see if there is anything we can use to put pressure on one or the other of them.'

Inspector Vellacott entered the room where Nigel Threlfall was seated and where a Detective Sergeant from the Metropolitan Police was waiting to control the recorder. When the formalities had been completed Vellacott began his questioning.

'You have been charged Mr Threlfall with falsifying the record of a death and giving false evidence at an inquest.'

'I have told you already that I was acting under instructions.'

'We know that the person who was killed was a man called Alan Vickery. In addition, we have proof that you altered the computer records of the Rainbow Centre to make it look as if the dead man was Patrick Tod Grimhausen. However, there is no evidence that Grimhausen was ever at the site in Cornwall.'

'I repeat that I was acting under orders.'

'Alan Vickery did not die in a hit and run accident on a country road near the Trescowen Cove site. He was knocked down and killed on the slip road leading from the site to the main road, having been sent out by you on a fool's errand. As a result, Threlfall, you are an accessory to the killing of Alan Vickery.'

'I had no part in his death' Threlfall protested.

'But you knew what was going to happen to him.'

'I thought he was to be taken to another site in the far north.'

'If that was what you thought why did you identify his body as being Tod Grimhausen?'

'I wasn't told whose body it was to be, simply that I was to identify it as the person whose name I had been given.'

'But you did know who it was didn't you when you saw the body?'

'I was obeying orders.'

'How did you choose Vickery?'

'I didn't. It was Walby, the Head of Security. He said he looked like this Grimhausen. It was necessary that people would think that man was dead.'

'Why?'

'He never said.'

'You say you were simply obeying orders.'

'That's the truth.

'But not necessarily the whole truth is it Threlfall.'

'I don't know what you are talking about.'

'A month after the death of the so called Tod Grimhausen you said that someone handed you an envelope that they had been holding.'

'That's correct.'

'Who was that person?'

'I can't recall his name off the top of my head.'

'Because he didn't exist, did he? That supposed envelope said that another envelope had been deposited with a priest.'

'Yes.'

'Then it might surprise you to learn that the priest has identified the person who deposited the envelop with him and that person was you.'

'I only did what I was told to do.'

'You have told us that you were promised promotion if you co-operated.'

'I was.'

'What sort of increase in pay would it give you?'

'I wasn't told a figure.'

'Are you saying that you did all these things without knowing what your reward would be? If you are, then let me say that I do not for a single minute believe you.'

'I was promised promotion.'

'I am not talking about promotion. I am talking about hard cash. How much were you to be paid Threlfall? After all, every labourer is worthy of his hire.'

'You will never prove that I have received a penny.'

'I don't suppose you have. Nor will you get paid. You see Threlfall, the Will you helped uncover has been proved to be a forgery. There is no money to come from Patrick Tod Grimhausen to the Arcus Foundation in Luxembourg – a foundation whose name in English is arch which is the shape of a rainbow..

Threlfall's face turned white and his hands began to shake.

'So, you see Threlfall, you are already charged with falsifying a death record and committing perjury. On top of that charges of being concerned in the fraudulent production of a Will and of being an accessory before and after the murder of Alan Vickery will be added to the list. You will be in prison for very many years Threlfall.'

'If I agree to help you how will it help me?'

'I am not here to make promises or bargains. However, if what you say is helpful to the prosecution that will be taken into account.'

'Twenty thousand pounds' Threlfall muttered. 'That was what I was promised on top of promotion.'

'Who made that promise?'

'Delaney, the man who gave me my orders.'

In another interview room, Inspector Seagrave and a Detective Sergeant faced Terence Paul Shebdon who seemed relieved that he was being questioned by a police officer from Yorkshire rather than one from the Met. After the initial formalities Seagrave opened the questioning.

'In your previous interview you acknowledged that you had repaired the offside front traffic indicator of a Land Rover with the registration number ELV15P. Is that correct?'

'I did what I was told to do, no more and no less.'

'You were told that this vehicle had caused the death of a man in Cornwall.'

'If it did, it was nothing to do with me. I wasn't in Cornwall.'

'You were told that the Land Rover was seen in the dales close to a spot where the body of a murdered woman was recovered.'

'You can't prove I was there.'

'The police having obtained a warrant have searched a rented unit in Darlington. The very unit that was used by you and other Rainbow personnel.'

'I only use it when told to do so.'

'You are a competent electrician?'

'I can put my hand to most DIY things.'

'You have already been charged with being involved in the manufacture of an explosive device. Among the items recovered from the unit was a leaflet entitled 'How to manufacture a bomb'. Also recovered was some metal piping, electric wiring and pieces of metal used in bomb making.'

'What would I want with a bomb? I am a security staff member at a craft centre.'

'Your finger prints were on that leaflet.'

'So? I can read you know.'

'The other things I mentioned have been brought to the bomb experts here in London who confirm they are similar to those used in a bomb addressed to a lady who is the half-sister of the woman whose body was found in the dales.'

'I'm not the only person who uses that rental unit.'

'Also found in the unit were ropes that were similar to those used to tie up the woman found in the dales and those used to tie up a man whose body was recovered from a reservoir.'

'Like I said, I am not the only one who uses that place.'

'We also found some black plastic sacks of the same type as were used to cover the body of the man in the reservoir.'

'Black plastic sacks are two a penny.'

'You know Shebdon, you may think you are clever but you're a million times less bright than the forensic scientists who are examining all these items. If you think we are not going to connect you to all these things you are very wrong.'

'You can be as clever as you like but you will never prove I sent a bomb to anyone nor that I killed anyone.'

'Just stop trying to be clever Shebdon and look at the facts. You are facing charges under the Terrorism Acts for the manufacture of a bomb that could have killed I don't know how many people. You are also facing charges of being an accessory before and after the fact in two murders. That adds up to a possible three life sentences.'

'Can't you get it through your thick head that all I have done is obey orders given me by my boss. The person you want is Walby.'

'How much did he offer you for your work Shebdon?'

'What are you getting at?'

'Come off it, man. Don't try and tell me it was all just part of your day to day work. How much did he offer you for your help?'

'Find out if you can.'

'Oh, just one more thing Shebdon. There is no pot of gold at the end of this rainbow. It was supposed to come from the estates of the two people that were killed but their Wills are fakes. So, that hen isn't going to lay any golden eggs. Not only have you backed a loser but you are going to have to pay a very heavy price for doing so.'

'Look', said Shebdon 'if what you say is true.'

'And it is' interrupted Seagrave.

'What if I said I would give you the full story? What would I get in return?'

'I am not here to do deals, Shebdon.'

'Then you can go to hell.'

'I am going to pause this interview at this point to give you a chance to reconsider what you have said and to decide if you want to alter or adjust anything.'

Kenneth Walby glared at Robert Thomasson as he entered the interview room. When the initial formalities had been completed Thomasson spoke to him.

'Kenneth Walby, you have been charged with causing the death of Alan Vickery by dangerous driving. I must warn you that it is most likely that further charges will follow.'

'What charges?'

'Firstly, that you did not kill Vickery in an accident but you did so deliberately. In other words that you murdered him.

'You'll never make that stick.'

'We know that it was you who told Threlfall at Trescowen Cove to send Vickery down that trackway as it was necessary to have a body that could be claimed to be that of Patrick Tod Grimhausen.'

'That's a lie.'

'Is it? I don't think so. But, let's move on. When we searched that rental unit in Darlington, we found some very interesting things.'

'That must have been nice for you.'

'These include a leaflet entitled "How to Make a Letter Bomb", some steel tubing and electric wires and other small pieces of metal.'

'So what?'

'A letter bomb was sent to the home address of the half-sister of the woman who was supposed to have died at Netherton. The experts tell us they consider that the items found in Darlington match those used in the bomb.'

Look copper, I am not the only person who has access to that place.'

'Who else has access?'

'My assistant for one. And he is a dab hand with electrics.'

'Anyone else?'

'Delaney our boss has a key as well.'

'Are you saying that either Shebdon or Delaney made a bomb in that unit?'

'I am not saying anything.'

'Also found in Darlington are pieces of rope that match those used to tie up the bodies of Bethany Mercier and Tod Grimhausen both of whom were murdered.'

'A few bits of rope don't prove I killed anyone.'

'I am not saying that you did. But I think you helped in the disposal of the bodies.'

'What you think and what you can prove are different things.'

'So, all you did was obey orders?'

'Yes. I did what my boss told me to do.'

'And what was to be your reward?'

'What do you mean – reward?'

'Come off it Walby, you're not trying to tell me you did everything you did just because your boss said so. How much were you to be paid?'

'That's for you to find out.'

'Then, let me tell you something. The money was to come from the estates of those two people who were killed and whose bodies you disposed of. They left Wills leaving hundreds of thousands to the Arcus Foundation.'

'Never heard of it.'

'Maybe not, but it's the fund that holds the Rainbow cash. It's the pot of gold. The only problem is that those two Wills were phoneys and are not worth the paper they are written on. There is no pot of gold and you, my friend, are going to get exactly nothing for your trouble.'

'I don't believe you. You're trying it on. Well, it won't work.'

'I am going to pause this meeting for the moment Walby to give you a chance to think over what I have said and to have a chance to alter or adjust your statements.'

Thomasson got to his feet and left the room.

The four men met up to review what they had learned and to assess the state of in the interrogations.

'What we have got is Threlfall was to be paid twenty thousand. Shebdon as good as admits he was to be paid but we do not know how much. Walby is still trying to bluff it out.'

'To what extent are we going to want or need either Shebdon or Walby to agree to talk?' asked Thomasson.

'I think we could get Shebdon if we are able to sugar the pill a bit. I have laid it on quite hard,' said Seagrave 'but if I were to hint that we might not go for accessory before or after the fact but simply for assisting in the disposal of a body, he might tell us what we want to know.'

'I have a feeling' said Buxton 'that he was simply a sub-contractor in all this. The two principal villains are Walby and Delaney. If we can find out how much Walby was promised we might find that we can put even more pressure on Shebdon.'

'Right, I will get back to Walby and see what I can get out of him' said Thomasson.

Back in the interview room Thomasson looked hard at Welby for a minute or more before he spoke.

'Have you anything to add to or to alter what you have said'

'No.'

'Then let me sum up your position Walby. By your own admission you knocked down and killed a man called Alan Vickery. You state that you were acting on orders. Back in Yorkshire you arranged for Shebdon to replace the broken light. Not only that but you gave him a leaflet and other items and told him to manufacture a bomb that was sent to try and kill an innocent woman. Again, you maintain you only obeyed orders. Finally, you participated in disposing of the bodies of two people who were either killed by you or by someone known to you.'

'I never killed those two and you will never prove that I did.'

'So, where does all this put you Walby? You have already been charged with the death of Alan Vickery. By ordering Shebdon to make a bomb you can be charged under the Terrorism Acts. For disposing of two murdered bodies you became at least an accessory after the fact. I don't have to spell out for you what sort of sentence you would get for those charges. Now I don't for one moment believe that you did everything you did because your boss told you to do it. You were offered payment for your services. The figure doesn't actually matter because you are never going to get that money. You are savvy enough to know man, that the degree to which you provide information that leads to the conviction of the real culprit in all this is going to be valuable to your defence in pleading mitigation. Face the facts, you have been taken for a ride man. How much were you promised Walby?'

Walby sat and looked at Thomasson for five minutes without speaking. Then, with a shrug of his shoulders he muttered, 'Thirty grand'

When Seagrave went back to Shebdon he asked him, 'Well, Shebdon, have you anything to add to what you have said?'

'What's in it for me if I do?'

'That depends on the degree to which you help us. That is for you to decide. I have one other question I want you to answer. How much did Walby offer you for your help?'

'I was to get ten grand. We were to split what he got fifty fifty.'

'Interesting, because Walby was to be paid thirty grand. He was shafting you Shebdon.'

'Is that the truth copper?'

'It is the truth.'

'The dirty, twisting devil' snarled Shebdon. 'I bet he is trying to put all the blame on me. Well, he's not going to get away with it. Alright, Inspector, I will tell you all I know and I will give evidence against Walby and Delaney.'

And Shebdon began to give chapter and verse.

CHAPTER THIRTY EIGHT

BUXTON REPORTS

MARCH 1995

Buxton sat at the head of a table in the dining room at Peter Lewis' Guest House in Swaledale. In the other chairs were Louise Mercier, Gilbert Ravendale and Lewis himself.

'I thought that I owed it to you to bring you up to date with our investigations' he said 'as no small part of our success is due to the assistance that, between you, you have given us. As it's not possible for the Grimhausen family to be present I am delighted that Mr Ravendale has been able to join us and so be in a position to report the facts to New York. You will know from the media that arrests have been made and charges brought. There remains a great deal of detailed work to be done to prepare the cases for hearing in the Court and that is currently underway.

When it was decided to centralise the investigation, we were faced with solving potentially four murders, the forgery of two Wills, the building of an explosive device with intent to kill the recipient and perjury. Although the final control of the investigation was placed in the hands of the Metropolitan Police, I must emphasise the very considerable amount of work done by other police forces. This investigation has been a combined operation.'

'How did you ever start to unravel such a complicated problem?' asked Louise.

'The best way to start a story is at the beginning' smiled Buxton. 'This case began when two young people were making their way from Scotland down to London. By chance they came upon a community just outside a small town in North Yorkshire where they stayed for a couple of weeks. Both these young people had been used to living a nomadic existence and were used to stopping off here and there for short or sometimes longer periods of time. Bethany Mercier had given up her university course in the history of art and opted out of routine life. Tod Grimhausen, a young American, wanted no part of the family investment business and came across to Europe to get away from family pressure to conform in an effort to find the freedom he was looking for. One reason for his cutting loose was that he was an accomplished wood carver and there was no way his family were going to agree to his following that career.'

'Yes,' agreed Ravendale 'the Grimhausen family, charming as they are, could be classified as traditional WASPs.'

'The two of them seemed to have met in Scotland and a mutual attraction developed.' continued Buxton 'They had one particular thing in common. Bethany was due to inherit a large sum from her father's estate in the near future and Tod had a similarly generous fund available to him from his late grandmother. The community in Yorkshire was a self contained unit that allowed its members to develop their artistic talents. You could live there and be free of all the shackles of everyday life such as paying rent or mortgage interest. The fact that your food and accommodation was provided was an added attraction. Given this, it was not very surprising that, when they left London, they should decide to make their way back to North Yorkshire and this community. Bethany had already spent some time in a kibbutz so was familiar with that style of life. Tod, I suspect, was happy to go where Bethany led. However, they fairly soon found that being part of The End of The Rainbow was not the paradise they had thought. The price that members had to pay for their apparent freedom was conformation to a strict regime. In fact, it turned out to be more like a police state in that members were encouraged to report any slight divergence from the rules or any criticism of the system to the people in charge. This was done via the Security staff who, in turn, reported to the director of the site. It was hardly surprising that Bethany and Tod began to consider moving on. From what we have learned from other community members they quite freely talked about using the money they were due to inherit. They were planning, they said, on leaving Netherton to set up their own gallery in Devon or Cornwall. This information percolated back to the management who set in motion the tragedies that followed.'

'In other words, said Lewis, 'the motive was no more nor less than the oldest one in the world – money!'

'Exactly' agreed Buxton. 'There are quite a number of Rainbow communities scattered around the United Kingdom and, while on the face of it, they appear independent, they are all controlled by Netherton. The man in charge there and thus head of the whole organisation, is called Martin Delaney. A man who is not really driven by a desire to reinvent the world of William Morris but by the more prosaic object of making as much money as possible from his business ventures. When he learned that two of the members of his community were about to leave and set up on their own, he had their room bugged by his security staff. Originally, he wanted to know if they were likely to prove a serious challenge to his business but unfortunately Bethany and Tod were indiscreet in talking about how much money they had and that was how he found out about their inheritances. There was no way he was going to lose out on more than half a million pounds.'

'Bethany's trust fund was only about three hundred thousand' said Louise.

'And Tod's was not far short of that' added' Ravendale.

'More than enough working capital to set up their own gallery' continued Buxton. 'And more than enough to excite Delaney's greed, so he set about planning how to get his hands on the money. I think he started with the idea of trying to persuade them to buy into the Rainbow set up but any feelers he put out fell on deaf ears. It was then he decided on more drastic action. Delaney knew that to carry out his plan he would need assistance and he was prepared to pay for it. When he heard via the bug hidden in their room that they planned to leave Netherton on the fifth of April he set his trap and devised a plan which, if the luck had been with him, he would have got away with.

This is where he made his first mistake. He isn't the only criminal to have made such an error. The more complex the planned crime is the more chances there are of something going wrong and the more the perpetrator is tempted to try and close any gaps that become apparent. Very often the best thing to do is to keep it simple. Once you start to elaborate you increase the chances of being caught.

To avoid increasing the risk by basing all his action on Netherton, Delaney decided to lay a false trail by using a site as far away as possible from Yorkshire. He chose Trescowen Cove in Cornwall. One thing that influenced his choice was the knowledge that the head of that community, a man called Nigel Threlfall, was man with an eye for the main chance. He secured his support with an offer of twenty thousand pounds and promotion to Assistant Head of the organisation.'

'Not exactly a big slice out of more than half a million' observed Ravendale.

'But he didn't tell Threlfall how much was involved. He made it sound as if it was a fair price for doing little other than falsifying some records and lying about the identity of a dead man. You see what Delaney had decided to do was to stage two deaths; one in Cornwall and one in Yorkshire that appeared to be those of Bethany and Tod. It would be claimed that they left no information about next of kin so he arranged a quick cremation and scattering of the ashes. That way there was no risk of an exhumation revealing his fraud. Then, using a contact who specialised in faking copies of paintings and documents, he arranged for Wills to be prepared that left all the young people's estates to a foundation in Luxembourg which was a front for his own financial transactions. He then set about creating a complicated system regarding the discovery of the Wills. One was to be said to have been found taped under a drawer in the room occupied by Bethany and Tod. The other involved a series of plain envelopes that led to the Grimhausen's bank in London where Delaney himself posted the document into their letter-box. The clever part of this whole plan was that the wills were made to look more realistic by nominating family members as executors.

'But both Bethany and Tod had relatives' protested Louise. 'Why weren't their deaths reported to their families?'

'Because Delaney wanted the first bodies disposed of without the families having a chance to view the remains. He banked on the fact that their first intimation being from a solicitor regarding a Will would avoid their asking awkward questions.'

He also bought the services of his Head of Security, a man called Walby, This man had a criminal record for violence and there is little doubt this fact was the reason why Delaney employed him in the first place. The same applied to Walby's deputy, a man called Shebdon who was another with a criminal record. This gave Delaney a hold over both of them. Do what he wanted or risk losing a good job and free accommodation. Walby showed that he was more than ready to be recruited into Delaney's plans when he was offered thirty thousand pounds. For his part he realised that he was going to need help to carry out what was required. While Delaney agreed that Walby could make whatever arrangements he wanted, he told him he would have to pay anyone he used out of his own fee. Walby brought in his assistant Shebdon, who has an even longer criminal record. Shebdon was promised ten thousand pounds for his services. Delaney was now ready to put his plan into action. The first thing to be done was to get rid of Bethany and Tod. With them out of the way he could move on to stage two.

When he heard via the bug hidden in their room that they planned to leave Netherton on the 5th April he set his trap and devised a plan which, if the luck had been with him, he would have got away with. As I said, to avoid increasing the risk by basing all his action on Netherton, he planned to lay a false trail by using a site as far away as possible from Yorkshire.

'Fifty thousand is not exactly a big slice out of more than half a million' observed Ravendale.

'Didn't he realise' said Louise, 'that if they just vanished their next of kin would start asking questions?'

'You know that they had next of kin and, as a matter of fact, so did Delaney as they had named them on their application forms to join the Community in Yorkshire. To cover his tracks Delaney altered all the necessary computer records. Those for the real Bethany were exchanged for those of a Julie Cranston, after any reference to next of kin had been deleted. To cover up for Julie Cranston he created entries that showed she had left the site. His next step was to push Julie Cranston out of a third floor doorway. Having killed Julie, he claimed she was Bethany Mercier who had no next of kin. This identity was accepted and the inquest returned a verdict of accidental death. Julie's body was cremated and her ashes scattered.'

'But where was the real Bethany while all this was happening?' asked Lewis

I am afraid that both she and Tod were dead. They had been killed by Delaney before he killed Julie Cranston and arranged for a young man to be killed in Cornwall. Having dealt with the pseudo Bethany he turned to deal with pseudo Tod. The first step was to take him out of the Netherton records as having transferred to Cornwall which was why he bought the services of Threlfall in Cornwall. Tod's name was written over that of a young man called Alan Vickery. A new record for Vickery showed he had left the site of his own free will. Alan Vickery was killed by being run down by a vehicle driven by Walby who was visiting Cornwall. Threlfall identified the body of Alan Vickery as being that of someone called Tod Grimhausen who had no known relations. Once again, an inquest held that the death was accidental and the body was cremated and this time the ashes were scattered at sea.

In both cases, some weeks after the deaths of the so called Bethany and Tod, their so called Wills came to light. Delaney, through the help of Walby had paid a forger two thousand pounds to forge the documents. As I have said to make them appear more realistic; that for Bethany named her half-sister as executor and that for Tod named his father in New York both Wills left all the testator's money to the Arcus Foundation in Luxembourg. As clever as all this was Delaney had overlooked two facts. His first mistake was to assume that no-one would link the Arcus Foundation to him. It was Chief Inspector Thomasson's daughter, who is studying classics at Oxford, who told her father that Arcus is Latin for an arch, the shape of a rainbow, thus indicating a potential link with the Rainbow organisation in this country. In fact, we have discovered that the people nominally controlling that foundation were simply nominees for Delaney and his wife. The second, and much more serious mistake, was to think that simply deleting or altering a computer record wipes out completely the original record. By checking the records our computer experts were able to tell us exactly what the changes to the records relating to those four young people were and when they were made.'

'I should have thought of that' exclaimed Peter Lewis. 'I have had enough experience of computer systems in my past life to be aware of that fact.'

'Why should you think of it Peter?' asked Louise. It was odd, she thought, how easily she had slipped into the habit of using his Christian name 'Knowing something as esoteric as that is not very likely to spring to mind when faced with the question as to how Bethany could have died twice.'

'When the Will came to light Miss Mercier had no reason to suspect that it had not been written by her sister.'

'No, I had spoken to Bethany about the importance of her making a Will' agreed Louise.

'Not only that 'continued Buxton 'but the signature looked right. Delaney must have thought he had got away with the first part of his plan. The same applied when, via the somewhat roundabout route he had contrived that a Will in the name of Patrick Tod Grimhausen came to light and was apparently accepted as genuine. Once again this was the work of Walby's forger friend. Delaney must have thought that he had got away with the second part of his plan and all he had to do was sit back and be patient and over half a million pounds would fall into his lap.'

'You said Commander, that Delaney had killed both Bethany and Tod. How, when and where are the questions that I keep asking myself' said Ravendale.

'As I said, the couple planned to leave Netherton on 5th April. In an apparent show of friendliness Delaney invited them to his office to say goodbye and to sign off their agreement with the Community. In addition, he said that he had asked Walby to drive them to Scotch Corner where they could pick up a lift. What they didn't know was that the coffee he had offered them had been drugged. By the time they had been in Walby's vehicle for a quarter of an hour they were both unconscious. Instead of driving them to Scotch Corner he took them to Darlington to the rental unit registered in his name. He backed the Land Rover into the unit where Delaney, who had left Netherton by a fast car, accompanied by Shebdon, was waiting for him. We have

CCTV footage of both vehicles arriving at the unit on that day and at the right time. Delaney did not want Walby or Shebdon to know what he planned to do, I suspect he feared blackmail so he sent them off to a nearby pub for a drink. When they came back Bethany and Tod were dead. They had been hit over the head by a heavy metal bar while they were still unconscious in the Land Rover. The only consolation is that I don't think they ever knew what was happening to them. Delaney had wrapped the bodies in the seat covers of the Land Rover, having trussed them up at wrists and ankles. Together with his assistants he wrapped Tod's body in black plastic sacks and tied up the parcel with ropes. Bethany was left in the rental unit. While he returned home to set up an alibi, Walby and Shebdon drove across country to Bentwood Down Reservoir which was closed to visitors by that time. They took the body from the vehicle and carried it across to a place where looked isolated, lashed the heavy package to some tree roots and weighted it with some stones before dropping it into the deep water created by tree roots.

The next morning Walby and his assistant went back to Darlington to collect Bethany's body before driving across country to the northern edge of the dales. They searched for and found a suitable sinkhole in the rocks. Then satisfying themselves that there did not seem to be anyone about, they took the body from the vehicle and removed the wrapping before dropping it down the narrow opening. This concluded part one of the Delaney plan.

He started part two by sending Walby on one of his periodic visits to another Rainbow site to check up on their security arrangements. This time he visited Trescowen Cove in Cornwall. Delaney had already alerted Threlfall who had identified the young man who was to become the body of the supposed Tod Grimhausen. He was called Alan Vickery and Threlfall asked him to go down to the road very early one morning to take delivery of some special items of wood carving. Walby, having been alerted, ran down Vickery on the trackway between the site and the road and killed him. He put the body in his vehicle and deposited it on a nearby road to look as if the accident had taken place there. It was not until later that he found that, in hitting Vickery, he had broken the front nearside traffic indicator light. Back in Yorkshire he told his assistant to repair it as quickly as possible. Meanwhile Threlfall altered the computer records, claimed the body to be that of Patrick Tod Grimhausen and saw it through the inquest and cremation. The ashes were scattered at sea.

Back in Yorkshire Delaney wasted no time. He had selected a young woman called Julie Cranston as his victim and altered the computer records to show that she was Bethany Mercier and that Julie Cranston had left the site. He also made changes that showed Tod Grimhausen had been transferred to Cornwall. He next arranged that Julie Cranston should be asked to take some photos from the third floor of the Netherton building from a usually locked doorway. While she was doing this Delaney who had hidden himself on that floor, took a long pole used to open blinds or high up windows and shoved Julie off balance so that she fell to her death. At the appropriate moment he appeared to identify the body as Bethany Mercier, registered her death, attended the inquest to formally identify her and arranged for the body to be cremated and the ashes scattered at Netherton.

'The final stage of part two of his plan was for the Wills of both Bethany and Tod to come to light. In fact, the person who took over Julie Cranston's room never did find such a document. Delaney simply claimed that she had. Down in Cornwall, Threlfall claimed that he had been handed an envelope that said another envelope had been deposited with a local priest. That was true, but it was not deposited by Tod for the priest identified Threlfall as the depositor. That envelope led to a bank in London who had received a Will through their door that claimed to come from Tod.

Part two of Delaney's plan had been successfully completed.

CHAPTER THIRTY NINE

BUXTON CONCLUDES HIS REPORT

MARCH 1995

'Having set out how the various crimes were committed we can pass on to how the puzzle that had been created was solved' said Buxton after they has taken a break for coffee and French pastries.

'Having carried out his plan Delaney thought that all he had to do was to be patient and over a half a million pounds would fall into his lap' continued Buxton. 'You, Miss Mercier, did not see any reason to doubt that the Will was indeed that of your half-sister. While, as far as I am aware, the Grimhausen family accepted the other Will as being genuine. But, unfortunately for Delaney, the tide started to turn.

The first intimation that things were not what they appeared came when an unfortunate sheep fell down the hole in which Bethany's body had been deposited. The rescuer of the sheep noticed that just below it there was a skeleton. Whilst it was not possible to recover it in one piece. When the skeleton was reconstructed it proved to be that of a young woman. This is where forensic science came into its own. It is possible using scientific data to carry out various tests and this led to the creation of a drawing of what the young woman had looked like. To try and obtain an identity the police published the artist's impression of the face. Mr Lewis saw this and although he had never met Bethany he recognised a likeness to a photograph Miss Mercier had given him. When she saw the picture, Miss Mercier agreed that there was indeed a real likeness. So, with Miss Mercier's agreement, he contacted the local police and explained the likeness and the fact that Bethany had died at Netherton. The intention being to avoid the police looking for someone who was already dead. This led to further forensic investigation and the making of a full reconstruction of the head which immediately was recognised as that of Bethany. A small piece of jewellery found in the hole confirmed the fact. The question now was, how could the same person die twice?

The next thing that went wrong for Delaney was when a fisherman found a black sack floating in a reservoir where he planned to fish. It contained the body of a young man. This time a problem of identifying a partially decomposed body had to be solved. By sheer good fortune an American dental specialist was visiting this country and saw an x-ray of the body's teeth. He recognised that the victim had had American dental work. Thanks to the very capable investigations by Mr Ravendale a copy of Tod Grimhausen's dental record was obtained and a match was made. Here was a second person who appeared to have died twice.'

'At which point' grinned Ravendale 'enter Commander Buxton.'

'Thanks to the sterling work done by all of you I had a firm basis on which to build. We knew that the deaths at Netherton and Trescowen Cove were faked. We knew that the real Bethany and the real Tod were dead. We needed to prove who was responsible. The obvious step was to haul in Threlfall and Delaney for falsifying deaths and committing perjury. At the same time, we planned to raid the sites in Cornwall and Yorkshire to confiscate all computer equipment they held and to question every single person in both places. This produced several results. Firstly, the computers gave up their secrets and the false entries were uncovered. Secondly, Threlfall quickly admitted his part in the scheme more out of the fright of being charged with murder than regret for his other crimes. Robert Thomasson's theory that Tod Grimhausen had never been in Cornwall was proved right when no-one at that site recognised him. Importantly Thomasson also discovered that the Head of Security at Netherton was there when the young man was killed.

'The real identity of the two pseudo victims was established by a mixture of good police work and some luck. A young man sought details of a brother who he thought had gone missing. He wanted to find him because the young man's mother was dying and was asking for him. The missing man proved to be Alan Vickery and the post mortem examination carried out after the body was discovered provided enough medical evidence to confirm that it was Alan Vickery. In Yorkshire one of the cleaners at the police headquarters saw a picture taken at the post mortem mentioned a young woman called Julie Cranston who had disappeared. Cross reference between her medical records and the post mortem confirmed beyond doubt that it was Julie Cranston. Once again medical evidence obtained at the post mortem had allowed us to prove that the body was that of the young woman, who had fallen to her death. The next question was who had killed them? As far as Alan Vickery was concerned traces of a broken car warning light were found in grass near the track from the site and the road and on the clothes Vickery was wearing. When we found the Land Rover driven by Walby had had its front offside warning light replaced we knew who had killed that innocent young man.

A careful search at Netherton discovered that Delaney was about the premises on the day of the fall. Not only that but we found a long pole used to open and close windows which were out of reach or to raise or lower blinds. It had Delaney's finger prints on it and the metal at the end matched a bruise on the back of the young woman that had been noted at her post mortem.

While all this was happening, a white van tried to run down Miss Mercier in London. More by luck than judgement the attempt failed. But, why had it happened? It seemed to me that someone was worried that Miss Mercier might spot the Will was not valid. We subjected both Wills to expert examination and it proved they were forgeries. A fact that was not disclosed to Delaney or the others. The supposition about the reason for an attempt on the life of Miss Mercier was valid came when someone tried to send her a parcel which contained a bomb. Thanks to the alertness of Miss Mercier and Mr Lewis we were alerted and the bomb was made safe.'

'I never knew it was a bomb' exclaimed Louise. 'I was told it was just a mail order catalogue'

'We did not want to worry you unduly Miss Mercier' said Buxton with a smile. 'By that time, you were here in Yorkshire and there was no reason to suppose that Delaney knew that.'

The final piece of the jigsaw proved to be a storage unit rented by Walby in Darlington. When this was raided, we found a leaflet detailing how to make a bomb, items that matched those used in the construction of the bomb sent to your house and samples of rope of the same type that was used to tie up Bethany and Tod. There were also black plastic sacks of the same type as were used to wrap up Tod's body and a bloodstained set of car covers that fitted Walby's vehicle.

We had thought from the very beginning that our best hope was that one or the other of those involved would talk to try and lessen the charges against them. The first was, as I said, Threlfall. The second proved to be Shebdon the security assistant who thought he was going to get half of what was paid to Walby. When he found out that he had been tricked over the amount he was to be paid and the fact that there was no gold at the end of this rainbow he agreed to talk. '

'I must congratulate you and all your colleagues' said Peter Lewis 'for unravelling such a complex set of lies.'

'Indeed' agreed Ravendale. 'I have no doubt that Grimhausen family will be equally impressed.'

'There is still a lot of hard work to be done' said Buxton 'but for me, the most satisfactory thing about the whole investigation is the level of co-operation there has been between the various police forces. This was truly a team effort.'

So concluded the case of the double deaths. Delaney, Threlfall, Walby and Shebdon were all arrested. The defence tried to argue that the declarations that people had signed agreeing not disclose what they knew about the Communities should be treated in the same way as a religious confession. This was summarily rejected by both the high court judge at the trial and by the law lords at the appeal. Delaney was convicted and sentenced to thirty years in prison. Walby received fifteen years and Threlfall ten years. Shebdon, because he gave evidence for the prosecution only faced a lesser charge and received five years.

The End of The Rainbow communities quickly regrouped and replaced Delaney and Threlfall and revoked the policy of encouraging members to report one another. Although they feared the effect the trial would have on their business the opposite happened and more people than usual visited the sites if only to view the scenes of the crimes.

CHAPTER FORTY

POST SCRIPTUM

MARCH 1995

Shortly after Buxton had left Louise Mercier and Peter Lewis seated over a glass of wine and talking about the strange events of the last two years.

'I suppose the time has come' said Louise 'to start to pick up the pieces and get back to what used to be a normal life.'

'Is that what you want to do?' asked Peter.

'Well, I cannot stay here as your guest, indefinitely can I?'

'But you are not a guest. You have a job here. A job which I have to say you are doing as efficiently as you always did any job.'

'But it is not a permanent job is it, it's one you created so that I didn't feel a burden on you.'

'Maybe it was created for that reason, but it has proved its worth. It is entirely up to you Louise but if you would like to make your job permanent I for one should be very pleased.'

'But what about my house in London?'

'Why not keep that and let it out permanently. It could prove a valuable asset and it gives you a cushion if you should ever want to go back to London. On top of which you are going to inherit a nice amount from Bethany's estate.'

'I must admit that I hadn't thought of it in that way.'

'You know Louise, both of us have been through some quite big highs and lows these past two years. Sometimes you have to do that to get things into their proper perspective. That is certainly true of me. I may not be the big executive any more but I can honestly say that I am happier and more content today than I have ever been before. Not only that but I am looking forward to developing this business. In fact, I am considering turning it into a limited company. Nothing would give me greater pleasure than if you would agree to become my fellow director. We are a good team, you and I. No more of the boss and his secretary but a working partnership. How about it?'

'Thank you very much for the offer. It's come as a complete surprise to me. Can I have a little while to think it over?'

'Take as long as you need.'

'I think you may expect the answer to be positive 'Louise smiled.

MARCH 1996

Richard Buxton entered Robert Thomasson's room.

'I'll bet you a free lunch you can't guess what is in here' he grinned waving a newspaper.

'What is it?' asked Thomasson

'It's from our friend Seagrave in Richmond'

'They have not had another suspicious death at Netherton have they?'

'Not that I know about.'

'Then I might as well give up sir.'

'Read this and be prepared to be surprised' Buxton held out the newspaper.

Thomasson took it in his hand and looked at the page presented to him. At first there was no reaction. Then he gave an almost audible gasp.

'Well, I'll be damned 'he exclaimed.

Buxton took back the paper and read:

"Marriages "Lewis – Mercier. On Saturday 4th March at St Andrew's Weltby, Peter Graham Lewis to Louise Angela Mercier."

'Come on Robert' laughed Buxton 'let's go out and have lunch so that we can toast the happy couple. Oh, and I will pay!'

ABOUT THE AUTHOR

Brian Wright

The author is a retired banker. He is married with two children and lives on the Norfolk/ Suffolk border.

Printed in Great Britain
by Amazon

61707383R00159